PARASITE

Fuck you are the best words if you can't shut the fuck up!
Danny 4/19/97

VOLUME TWO
PARASITE REGAINED

Edited By
D M Mitchell

APOPHENIA

This book is a work of fiction. The characters and incidents portrayed in it are all drawn from the authors' imaginations. Any resemblance to real persons, living or dead, events, or localities is purely coincidental.

PARASITE: VOLUME TWO: PARASITE REGAINED
All stories Copyright © 2014 the respective authors.
Cover art Copyright © 2014 Pablo Vision.

First published in the world in 2014 by Apophenia

ISBN: 978-0692289839

QUESTIONAIRE RE: THE MAIN SIGNS OF PARASITE INFESTATION

- Feel tired most of the time / Chronic Fatigue / Exhausted/ Chronic Fatigue Syndrome?
- Digestive problems / gas, bloating, constipation or diarrhoea?
- Chronic constipation / Irregular bowel movements?
- Low energy / Low stamina?
- Always getting sick / Feeling down / catching flu?
- Food sensitivities and environmental intolerance / Food Allergies?
- Developed allergic-like reactions and can't understand why?
- Have joint and muscle pains and inflammation often assumed to be arthritis?
- Suffer with anemia or iron deficiency (pernicious anemia)?
- Have hives, rashes, weeping eczema, skin ulcers, swelling, sores, papular lesions, itchy dermatitis, itchy anus?
- Suffer with restlessness and anxiety?
- Experience multiple awakenings during the night particularly between 2 and 3 am?

- Grinding teeth?
- Have an excessive amount of bacterial or viral infections?
- Depressed?
- Difficulty gaining or losing weight no matter what you do?
- Did a Candida program which either didn't help at all or helped somewhat but you still can't stay away from bread, alcohol, fruit, or fruit juices?
- Just can't figure out why you don't feel really great and neither can your doctor?
- Itchy ears, nose, anus?
- Forgetfulness, slow reflexes, gas and bloating, unclear thinking?
- Loss of appetite, yellowish face?
- Fast heartbeat, heart pain, pain in the navel?
- Eating more than normal but still feeling hungry?
- Pain in the back, thighs, shoulders?
- General lethargy?
- Numb hands?
- Burning sensation in the stomach?
- Drooling while sleeping?
- Damp lips at night, dry lips during the day, grinding teeth while asleep?
- Bed wetting?

Diagnosing human parasites can be difficult because parasite symptoms mimic many other diseases. Most health professionals aren't familiar with parasite disease and don't ask for the complete travel and lifestyle history that could identify a possible parasite infection.

TRAVEL – PARASITE DIAGNOSIS

- Have you ever been in Mexico, Africa, Israel, China, Russia, Asia, Europe, or Central or South America?
- Have you traveled to Hawaii, the Caribbean, the Bahamas, or other tropical islands?
- Do you swim in freshwater lakes, streams, or ponds while abroad?
- Did you serve overseas while in the military?
- Were you a prisoner of war in World War II, Korea, or Vietnam?
- Have you had intestinal problems, unexplained fever, night sweats, or an elevated white blood count during or since travelling abroad?

WATER – PARASITE DIAGNOSIS

- Is your water supply from a mountainous area?

- Do you drink untested well-water?
- Have you ever drunk water from lakes, streams, or rivers on hiking or camping trips without first boiling or filtering it?
- Do you use plain tap water to clean your contact lenses?
- Do you use regular tap water that is unfiltered for colonics or enemas?
- Can you trace the onset of symptoms (intermittent constipation and diarrhoea, night sweats, muscle aches and pains, unexplained eye ulcers) to any of the above?

FOOD – PARASITE DIAGNOSIS

- Do you regularly eat unpeeled raw fruits and raw vegetables in salads?
- Do you frequently eat in sushi bars or salad bars; in delicatessens; vegetarian, Mexican, fish, Indian, Armenian, Greek, Pakistani, Ethiopian, Filipino, Korean, Japanese, Chinese, or Thai restaurants; fast food restaurants; or steak houses?
- Do you use a microwave oven for cooking (as opposed to reheating) pork, fish, or beef?
- Do you prefer fish or meat that is undercooked, i.e., rare or medium rare?
- Do you frequently eat hot dogs made from pork?

- Do you eat smoked or pickled foods, e.g., sausage, lox, herring?
- Do you enjoy raw fish dishes like sushi or sashimi, Latin American ceviche, or Dutch green herring?
- Do you enjoy raw meat dishes like Italian carpaccio, steak tartare, or Middle Eastern kibbe?
- At home do you use the same cutting board for chicken, fish, and meat as you do for vegetables?
- Do you prepare sushi or sashimi dishes at home?
- Do you prepare gefilte fish at home?
- Can you trace the onset of symptoms (weight loss, anaemia, bloating, distended belly) to any of the above?

PETS – PARASITE DIAGNOSIS

- Have you gotten a puppy recently?
- Have you lived with, do you currently live with, or do you frequently handle pets?
- Do you forget to wash your hands after petting or cleaning up after your animals, and before eating?
- Does your pet sleep with you in your bed?
- Do your pets eat from your plates?
- Do you clean your cat's litter box?

- Do you keep your pets in your yard where children play?
- Can you trace the onset of your symptoms (abdominal pain, high white blood cell count, distended belly in children, unexplained fever) to any of the above?

WORKPLACE – PARASITE DIAGNOSIS

- Do you work in a hospital?
- Do you work in a pet shop, zoo, experimental laboratory, or veterinary clinic?
- Do you work with or around animals?
- Do you work in a day-care center?
- Do you garden or work in a yard to which cats and dogs have access?
- Do you work in sanitation?
- Can you trace the onset of symptoms (gastrointestinal disorders) to any of the above?

SEXUAL PRACTICES – PARASITE DIAGNOSIS

- Do you engage in oral sex?
- Do you practice anal intercourse without the use of a condom?
- Have you had sexual relations with a foreign-born individual?
- Can you trace the onset of symptoms

(persistent reproductive-organ problems) to any of the above?

MAJOR SYMPTOMS – PARASITE DIAGNOSIS

Although the following symptoms can be related to parasite-based diseases, they could also be occurring as a result of other illnesses.

ADULTS

- Do you have a bluish caste around your lips?
- Is your abdomen distended no matter what you eat?
- Are there dark circles around or under your eyes?
- Do you have a history of allergies?
- Do you suffer from intermittent diarrhea and constipation, intermittent loose and hard stools, or chronic constipation?
- Do you have persistent acne, anorexia, anemia, open ileocecal valve, skin eruptions, PMS, bad breath, itching, pale skin, chronic fatigue, food intolerances, sinus congestion, difficulty in breathing, edema, bloody stools, ringing of the ears, anal itching, puffy eyes, palpitations, vague abdominal discomfort, or vertigo?
- Do you grind your teeth?

- Are you experiencing weight loss or weight gain, loss of appetite, insomnia, depression, moodiness, sugar craving, lethargy, or disorientation?

CHILDREN

- Does your child have dark circles under his eyes?
- Is your child hyperactive?
- Has your child been diagnosed with 'failure to thrive'?
- Does your child grind or clench his teeth at night?
- Does your child constantly pick his nose or scratch his behind?
- Does your child have a habit of eating dirt?
- Does your child wet the bed?
- Is your child often restless at night?
- Does your child cry often or for no reason?
- Does your child tear his hair out?
- Does your child have a limp that orthopedic treatment has not helped?
- Does your child have a brassy staccato-type cough?
- Does your child have convulsions or an abnormal electro-encephalogram (EEG)?
- Does your child have recurring headaches?

- Is your child unusually sensitive to light and prone to eyelid twitching, blinking frequently, or squinting?
- Does your child have unusual tendencies to bleed in the gums, the rectum, or nose?

INFANTS

- Does your baby have severe intermittent colic?
- Does your baby consistently bang his head against the crib?
- Does your baby show a blotchy rash around the perianal area?

METAPHYSICAL

- Are you happy with your life?
- Do you feel that you have reached the place in your life where you thought you'd be at the age you've reached?
- Do you ever feel as if the thoughts in your head aren't really yours?
- Can you remember when the colour went out of everything?
- Can you remember the last time you really tasted your food?
- Do you love anyone; do you trust anyone?
- Are you happy with your life?

- Ever felt like you'd been cheated?

MENACING DAZE
Michael Roth

Public bathrooms are for fucking, shitting and fighting, in that order. David Michael K. knew the score very well, being an experienced cruiser and street fighter. Walking past the Firkin Pub, he could hear the din of voices and Lee Perry music pouring out the front door.

The fucking Firkin, he thought, running his hand over his cropped scalp. Should be able to pull a bird there. That's if nothing's changed. He shoved his hands into the pockets of his sta-pres and counted the coins with his fingers. Should be enough for a pint or two, he thought. Let's give this a go.

He stepped in and headed to the bar. There was a raucous roar from a dark corner. He turned towards the loud shouting and saw a table of skinheads slamming their fists onto the table and laughing. Against the bar, waiting for a pint, he spotted an attractive woman with cropped black hair. She turned and he recognized her from his youth - they used to meet up at punk gigs years ago. While he had never fucked her, he always wished he had. From the look in her eyes, he knew that he had been recognized as well.

"David?" she said, "That you?"

"Glory, yeah, been awhile."

They exchanged a few more pleasantries, then he excused himself.

"Going so soon?"

"Just to the loo. Want to come along?"

"Of course!"

The bathroom floor was covered with piss and had that familiar odor of shit and anti-septic cleaner. They headed straight to the single stall, closing and latching the door. She lost no time in taking down his trousers and falling to her knees, swallowing his hardening member with a single gulp. Her technique was expert and she worked him like a vacuum cleaner. He wanted to get at her pussy. He sat onto the cold, stained toilet, lifted her short skirt and pulled off her cottons. She leaned back against the metal door, legs spread. She had a hammer and sickle tattooed across her pubic mound. David Michael nodded silent approval, no wonder she tasted so good. He hated fucking Nazis and refused to participate in giving them pleasure. Here was a group of people who wanted to control who he could or could not fuck. Besides, most were rampant coprophiliacs, a practice too messy for every day shagging. He dove into her shaved pussy, tongue swiping across her hard clit. She shrieked in pleasure, banging her hands against the metal walls. After a couple minutes of receiving oral, she pushed David back onto the toilet and straddled his hips. She lowered herself onto his throbbing member, sliding in easily from the wetness of her hole. She gyrated vigorously, grunting and growling, pushing his body back into the damp plumbing.

He felt a twisting in his bowels. He held back the shit poking out of his asshole. The million year old DNA codes were unraveling in his brain and within seconds his genetic wealth was exploding into her cunt while at the same time he released his anus, sending the shit into the toilet with a splash and a loud fart. She fell forward, muscles tensing then relaxing as waves of multiple orgasms went through her body.

"That's what I needed." She said, standing up and stepping back into her panties. David gestured with his eyebrows, giving a surprised look. "Oh, I love the feel of hot spunk in my underwear." she said with a wink before leaving the stall. "Stop by our table, my friends will definitely want to meet you." She called as she left the room.

K. cleaned up, congratulating himself on the bit of luck and looking forward to some more prolonged shagging later that night. Hopefully, a group session with Glory and her friends. He heard the door open and the click of boots on the tile.

"Back so soon. Hope you brought a friend."

David Michael K. said stepping out of the stall.

"What the fuck you looking at?" the large skin said with a sneer. "Fucking pansy." On his right arm was a tattoo of a deer jumping across a swastika. On his other arm, 'White Pride' was tattooed in a gothic style. The skin was looking for a fight. David Michael had seen yobs like this before. Guys who think they're tough because of their size without realizing that at least half of fighting is a mental game. I'll dispatch with this one quickly, he thought, and then it will be on to a brilliant all night fuck session.

Stepping forward, arms raised slightly in a surrender position, David hoped to get in a quick head butt. The skin clenched his fists, ready to strike. So, it was not going to be that easy, he thought. He feinted with his right and shot out a quick left hook. A classic move and if executed properly could bust a jaw or at least stun the opponent so a further beating could be meted out. David Michael loved this move because if he missed with his fist he could follow through with his elbow. But now he would have to rethink this tactic. The skinhead ducked to the left, not taken in by the feint and punished David's ribs with a couple of hard upper cuts. Quickly followed by a leg sweep. David Michael, already stunned and breathless, hit the floor hard, head bouncing against the wet tile. As an experienced fighter,

David knew how to take a fall, but this attack caught him off guard. Instinctively, he threw out his legs for an ankle sweep but there was nothing but air. Arms up David was waiting for the inevitable kick in the ribs as he snaked his way along the floor on his back. Instead came a stomp to the stomach by a size 12 Doc Martin followed by a stomp to his face, which fortunately glanced off his arm. Otherwise, his face would have been driven to the other side of his head.

The door to the bathroom opened. "What the fuck!" came a man's voice.

"I'll do you next if you don't fuck off!" the skinhead retorted.

This distraction was all he needed. He thrust both his legs, heels first, into the skinhead's groin. The skinhead was pushed two feet into the air, howling, clutching his swelling balls. David Michael got up, one arm holding his ribs, and drove a knee into the opponent's face. He could feel the nose collapse and twist, splattering blood across his pants. The skinhead, obviously an experienced hooligan and one tough customer to boot, pushed David back against the washroom stall with his shoulder. David knew he had to end this soon before the Nazi's friends showed up to stomp him into a pulp. He extended his thumb and drove it into the skinhead's eye. He could feel this digit burrowing into soft flesh and warm liquid. The skinhead collapsed to the piss- covered floor of the washroom stall.

David Michael grabbed a wad of paper towels and walked past the stunned observer. Next time none of this fancy stuff, he thought sneaking out the back door, I'll just ram my fist into his throat. I'll have to let that shag session go for now. I don't want to be around when the other skinheads find their friend. Of course, he enjoyed the fight game and rarely turned down the opportunity for some ultra violence. But there were other matters at hand.

David Michael stepped out into the alley. Thinking of the fight brought back fond memories of his time with the Dumb Fucks, a firm dedicated to street fighting and poststructuralist theory. He formed the Dumb Fucks after reading *Anti Oedipus* by Deleuze and Guattari. His enthusiasm for the book, and his ultimate disappointment with the follow up *Thousand Plateaus*, led him to take the work directly to the people with violence. Punch ups with anyone, academics and soccer fans alike, followed. But those times had passed. He turned the corner out of the alley and walked up the street with confidence.

Cracking his knuckles, he felt good after the fight and fuck. He could feel the energy around him, as he was in tune with his surroundings. Things slowed down and he could navigate the chaotic flow of the streets. People were out of touch with their realities. They were alienated by capitalism, not to mention other forms of simian governing structures. And they had lost the desire to transcend these illusionary surroundings and explore deep surrealities.

K.'s attention was drawn to the Tesco. Overhead, he noticed two pink saucers, just floating in the sky. They shimmered in the sun and had an almost translucent but metallic quality. No one else seemed to be aware of their presence.

"Fuck me." He said. "Not again."

K. decided to contemplate the return of the pink saucers over a fry up and a pint. The first time he saw them was during some intense experimentation with mushrooms. He was using them as he worked with the Enochian calls as well as some higher circuit work he picked up from Robert Anton Wilson's *Prometheus Rising*. In his downtime, he was reading *Simulacra and Simulation* by Baudrillard, *Book of Pleasure* by Spare and *Eden, Eden, Eden* by Guyotat. He discovered that by pushing his mind with magickal practice and drugs, he was able to contact alien entities. At the time, these entities did say that they would return...

"Mr. K."

A distinguished gentleman, probably in his mid-50s and dressed in a designer blue suit, looked at K. while holding the back of the chair.

"Can I have a seat?"

K. looked at him stone faced. It wasn't the first time that he'd been cruised by a geezer. He nodded to the chair and resumed stuffing the eggs and ham into his mouth. See what this geezer has to offer, he thought, taking a sip of his pint of bitter to wash down the grease.

"Mr. K., yes I know who you are? We've been watching you, and think you would be a suitable candidate for a job opening we have with the Company. It's certainly a promotion from what you have now."

"Look mate," K. gestured with his fork, "Number one, I'm not a rent boy. Number two, who the fuck are you?"

"Sorry for not introducing myself, but I'm sure we may have met before. I'm the Doctor. And, I'm afraid that you misunderstand me." The Doctor placed a manila folder onto the table. "We are conducting an ongoing work, an experiment if you will. It's centered around the transmission of memes, the use of morphic resonance and morphic fields for their transmission and the utilization of waking dream-states or altered states of consciousness to tap into these transmissions. I can't go into details right now. It's all here in this folder."

K. picked the blood sausage from his teeth with

his tongue as he eyed the folder. He became interested in magick at a young age. He loved the idea of psychic attacks and peppered his workbooks with sigils that would charge when viewed or read. Later, he realized that most politicos and academics were essentially conservative, close-minded ideologues, no matter how radical their beliefs may be. He could take them out of their element by incorporating magickal theory in his discussions of Marx or Deleuze. Not one for just talk, he took action and dove into full experimentation of Austin Spare's sigils, the Enochian calls and the Abremelin working. He wanted to be well versed in all elements of combat, and these magickal weapons came in handy when he couldn't use his size twelve boots.

"Okay." This has State asset all over it, he thought.

"Any questions?"

"Will I be paid for this?"

"Of course, nothing comes free after all." The Doctor said with a chuckle, although there was no laughter in his eyes. "Don't worry, just come by my office. We'll discuss things further. All the information is right there in the folder." The Doctor stood up, ready to leave.

"And what if I'm not interested?" K. said, staring at the Doctor, arms crossed.

"You will be." He turned to leave. "Just read the file."

And he left the restaurant.

David Michael K. stood outside a closed curry take-out. Glancing up the street he noticed a pudgy man in hip clothes walking up the sidewalk towards him. A person K. recognized.

"That bastard!" K. hissed. It was Don Draper, an ex-comrade from Trotsky's Hammer. Draper had not clocked him yet and he took the opportunity to slide into the doorway. Draper was an elitist, a sexist, and an asshole. These qualities have taken him far up the Trotsky's Hammer hierarchy. K. was a member in his youth, before forming the Dumb Fucks, when he believed groups like this could lead the way for a revolutionary transformation of society. But their priority was the weekly paper sales they forced their members to do. Selling the party rag was considered a revolutionary act, and at each party meeting there would be a detailed account of the week's sales with each comrade describing who they sold to, who they almost sold to, who they would have liked to have sold to, and who they did not sell to. The women fulfilled their roles by serving coffee and taking notes. The meeting would draw to a close with an accounting of the money taken in from the paper sales and a red star pin presented to the person who sold the most.

The comrades would then withdraw to a local pub where they would argue the finer points of Trotsky, the Left Opposition and the Fourth International, while the female members stayed behind and took care of the children.

K. refused to participate in the paper sales and this made him a pariah among the party functionaries. He remembered an incident well.

"Where were you yesterday? There was a paper sale on Commercial?" Draper accused him in a loud voice, drawing the attention of other members in the room.

"Getting my new boots…" he said. Draper let out a whistle.

"Nice." He said sarcastically. "How much did they cost you?"

"40 quid."

"That much for boots? A bit extravagant, don't you think?" he commented, gesturing with his cup of designer coffee. "You can spend 40 dollars on boots, but you can't spare a couple of dollars for the dues box or bother to show up to the weekly sale. These are important activities. You will have to reexamine your life and determine your priorities."

A wave of disgust swept through K. as he resisted the urge to ram his fist into Draper's face. He was still young and intimidated by those in authority.

"I hear what you're saying," he said, deliberately, fixing a hard stare. "By the way, that Sawbucks coffee you have there. Isn't that a bourgeois luxury?"

He raised his eyebrows slightly, not understanding the accusation.

"Well, by buying a coffee from Sawbucks aren't you supporting a multinational company listed on the stock exchange and well known for its aggressive capitalist tendencies. A company that routinely exploits its workers, that pushes any local independent ventures out of a community to dominate unquestionably. Not to mention the issue of perpetuating the squalor of the Third World by forcing them to produce cash crops like coffee for the privileged Western world instead of food for their own people. So Don, how much did you pay for that coffee?"

Don shrugged his shoulders. "It's just coffee."

K. left the meeting and never returned. Now here was the fat fuck walking towards him, a cup of Sawbucks in hand. He stepped out to face him. Draper's face lightened with recognition as he saw K.

"David," he said smugly, lip curling into a sneer. "Dropped out of the struggle, I see."

K. answered by thrusting his size 12 Doc Martin boot hard into Draper's groin. The fat cunt lurched forward, face red, fingers crushing the paper cup, soaking his hand with hot coffee. A gurgled croak came from his throat as the air left his lungs. Grabbing his hair, K. slammed his knee into his face. He felt the nose collapse. As Don fell to the ground, K. took the opportunity to put the boots hard into the comrade's ribs, each kick landing with a satisfying thud. Standing back, he observed the twitching body of the ideologue, panting heavily, gurgling from the blood in his mouth and throat.

"Scum like you create power structures that mirror those of the dominant culture. You wield control in the name of the oppressed against the oppressed. Remember, the Bourgeoisie produces its own grave-diggers."

As if his body and mind were operating in automatic, he raised his leg up to near vertical as he executed a perfect ax kick down onto the back of the aging hack's neck, snapping it instantly. Satisfied, he nudged the lump of flesh on the sidewalk with his foot. However, what was the body of Don Draper now appeared to be the body of a large monkey with sunglasses. Looking closer, he recoiled as he saw the lump was actually Bingo from the Banana Splits. It was not a person in costume. The character bleeding out before him was real.

David Michael K. shoved his hands into his stapres and quickly walked up the street. He did not look back. He was afraid that thing would still be there if he did.

David Michael K. felt disoriented. First, the pink flying saucers, then the Doctor and the Building, and now Bingo. This was unusual for him. His practice had given him nerves of steel, but everything that had transpired over the last few days had caused a visceral reaction. If he had not carried out such intense experiments with psychedelics and occult ritual practice in his youth, he might have thought he was going crazy. Instead, he knew that he has entered a shamanic space as this feeling felt similar to DMT experiences from years ago. At that time, the entities he encountered under the influence informed him that they would come back to visit him periodically at unspecified times. He had no idea that they would manifest in this way. He navigated the streets by pure instinct, eyes closed, until he fell through the door of his flat.

"I just killed one of the Banana Splits" he spat, lying on the couch.

"You what?!" Cassie said, laughing. "Which one, goofball."

"Bingo."

"Good, he probably deserved it."

"I thought it was Don Draper."

"Either way. He had it coming." Cassie laughed even harder. She hated Draper from the old activist days. He resented her membership in S.C.U.M., because he knew that he had no chance to molest her on party retreats. She joined it to take the piss out of other so-called activists, especially men even though the organization's gender prejudice grated against her class consciousness. She tossed K. a warm Boddingtons.

"Drink up. Relax."

K. knew he just had to go with the experience. Ride it out and it would lead him to understanding. He put the Scotland vs. England Six Nations match on the TV and melted back into the couch.

"You got to see this!" Cassie shouted, pointing out the window.

Outside, the street was filled with a mob of clowns. More precisely, they were skinheads with clown makeup. Years ago, a number of gangs came together in their enthusiasm for the film *The Warriors*. Factions took up the looks of their fictional movie counterparts. Outside were the Turnbull Furies - an alliance between the Baseball Furies and the Turnbull ACs. Everyone else just called them the Clowns. He knew that the Clowns were controlling the drug trade throughout the North. He did not realize that they had made their way this far south.

"Did you buy anything from these freaks?" K. said to Cassie, surveying the street below.

Cassie shrugged. "Yeah, some hash. I needed some quick as I was doing some workings with Crowley and I wanted the right vibe." She muttered.

"They don't look too happy. Did you stiff them?"

"No! I just had to get physical with one of the blokes who wanted to take a bit more than my money."

"Fuck me." K. said. He never dealt with gangs when it came to drugs.

Too dangerous. Hippies were easier because they were all money and business, without the violence. That way, he could bring the violence if necessary.

K. cracked his fingers, gearing for the inevitable punch up. He nodded to Cassie, who was now holding a collapsible baton. She grinned. He knew she was ready for some violence.

There was a knock at the door. K. turned to Cassie. "Let's do this." He said, the excitement of an impending fight rising in every muscle. Cassie hurled open the door and swung her baton hard, anticipating a clown's head. The pleasant thud was the answer she was looking for.

"Take that, childfucker!"

As their eyes came into focus, K. and Cassie noticed that instead of a gang of clowns standing in their doorway, there was an attractive blond woman in a dark dress suit and her partner, a burly man who was now crumpled on the hall floor, blood pumping from his face.

"Don't you people look first before you hit somebody over the head." The woman said with a sneer.

"Fuck me." Cassie said, bewildered. "Who the fuck are you, then?"

"Yeah, what's a posh bird like you hanging around this part of town." K. laughed, eyeing the fit bird, imaging a round of sexual athletics with her, Cassie and himself.

"I'm Ms. Davenport. I'm an associate of the Doctor." She said. "He didn't want any distractions for you, so he arranged to pay off your drug debt. The clowns want to assert a sense of authority and control. But, don't worry, it's just theatre."

"Oh, we weren't worried at all." K. said. "How did you know about Cassie's situation?

"We know things, Mr. K. It's our job. And before you feel the need to indulge, think twice about who you associate with." She said with a sideways glance to Cassie.

"We'll be seeing you, Mr. K." Ms. Davenport kicked the man, who was stumbling to stand. He held a now blood soaked handkerchief over his face. "Walk it off." She said dismissively. The two disappeared down the hallway and into the staircase.

"That was fucking odd."

"Well, they're gone." Cassie said, looking back out the window. "But they've left a calling card."

On the sidewalk was a very large set of balloons twisted to resemble a hand with two fingers raised.

"Yeah, up yours, too."

K. stared out the window of the Marine Pub, a quiet place where he could go, have a pint and think. The more he thought about the Doctor, the more believed that he was being groomed as a State asset. The psycho-dynamics and the magickal nature of the work were interesting, but there was something a bit dodgy about the whole thing. As if there was something more to it all. Something he was not being told.

Also, the strange visions he had been having lately had him unnerved. He had read somewhere that being held in captivity can sometimes induce hallucinations. That's what he felt like. There was something definitely claustrophobic about the place, he thought. Also, he could not shake an intense feeling of déjà vu…

"Mind if I join you?" David Michael's train of thought was interrupted by a well-dressed woman, probably late forties, long black hair. He gestured with a nod to the chair opposite him. She sat down still looking at him. "I've been in this country for a couple of days but I haven't had any excitement yet."

"Oh, really?"

"My husband is over here for business. It's just meetings and more meetings, not that it matters. He just cares about the Company."

David Michael looked the woman over. Attractive and stylish, she resembled an upper class version of Leila Waddell in an odd sort of way. He was not normally attracted to posh birds but he was intrigued.

"That's too bad, a woman like you left all alone. What's your name?" He felt something between his legs. He looked down and saw her shoeless foot. Her toes massaged his groin through his pants.

"Let's not complicate things." She said, smiling. "I'm staying close by, in the Boleskine Hotel."

David Michael K. surveyed the posh suite. The woman closed and locked the door. Turning around, she had a fiery look in her eye.

"No one to bother us here for a while." the woman said, walking over to the bed. David Michael, reading her mind, began to take off his sta-pres, exposing his red underwear. His passion for red underwear was an old habit from when he was younger, and fell into a life-stylist mode of political expression. After years of street fighting and hardcore politics he realized the fetishising of material symbols placed one into a dogmatic box. While this can be used tactically to bring dominant culture symbols into disrepute, he now expressed his beliefs through action, which he was going to do now by getting a good blowjob. The posh bird understood what he wanted as he leaned back slightly. Pulling down the Y-fronts, she took his hardening cock into her mouth. Swirling her tongue around the head before plunging the whole member down her throat. She started to hum, the trembling of her lips sending shivers through David Michael's body. Starting from his cock up to the base of his neck. From her exceptional technique, he felt his chakras opening one by one. He wanted it to last longer so he grabbed her by the hair and pulled her head up.

"What's the matter?" she inquired.

He didn't answer but grabbed his belt and strapped it around his neck. Then he tied the opposite end around the headboard of the bed. David Michael could feel his face become flushed from the pressure around his neck. She removed her clothes, frigging herself as he got ready. When he had finished his adjustments, she began to work again on his swollen member. David Michael got a nice surprise as she stuck one finger, then two, up to the second knuckle into his arse. No need for lubrication as that was provided by the sweat. David Michael lied back to enjoy the sound of Psychic TV's 'Infinite Beat' looping through his brain. It was the perfect tune to be blown to while working astral and neural pathways. With the strains of this tune going through his head, it did not take long for the million year old DNA codes to unravel and before long he was out on the mud flats. He came back to reality with the woman stroking his cock, his genetic wealth spraying over his stomach.

"You didn't take it in your mouth!?" David Michael said, untying the belt from his neck.

"Why?"

"So, I can taste myself when I kiss you."

David Michael ignored this obvious breach of sexual etiquette, as it was time to continue with the sexual athletics. The posh bird walked over to the window and stood there naked. She opened the window and leaned out, her breasts resting against the sill.

"I liked to be watched," She said, "Unfortunately, my husband doesn't share this passion. While he can talk big with the cronies at the Company, he's actually sexually self-conscious and awkward. That's why I always like a bit of trade when I can get it."

David Michael nodded approval with a wry grin and settled in behind her, kneeling on the floor, his face between her cheeks. He poked his tongue into her hole then down to her clit in one long fluid motion. She moved her hips in response, all the time watching the people on the street below.

David Michael stood up and guided his still hard member into her, thrusting deep as she gave a shout. He continued to pump vigorously, slapping her backside and peering over her shoulders to see how many people had gathered below. Most people did not notice the couple above. Some, who did, pretended they were not there. Others stopped to watch the action, leaning against the storefront windows across the street, drinking coffee and talking about the latest Six Nations match.

She met his thrusts with enthusiasm. Her tight cunt told him that her husband did not take care of her in the sex department. A job he didn't mind doing. He looked over to the night table and noticed a novel, *Prelude to an Orgasm* by Michael Roth. He had never read Roth before, avoiding popular literature meant for pseudo-intellectual snobs.

"Time for a change." She pushed him back onto the bed, and pinned his arms down before mounting him. She rode him hard.

For a second time, he left his body and traversed the familiar mud flats a million years away. In this altered state, he noticed that the room was actually a representation of late nineteenth century London and that various personal effects were situated geographically where the victims of Jack the Ripper would have been. The woman began to chant the 18th Enochian aether and David Michael could sense the air around him begin to ripple. Soon the room disappeared altogether and the two of them were in a dark alley. Undeterred by the cold, damp pavement, the woman continued to fuck him hard and he responded in kind.

He could feel the genetic material welling up in his cock when suddenly he was brought back to present time by a loud crash. The window had shattered, spraying shards of glass onto the floor and across their naked bodies. Something else whistled past his head and into the wall with a thud.

"Take cover, we're being shot at!" the posh bird shouted, rolling to the side, K. jumping with her. Two more shots ricocheted around the room before becoming imbedded in the wall.

"What the hell's going on."

"Someone's taking shots at us, obviously trying to kill one or both of us." She said.

What a waste, David Michael thought as he looked at his limp cock and the dribble of cum seeping from the tip.

K. opened the door to his flat. The first thing he

saw was Cassie's face, eyes staring hard.

"This a mate of yours." She growled. K. looked past her to see a tall, well-dressed man lounging on the sofa. He grunted a no.

"Who the fuck are you then?" he said, walking past Cassie.

"I'm Magus." he said. "Sorry to be a bother, but I believe we know someone in common."

"Who?"

"The Doctor." Magus continued. "I believe you were, and no doubt still are, whether you know it or not, part of the experiment. Once you're in, you stay in. There's a saying around the Building - you don't leave it, it leaves you. Unless you know where the exits are. Metaphorically, of course."

"What are you talking about?"

"He's been rambling like this since he got here." Cassie said. "Told him to fuck off but he insisted he knew you. I threatened to punch him in the throat if he kept it up."

She sat in the kitchen chair, throwing her feet up on the table. "This all about that job? Easy money, you said." Cassie sat back with her copy of *Medical Apartheid*.

"Yeah." K. drawled, not taking his eyes off the other man in the room.

"I've recently escaped from the Building and the good Doctor. And I've come to get you out as well."

Now K. became interested. He joined Magus, sitting in a chair across from him. Magus held out his hand as introduction to K., who ignored the gesture. Magus sat back on the couch and continued.

"You've read the documentation, right? You've met the Doctor, right? Well this experiment was actually to test some magickal weapons. See how they would work in population control and compliance, civilian defense, black ops ... well the list goes on. The scope is broad and the applications are many. To put it crudely, these are magickal weapons to attack on an astral plane, or shamanic space or magickal realm or whatever you want to call it. Of course, we know that there is no true separation between the magickal and consensual reality. It's just a matter of perspective."

"So what's this got to do with me?" K. said.

"See, in this experiment, you are the Heirophant." Magus said, handing him the corresponding card from the Thoth deck. "They needed an enforcer. You know how things can get chaotic quite quickly sometimes in a ritual space, astrally or physically. Your role was to keep things in line."

"Let me guess, you're the Magus."

Magus nodded affirmative with a slight bow.

"I had the feeling that I was being recruited to be a State asset." K. said.

"The only thing wrong with that is the Building and the experiment are beyond the State." Magus said.

"Right. Why don't we just head over to the Building and give the good Doctor what he has coming to him. Then we burn the whole place down." K. said. He always advocated direct action over sitting around talking.

"I must urge discretion. As you may already know, the Building is a golem. It's watching our every move. So we don't have long."

"Well, how long is this going to take?"

Magus shrugged. K. got up and grabbed a couple of Boddingtons from the fridge. He offered one to Magus. Magus declined with a slight wave of his hand.

"You don't drink?"

"Of course not."

"You a church society teetotaler type, are you? 'Cause if you are, I don't want anything to do with you."

"No, no. I don't imbibe any beverage. Or food for that matter. Or…"

K. regarded him quizzically.

"I'm sorry, Mr. K." Magus said, "You didn't think I was real, did you? I don't really exist."

K. leaned back in his chair. He knew it was going to be a long night.

Cassie pressed her finger to David's lips. David stepped back, out of sight as she opened the door into a posh reading hall. He surveyed the hallway. There were lots of dark wood and portraits in oil hanging on the walls. Smell of stale rot hung in the air.

"Are my guests here?" Barbara Radford Salisbury, bestselling author of royal romances said, straightening her trademark pink dress. The 95 year-old woman was awaiting the arrival of some members of the lesser nobility for tea. With any luck, one of the young Dukes would be convinced to strip and flog his member for her, all research for an upcoming book, of course. She never lacked volunteers to molest her thin, wrinkled body. People knew she was well connected with the royal family and would bow to her whims on the off chance she would put in a word for them with the Queen.

"There has been a slight change of plans, mum." Cassie said, entering the room.

"Oh, the young Duke couldn't make it?" Salisbury stated, day dreaming about the 18 year-olds hard body before becoming annoyed, swinging her thin arm toward her servant's face. "What am I to do now!?"

"Die." Cassie growled.

On cue, David Michael entered the room, cracking his knuckles, staring down the old tart.

"Your books have poisoned the minds of working class women with bourgeois fairy tales, convincing them to turn against their own class to aspire to the ideals of another class whose aims are contrary to their own. You are highly recognized in the literary world. We seek nothing less than the destruction of this occult establishment and to extinguish the stench of literature once and for all."

"My word, what is the meaning of all this!" turning to the young woman for an explanation.

The woman's answer was in the carving knife she had unsheathed and thrust into the wrinkled white face. Salisbury shuttered a last shallow breath as the knife penetrated her eye socket and buried itself into her brain. A thin arc of blood pumped from the wound over the maid's uniform. Having recovered from the momentary shock of murdering her former master, the maid proceeded to stab the withered corpse repeatedly, memories of years of humiliation and abuse finally being released. She had planned to sell the corpse to the Man/Corpse Love Society for further humiliation. She remembered the contact sputtering over the phone "Ah, we've never had a posh bird like that before!" Now, it was all but useless.

David Michael grabbed Salisbury's books and

piled them on the floor. In an instant, they were a blaze. Cassie tossed the bloody knife into the fire and tore off her bloody uniform.

"Show me another rich cunt, and I'll stick her too." she muttered.

David wanted to fuck her right there in the growing pool of blood and meat.

"Wake up, David Michael K."

ABATTOIR
William Whitehouse

Mary met him on the bridge near her flat, under a treacherous sky like a dirty bruise. Her period had just ended and she'd celebrated with a handful of pills. None of her friends had answered her phone calls; maybe they were out already, in which case she'd bump into them eventually. But she suspected that they were in fact, simply not answering the phone, avoiding her. She was becoming needy. She decided to walk for a while on her own, then check out a few clubs when they opened for the nightly meat-trade.

"In this city everyone preys on everyone else," she thought, adjusting the dark glasses which she habitually affected as they hid the bags that had grown beneath her eyes. She liked to think the glasses made her seem almost tragic, like a doomed heroine in a film-noir. No! She decided she wasn't tragic. She was predatory – a nocturnal beast, never waking up until at least four in the afternoon, just like her friends and acquaintances whom she only ever saw after dark. Vampires. She was glad she'd left her job, even though the money was starting to get tight.

Half of the world's human population is infected with Toxoplasma, parasites in the body-and the brain.

Remember that. Toxoplasma gondii is a common parasite found in the guts of cats; it sheds eggs that are picked up by rats and other animals that are eaten by cats. Toxoplasma forms cysts in the bodies of the intermediate rat hosts, including in the brain.

He was standing with his back to her – short blonde hair, tight arse. Once upon a time she had suffered from chronic shyness, but years of drink, drugs and casual sex had given her the predatory, self-assured character that she had always admired in women. She walked over and stood next to him as he swiveled a face as placid as an insect's towards her. "What's your name?" she asked – not really interested – just a formality.

"Johnny..." he grinned, playing her game. Joining in, following the rules on an autonomic level, she reached over and brushed a fly from the corner of his mouth. She knew that wasn't his name, but the lie actually reassured her.

His teeth looked quite sharp and glistened in the streetlight like those of a deep sea angler fish. She realized, with some surprise, that she violently wanted this man and it surprised her. Men, for her, were nothing more than an idle pastime – a habit long since emptied of any real pleasure, which came more and more often from a bottle or from pills.

Since cats don't want to eat dead, decaying prey, Toxoplasma takes the evolutionarily sound course of being a "good" parasite, leaving the rats perfectly healthy. Or are they? Oxford scientists discovered that the minds of the infected rats have been subtly altered. In a series of experiments, they demonstrated that healthy rats will prudently avoid areas that have been doused with cat urine. In fact, when scientists test anti-anxiety drugs on rats, they use a whiff of cat urine to induce neurochemical panic.

Beneath the bridge, shopping trolleys lay rusting in the mud of the riverbank. Drained of former associations and context, they had become abstractions, devoid of meaning – manifestations from the collective unconscious of a city that had been drained of feelings. Under a broken neon advert that read 'L VE S X,' a lurid spray-painted voodoo face watched them inscrutably.

"Buy me a drink..." she said, putting her hand on his crotch. Beneath the material of his jeans, she felt him respond, and was delighted to find he was quite well hung. In the darkening sky above the factories, a black kite fell like a wounded bird – a sudden flurry of sewer rats in the dark green water of the river below.

"Do you often pick up strangers?" he asked, a lupine grin twitching the corner of his mouth.

"I don't believe in wasting time on bullshit," she smiled in a way she hoped looked seductive but which felt lopsided on her face, her tongue thick from the drugs.

"What ever happened to safe sex?" he asked.

"No point in that is there? Like alcohol free lager."

He stared piercingly at her for a second, then, seeming to have made up his mind, took her wrist roughly. On the palm of his hand she saw a tattoo of a double swastika designed to resemble a black sun.

"Let's have that drink..."

As they left the bridge, the dying sun tinged the clouds of industrial smog purple. Sodium lights came on here and there. At the entrance to an Underground station, the chaffing noise of the rubber handrail pattered ghost-words into the back of her tripping brain. An automatic advertisement hoarding changed at intervals and, for a second, she thought she glimpsed the black solar design she'd seen on his arm.

However, it turns out that Toxoplasma-ridden rats show no such reaction. In fact, some of the infected rats actually seek out the cat urine-marked areas again and again. The parasite alters the mind (and thus the behavior) of the rat for its own benefit. If the parasite can alter rat behavior, does it have any effect on humans?

In her flat, he impaled her brutally with no attempt at giving her pleasure. The sweat ran from her numb body as he treated her like a slab of meat. This was what she really wanted – annihilation, pure and beautiful. She slipped into and out of a blank space beyond awareness, each blow penetrating to her core, removing sensitivity until she felt as drained as a black sun...

......her eyes shot tracer lines.......

.........a dark halo appearing behind his head, pouring over them like ink,

the bed rolling like an ocean of jelly as she blacked out.

Her last impression was of his jaws opening impossibly wide....then a vision of rows of carcasses swinging on hooks. She smelled blood and woke gagging at the taste of her own bitten-through tongue.

Dr. Torrey got together with the Oxford scientists, to see if anything could be done about those parasite-controlled rats that were driven to hang around cat urine-soaked corners (waiting for cats). According to a recent press release, haloperidol restores the rat's healthy fear of cat urine. In fact, antipsychotic drugs were as effective as pyrimethamine, a drug that specifically eliminates Toxoplasma.

When clarity reasserted itself, her whole body was aching as though she had severe sunburn. The sheets were sticky with her own blood. Something reptilian and insect-like moved in the back of her brain with sticky little feet. Storm clouds gathered in the muscles of her cramped thighs and shoulders. There was no sign of her date. There was also no trace of semen (for which she was grateful).

As she tried to sit upright, she was violently

sick. Her whole torso had been tattooed with snakes and black solar images. In the centre of the design were two figures joined together like an alchemical Rebis.

When at last her stomach settled she decided to look around the flat to see if he'd walked off with anything. Not that she had much – some CDs, a handful of books and a shell-collection. She rolled up the bed-sheets disgustedly, throwing them in the bin by the door. Then, glancing up, she noticed that the door was still locked from the inside and sudden visceral terror hit her in the guts. She put a hand over her mouth to keep from screaming, realizing that the lunatic was still in her flat.

Her first impulse was to open the door and leave but the noise of slowly running water from the bathroom drew her. She'd not noticed it before, probably because she'd been throwing up. If he was still in there she could lock him in and have a better chance of escape. Someone who tattooed your body while you slept was bound to be at least a little dangerous.

Still not sure that parasites can manipulate the behavior of host organisms? Consider these other cases: The lancet fluke Dicrocoelium dendriticum forces its ant host to attach to the tips of grass blades, the easier to be eaten. The fluke needs to get into the gut of a grazing animal to complete its life cycle. The fluke Euhaplorchis californiensis causes fish to shimmy and jump so wading birds will grab them and eat them, for the same reason. Hairworms, which live inside grasshoppers, sabotage the grasshopper's central nervous system, forcing them to jump into pools of water, drowning themselves. Hairworms then swim away from their hapless hosts to continue their life cycle.

As quietly as she could, she crept to the bathroom door which was slightly ajar, and reached for the handle. Her hands shook so badly that she fumbled and accidentally pushed it wide open.

He was hanging from a water pipe by a piece of wire that cut deeply into his throat. His tongue protruded blackly.

She sat numbly for a while, unable to think. After some time she decided to cut him down. She severed the wire with some pliers and dumped his body onto the tiled floor of the shower unit, but his weight made her overbalance and fall and for several seconds she lay with her face mere inches from his... her attention sucked into the vacuum of his dead eyes.

In a blind panic she hurled herself backwards across the floor, smacking her shoulder against a water pipe. Hauling herself up, and gripping the sides of the sink tightly, she began to throw up again. Looking into the mirror above the sink, she saw her retina split laterally ....

.............revealing a space – blank – void of substance inhabited only by a rippling magnetism....

Within her, new matrices began to form, new co-ordinates to mesh, new juxtapositions to fix.

The stars above her formed a cipher unlocked by her pain and his death.

The indices of her identity crumbled, pouring from her ruptured eyes to the surface of the mirror like crispy insects, overwhelming her with myriad images...

She heard the beating of titan wings, the roaring of flames as she crossed the threshold of being and a strangely familiar faceless face vaster than time loomed over her...

Her yearning was finally answered by the extinction she'd desired so badly.

A new head protruded from the wound and shed her the way a snake sheds its skin, dripping wet from its birth. The old husk whispered to the floor.

Johnny looked in the mirror at his new beautiful face - serene, cold and hungry.

Later he left the flat, it would be days before anyone came looking for her – and what would they find? Something barely resembling a human.

His new face was the sort that people didn't remember – too perfect, with no clearly distinguishing features. He could be a thousand different people.

He turned left at the end of the street and passed a builder's yard. Silence trickled down the walls, laying in coils at the bottom. Two large Dobermans in the yard sprang into action, barking and throwing themselves against the wire mesh of the gate. He smiled and placed his palms against the wire. The dogs began to lick his hands.

In her flat, the tap dripped...............

"He reached past my shoulders with a rod. I felt a shocking, unbearable pain. The room blacked out as if a switch had been thrown... I was split apart by it; for the moment I was masterless.

The pain left, leaving only its searing memory behind. Before I could speak, or even think coherently for myself, the splitting away had ended and I was again safe in the arms of my master...

The panic that possessed me washed away; I was again filled with an unworried sense of well being...

"What are you?"

"We are the people... We have studied you and we know your ways... We come," I went on, "to bring you peace... and contentment-and the joy of-of surrender." I hesitated again; "surrender" was not the right word. I struggled with it the way one struggles with a poorly grasped foreign language.

"The joy," I repeated, "-the joy of . . .nirvana." That was it; the word fitted. I felt like a dog being patted for fetching a stick; I wriggled with pleasure."

(The Puppet Masters – Robert Heinlein)

IN THE SHADOW OF THE FISH
D M Mitchell

Entering Seraphis, The Assassin dreamed again of the great fish – its enormous wooden jaws opening and closing, moved on brass hinges and supported with sticks by a milling throng of worshippers. Its great glass eyes rolled freely on swiveling supports and he shuddered involuntarily whenever the beast's gaze chanced in his direction. Gongs and sistra assailed his sleeping ears and smoke stung his nostrils as the chanting, undulating procession passed him. The sides of the Fish were dilapidated as if through much use and he could make out lights moving inside. For a brief moment he fancied the Fish was an enormous moving city filled with inhabitants going about their business. He awoke to the smell of strawberries, sweating, and instinctively felt for his guns.

Molten light poured in at a window, blinding him. He groped for the mirrored glasses he found himself relying on more and more, and fixed them over his clear pupil-less pink eyes. Relieved of the worst of the glare, he got up and walked, naked to the window, strapping on his gun belt as he walked. Across the street the doors of the Midas

Touch Saloon were swinging, indicating (as the street was empty) that someone had just gone inside. He'd need to go across there soon. He had no idea when the Sisters would catch up with him and had no desire to be taken by surprise.

The young boy-girl creature was still asleep in the corner under its filthy blanket. Its crimson hair spilled across its chalk white shoulders and The Assassin saw the blood-red gills on its neck move as the creature dreamed. He had no idea where the thing had come from, how old it was or if it had ever had a name. It could neither speak nor write. After leaving Thebes in disgrace, it had appeared outside the circle of illumination cast by his campfire, its huge fish-eyes staring at him. He'd offered it food which it had refused, seemingly grateful merely for the warmth. In the morning he'd taken it with him. He'd soon discovered that it fed on semen, with which he'd been happy to supply it.

He pulled the blanket from it, exposing its small breasts, and pushed it with his foot. It rolled over, opened its eyes and yawned. He indicated his erect penis with one hand and the thing crawled across, fastening its mouth around his thick shaft, milking him expertly.

When it had finished and sat there licking its fingers, he dressed in his dirty black clothes, fastened on his spurs (like some fighting cock) and placed his wide-brimmed hat atop his head. The boy-girl followed him sleepily out into the cruel sunlight. Flies buzzed. From somewhere near came a smell of shit. The street was deserted; a sign of impending violence if ever there were one. A slight movement to his left caught his attention; someone fastening their shutters at the sight of him. The Sisters had arrived already, then. He unclipped his holsters, slid the guns out and back in to ensure their free movement and turned to the Midas.

At the door, he gestured to the hermaphrodite with his chin. The thing walked across and crouched beneath a water-trough, chin on knees, the double set of genitals touching the dust. He shoved open the doors.

It was impenetrably murky inside, sawdust on the floor, "Sweet Dreams Baby" playing on a jukebox somewhere. Several hands of death-cards and a half empty bottle lay on the table nearest him. He gazed around, grinning in spite of himself. Cliché heaped upon cliché. A pungent scent like cat piss, sharp and acrid, wafted from the back of the room. He liked that for its sharpness, hated whatever was dull and vague and nebulous. This was a good sharp, clear day, a good day for dying.

He upended the bottle without looking at it. His senses were assailed more sharpness, the smell of wormwood. Ok. He was in the mood, now. He liked this feeling. He enjoyed killing. It removed uncertainties from the world.

Overturned chairs, a lingering wisp of cigar smoke, more abandoned drinks. This saloon was popular. The owner, an ex-Vegas Mafioso , had the magical gift for business, the alchemist's touch for making shit into gold.

Above him were quiet footsteps. He sank as far into the shadows as they would allow, one gun drawn and ready. A scent of lavender like some little old granny's front room. From where he stood, he could see most of the first floor balcony in the large mirror over the bar. The staircase was out of view. His breathing shallowed. They knew he was here.

Arms around each others' shoulders, the three sisters shuffled slowly across the landing, their long black dresses dragging the dust. Beneath their little old lady hats, black veils obscured their faces – Mercifully. They vanished at the farthest extremity of the mirror. The Assassin knew he had to split them up, if he were to have any chance. Outside, in the dust, a horse whinnied in terror; confused hoof-falls. The Sisters' steps faltered. He imagined them there frozen, smelling for him and decided to make his move.

Slowly and softly out through the rear door into a back room, across to the exit and thence to the back alleyway. Locked. He cursed silently. He couldn't let them find him here, cornered like a shithouse rat. Moving quickly, he kicked the door open and slid like a shadow outside. As the reverberations died away, he heard a noise from within as though someone were shaking a huge wet canvas out. They were onto him.

He ducked into the next building and waited. Almost immediately, he heard scuffing and snorting reminding him of the great brass bulls he'd tamed so many months ago. For a moment, he worried about the boy-girl but quickly put it from his thoughts. He had enough trouble pressing. He wished the sisters would talk to each other, but they never seemed to need to. Then, he grinned, revealing too many teeth, sharp like those of a shark, grouped in several rows. The Sisters had split up, one left, one right, the other more than likely straight up. He realized this was the only chance he was likely to get.

He opened the door, aimed and fired in one mercurial movement. His aim, as ever, was perfect. The black clad shape was thrown against the wooden wall of the saloon, cut almost in half across the stomach by his shot.

The figure slid down the wall leaving a broad red swathe on the white painted surface. Hitting the ground, it began to scream like a cat, kicking and clawing at the ground with great steel claws emerging birdlike from the sleeves of its dress.

"Gabriel!"

He spun round. Another of the Sisters faced him, arms stretched to either side of the alley, blocking his exit in that direction. Her veil had fallen away revealing a beautiful female face.

"Alecto, leave this now. This can't end well!" he croaked in a voice little used. The creature cocked its head.

"Say first, did you kill your mother or did you not?"

Her voice spilled from her like music.

"Yes. I killed her. There should be no denial of that."

"So, then how did you kill her? You are bound to say."

"I cut her throat." His face was expressionless..

Alecto was slowly drawing closer, dragging her long hooked fingernails along the walls. Curled shavings of wood fell to the dirt.

"By whose persuasion and advice did you this?"

"Oh fuck off! I've got a headache!"

White hot nuggets of lead followed a deadly trajectory. Alecto was faster, throwing aside the black dress as she leaped a great leap over his head. Black bat wings spreading wide, a flash of steel talons at hand and foot like a great eagle's and a sharp pain raked the side of his head as she passed over.

Fenton fell to the dust holding the side of his head. The ear was still there but the gash was very deep. He rolled over onto his back as Alecto made another pass. She veered away to avoid his gunshot, opened her black mouth enormously wide and screamed with a sound like the rending of metal. Atop her white face, snakes writhed.

And now the third Sister joined her. They swooped and circled just out of reach, waiting their chance. He risked a glance to the side; the building next to him was raised with a two foot crawlspace. He had three bullets left before he'd need to reload. Bad odds. He decided to sacrifice another bullet. They veered crazily to avoid it and he dived for the gap, just making it, scuttling along under the rotten wood like a crab. Claws struck the dirt a fraction of a second after he'd reached safety.

"Come on sweethearts. Come in and get me."

They screeched in their fury and it was enough to freeze a man's blood. Breaking glass and rending wood. They had vile tempers. He smiled but at the same time realized he was losing blood.

The wooden fish head snapped at him in the darkness. Cold enclosed him. He tried to stand and banged his head. It brought him back from his delirium. It took him several more minutes to reorient himself, then he wriggled towards the light coming from the far side of the building.

A voice – one of the Sisters;

"So, here the man has left a clear trail behind..." The other side of the building. Good. The light stung his eyes and he realized he'd lost his glasses. Squinting, he slipped from cover and ran across the alley to the blacksmith's forge. A huge iron wheel stood propped against the rear wall, manacles attached to it at intervals. Fenton ducked through the workshop into the house at the back. As he opened the door, three people turned to look at him, one of them a huge man with almost no neck, his skin scarred and cured like leather, tartar eyes like black flints. A woman and an older man also sat at the table. The blacksmith stood up.

"Take your dirty business out of my house, stranger!"

"Certainly," smiled Fenton. "But you won't mind if I use your other door?" The man growled moving forwards, muscles rippling like a tiger's. Fenton saw the shadow on the window before anyone else even glimpsed it. He fell to the floor, reloaded gun in his hand as the window shattered inwards. The woman screamed and fell backwards, hands to her eyes; countless glass shards making her look like a porcupine. The dark Sister flew in and the giant man bellowed, shovel-like hands closing on one leg and a great wing. Despite his enormous physical prowess, the Sister cut him to ribbons. Fenton was amazed at how much blood the man must have had in his huge body. And how much a person could lose and still go on struggling. Finally the man swayed and his grip seemed to relax. Fenton, who had stood watching with amused fascination, raised his gun and emptied it indiscriminately into giant and Sister alike. By the time he had finished there was a jigsaw puzzle in flesh for whoever cared to try to solve it.

Blood.

There was always blood.

The Great Fish turned and he could smell its breath now. The music of the worshippers was almost deafening.

He looked down at the ruined bodies in front of him. There was still the last Sister to deal with before he could leave this town. His guns were empty. The mutilated woman lay on the floor screaming, blood pouring between her fingers. The old man merely whimpered, staring at him in abject terror. He filled the chambers of his guns, counted out his remaining bullets. He decided he could afford to be merciful. A bullet through the woman's head stopped her noise. He smiled at the old man and opened the back door.

The street was empty. Quiet. He stepped out.

Not five paces from the door he was knocked flat to the ground by an immense force, both guns spinning from nerveless hands. As his gaze cleared he found himself staring into the inhumanly beautiful face of the last Sister. She had him pinned to the ground, her mouth inches away from his. She licked his face.

"I expected to taste guilt on you, murderer. But it is a feeling alien to you, am I right?"

"I have no guilt. I go about the world doing the God's work. I kill only at his decree or to defend myself from those who would harm or impede me."

"This God of yours. Is he flesh? Does he speak to you with a mouth or with noises in your brain?"

"He is as solid as you or I. He showed me the films of my mother and her crimes. Crimes there were no possibility of bringing to human account. I did the God's bidding."

"You know that we Sisters are answerable to no God with a cock? That we are of the Mother and defenders of the Tree that springs from her womb?"

"My earthly mother had no womb. I sprang from no womb. I was ejected from her bowels in a stream of running shit. She was no woman and gave up any right to be called so, long before my lamentable birth."

The Sister stared for a while, eyes golden,

flecked with green. She shifted her weight and Fenton found he could move one hand. He slid it down his stomach between them until he touched her crotch beneath her black dress. She made no protest. Gaining a handful of material, he drew the dress upwards, bit by bit until he could touch her skin. She wore no garment underneath the dress. His hand touched her warm cunt. He was relieved to find it wet and parted easily to his exploring hand. She hissed and her split tongue emerged again, swollen.

Suddenly in a flurry of movement she rolled over, dragging him on top, her hands scrabbling at his trousers. His cock emerged erect and she clutched it tightly, almost shoving it into her cunt. There in the dust with the frightened townspeople watching from behind shuttered windows, he fucked the last of his pursuers to exhaustion.

He left by sundown, the boy-girl trailing a few paces behind him. The sun made his shadow long before him. He never liked traveling east but the West contained a past from which he was fleeing.

After leaving the sisters he travelled towards _____ for three days, through the mountains of _____. It was at the end of the second day that he realised he was being hunted. Three figures on horseback, not making any efforts to conceal themselves, dogged him along the horizon. To be so brazen, they must be good, he realised. He slowed down to give them a chance to catch up. Good or not, they didn't stand a chance.

The boy/girl, as ever, trailed several paces behind him peering through the curtain of its hair. It had begun to annoy him and he had considered eating it. Perhaps he could sell it or give it to some whore as payment. It would be a long time though, before he reached anywhere where he could indulge either of those options.

He detoured behind the first large outcrop of rock that he thought would suit his purpose and set to making a fire, not for the heat but as a lure for his pursuers. Placing a small metal cube on the rock he passed his left hand over it and flames erupted out, forming a globular mass of flame almost five feet in diameter. Next he would need a tulpa.

He focused on a point somewhere above the top of his head. There was a liquid 'click' in his neck just below the atlas vertebra and he took two steps backwards. He found himself looking at his own back. The tulpa took considerable energy to sustain but this one wouldn't be needed for long. He pointed to the hermaphrodite which sat near the fire, obediently. Then he unslung his bags and removed a series of metal tubes which he assembled into a long-barrelled gun. He wished he hadn't lost his mirror-shades in his tousles with the Eumenides. The light hurt his eyes.

I took them two hours to reach his camp-fire; longer than he had expected and he was drained by the exertion of maintaining the tulpa, which was why he didn't at first notice that only two of his pursuers were below him. Normally he wouldn't have opened fire until all three were visible, but exhaustion tipped his hand. As the tulpa faded and his pursuers realised they had walked into a trap he blew one man's brains out and shot the other through the crotch. Then he cursed as he realised he was a man short.

Leaping from rock to rock he reached the man rolling on the ground in a pool of his own blood and shredded intestines and genitals.

"Where's your friend?" he asked.

"For god's sake, kill me" the man pleaded.

"I have drugs here that can keep you alive for days." Said the assassin, "without lessening your pain in any way."

"I don't know. Don't even know who he is. We were paid to follow you. We were told that's all we had to do – he was sent to do the rest." The man moaned.

"Ok. Thanks," said The Assassin and fired point blank. The man's head disappeared above the lower jaw.

The Assassin looked around at the rocks rising on either side of him. Silence – unnatural silence. Not an insect song, no birds or animals, he realised he was in deep trouble. He gestured to the hermaphrodite to take cover. It scuttled on all fours behind some large basalt formations.

A pain hit him in the pit of his stomach, as though his internal organs were rubbing against each other. Something wet hit the back of his hand and he knew it was blood from his nose without even looking down. The rocks beyond him rippled and he realised he was about to be hit by the waves of an infrasound shock.

There was no defence, no escape. He nevertheless threw himself down on the ground as the sonic attack ripped through him, forcing the vomit from his mouth in an acid spray. He dug his fists into his eyes to keep them from being ruptured or popping from the sockets. His eardrums had long ago succumbed to the tortures of countless enemies and replaced by Kevlar implants. He instinctively dropped the input levels to zero, but the shock was too low to be heard anyway. It was something only felt at a visceral level.

Time ceased to exist in the realm of agony and dislocation he had entered.

He rolled over and looked up into the most beautiful inhuman face he had ever seen, gold and green lights flickering over exquisite scales like masterly beaten copper. Small slanted eyes stared at him above cheekbones that were almost shelves, the eyes golden, split vertically by thin black pupils. He could only see the face framed by a hood of some soft dark green material. The rest of the body was concealed beneath a cloak. Behind this vision of inhuman exquisite loveliness was a black diminutive figure whose skin crawled with worms of blue orgone energy, its otherwise blank oval of a face punctuated by huge compound eyes like those of an insect. It had hit him with an infrasound blast from its sonic core. He realised he was lucky he hadn't been targeted by the creature's D.O.R. (deadly orgone radiation) system.

"Echidne of the Snakes, mother of monsters," he managed to croak out to his enemy above him. "Grim Echidna, a nymph who dies not nor grows old all her days."

"And you, my ugly little friend, feeder of carrion, ravisher of women, matricide, defier of gods. We meet again. And yet again my hands are bound and you must live. And still the injustice against my sex goes unpunished."

The Assassin pushed himself to a sitting position.

"You've been slumming, haven't you?" he indicated the Black Dwarf. "What service did you provide that you were given a thing such as that?"

Echidne smiled a smile that would make most men come and shit their pants at the same time.

"I was given it by someone who wants to see you fucked as badly as I do, but for now the three sisters have you woven into their tapestry so I'll just content myself with making your life as miserable as possible."

She opened her cloak. Beneath it she was naked and her sinuous body moved as though it were boneless. Two long, dark green serpents twined around her limbs, their heads fastened to her breasts.

"These children of mine have been suckling on my venom for a long time, and my venom has been infused with thoughts of you my old lover. Here, meet your children!"

She plucked first one and then the other and tossed them onto his lap. He froze as they insinuated themselves towards his face.

"They are imbued with a toxin that will send you into agonies of sexual rapture that will last for days; lip-froth of Cerberus, the Echidna's venom, wild deliriums, blindnesses of the brain, and crime and tears, and maddened lust for murder; all ground up, mixed with fresh blood, boiled in a pan of bronze, and stirred with a green hemlock stick. You will experience exquisite orgasms until you teeter on the edge of death. But that is something I am saving for you for a later date.

"The Eumenides disappointed me. I really thought you were getting your come-uppance, you male pig! But the Fates cannot be cheated. Although Fate is a woman, the whole lousy book was written, or at least rewritten by some inadequate man. For now, though, crow man, enjoy your little orgy. I will see you again."

She swirled her cloak about her body and turned her back on him.

The snakes sank their fangs into his skin and he started to scream as he came again and again.

The submissive hanging on the wall emitted a low moan that could have equally been of pleasure or pain. Mistress Claudia paced impatiently and nervously. The man lounging in the huge ornately carved chair in the corner made her nervous; not something she was accustomed to feeling in the presence of the male half of the species. He exhibited no body language that she recognised and he gave off no body scent of his own other than what adhered to him from his environment, not even the slightest subliminal traces of pheromone. His whole demeanour, especially the way he lay back, one leg thrown carelessly over a chair-arm, was calculated and artificial, revealing nothing of the real person who sat watching her.

Her whole career had hinged on being able to 'read' men, preferably at first glance. At times her life itself had depended on this skill. After several decades of careful manoeuvring, adroit planning and sucking the right cocks, she had found herself in a position of total security and control, which is one she liked and where she planned to stay for the rest of her allotted time. Then why had she let this enigma stroll so nonchalantly in here and arrogantly call into question all the things she'd slotted together to protect her from the miserable world outside of suffering, toil and imbecilic hatred?

He'd casually ambled in past ninety percent of her security personnel before they'd even realised. When they had spotted him, he'd casually hospitalised twelve of them before Claudia had called them off and invited him to her inner sanctum. She realised that had he meant her any harm he could just as easily have reached her suite of rooms without anyone even noticing him, gutted her and walked out like a tourist and nobody would have found her corpse for at least an hour. No – this fucker wanted an audience; that much she could tell, but very little else, and that only so because he wanted her to know it.

Idly she flicked her electrically charged stinger at the submissive on the wall raising another red weal across its skin. The noise it made barely registered on her consciousness, so preoccupied was she with her visitor. She stopped and glared at him. In reply he raised his half empty bottle of Stolichnaya in a mocking salute and smirked. Claudia kicked the living table which scuttled frantically out of view, squeaking like a kitten.

"Okay, fuckwit. You've invaded my sanctuary, maimed a dozen of my staff (all of whom, by the way, I have a reputation for taking care of), drank my vodka and wasted hours of my precious time. So far I haven't gotten a sensible sentence out of you. You've only gotten away with this so far because I've never seen anything quite like you and I've always had a soft spot for freaks but my patience is wearing thin so you better spill soon or I'm going to make some phone calls to some friends of mine and you'll be spilling your secrets in a different way. One particular ... acquaintance of mine would be very interested in stripping you down to see what makes you tick."

For a split second she thought she'd gotten a reaction when the man's face shivered almost imperceptibly. Then he stretched and smiled.

"Ahaha. Is there a doctor in the house?"

Claudia realised she'd found an opening.

"I see you know whom I'm talking about. Then you'd also better know that the Doctor and I have an understanding... an arrangement."

The man leaned forward with such effortless intensity that Claudia found herself taking a half step back; the first time she'd retreated from a man (if this were indeed a man after all) in a long time.

"I know the man very well. In fact you could say we have a professional relationship."

It hit Claudia like a thunderbolt. The 'man' opposite her was in fact the product of Zeus Industries, maybe even an example of the doctor's personal handiwork. She had heard rumours through her contacts – more than the world at large heard these days. What she heard was chilling in the extreme.

"You're one of his, aren't you?" The question was redundant.

"The orange never rots far from the tree." The man swigged from his bottle. "But it was my mother you should have seen. What a gal. Shit anywhere – watch your pockets!"

"Listen, stranger, whatever business you have with Dr Zeus is none of my concern. I happen to be on good business terms with him and at the end of the day I am a businesswoman."

"Nothing personal eh?"

"That's right."

He took a deep swig from the bottle and leaned forward in the chair.

"You provide the doctor with services and he provides you with protection, eh? Meaning he leaves you more or less alone?" He raised one eyebrow above his mirror-shades.

"In a nut shell. Now, I'd appreciate it if you'd…"

He stood up so swiftly and effortlessly that she found her back against the wall involuntarily without even realising she'd budged.

"Mistress Claudia, I do believe you are sworn to protect women and offer safe haven and gainful employment to any who come to your doors. Let me just ask you – what happens to those girls of yours whom you occasionally send over to the doctor's establishment and who never return? You must have wondered."

"They moved on, went to work elsewhere. We had no written contract and anyways, even if we did, where would I go to get it upheld, these days? There's no law outside of Power and Zeus holds more power than almost anyone."

The man pushed his shades up and rubbed his eyes. When he opened them they were pure, pupil-less silver orbs.

"Sweet, Claudia, sweet." He sighed and suddenly seemed to shrink into himself, tired.

"I don't imagine you've seen the things that end up in the Zeus Industries landfill site? I'm sure that there may be one or two items of twisted organic debris that turn up there that you might recognise. But what the hell? You're a businesswoman, right? Everyone has to oil the wheels now and again and you can't make an omelette without killing a few whores."

It was his grin that tipped her over the edge. She'd been very aware of the disappearance of some of her girls and it was a sore point with her.

Nonetheless, there had been nothing she could have done without jeopardising her whole establishment and the safety of the majority of her girls. Much as it pained her (and it did so deeply) she'd had to turn a blind eye to it all for the greater good. Still, the pain of knowing what was probably going on and being powerless to do anything to stop it was a deep ache for her and this bastard had just rubbed salt in it. She reached for the stiletto in her garter…

…but it was in his hand and he was up close to her, so quickly she'd not registered it. One of his hands was around her jaw, gently yet firmly holding her immobile. He slammed the stiletto into the wall next to her head where it hung quivering. His breath smelled faintly of aniseed and she wondered (in one of those stupid moments of lucidity we have in situations of extreme peril) why she had previously thought him odourless. Then the smell changed to cinnamon and she realised that he was controlling it.

"I'm going now Mistress C, but something tells me we'll be in touch again soon."

His free hand slid down her body and between her legs, sliding the material away from her flesh. Her breath hissed from between her teeth as three of his fingers slid between the lips of her labia. She closed her eyes.

"Nice cunt, really nice. Better than the real thing, eh? Bet you have a choice selection of them – state of the art? Do you mind my asking where you got them?"

He released her and one hand moved to her throat involuntarily even though he had inflicted no discomfort there.

"See you soon Mistress Claudia. Sleep well."

His swiftness and prowess in combat was more than a match for any man (or woman) she'd ever encountered previously, but in the nanosecond it took her to jerk the stiletto free from the wall, he'd vanished leaving behind nothing but a faint aroma of coconut.

THE MAGGOT
Cunt Fuckula

'You've got to be fucking kidding me!'

The cretin squirmed, perspiration slickening its jelly-coated skin, ridged and worm-like as it writhed under the pressure of my hand against its oesophagus. Beneath my extended thumb and forefinger, his throat's taut musculature felt awkward, bulbous.

'Don't fuck with me,' I warned. The words emerged as little more than a strained hiss as I concentrated my focus and energy on maintaining my stranglehold.

The maggot was excreting its foul-smelling viscous slime from glands beneath its epidermis at an alarming rate, the lubricant now slapping around and working its way up my wrist and the lower reaches of my forearm.

The fucker that twisted and undulated as it tried desperately to break free of my grip made an impenetrable gurgling sound, unintelligible, barely an approximation of human speech. And yet, as I studied its contorted featured, I sensed its meaning. For a moment, it went limp and I allowed myself a second to regain my breath, but didn't dare relax my grip or my attention, and rightly so: it was a ruse. Seconds later, it redoubled its efforts, thrashing violently in all directions, emitting monstrous polytonal shrieks from its constricted larynx. It took all of my strength to keep it pinioned, but it took more strength than I had to keep from looking into its eyes. Those eyes, bugging, bloodshot.

I landed a fist between them and winced as I did so.

'I fucking warned you...'

My own vision was beginning to swim slightly. I continued to curse and stutter like a Tourette's sufferer with a particularly extreme tic, landing further blows into the scab's pale, slimy features.

'Trust me, this is fucking hurting me more than it's hurting you,' I snarled. While the dialogue may have been cliché, the words I spoke were true. Every blow fired spasms of pain like electric chocks through my nervous system. This was the script I had been given and I was drilled to perfection, every breath, the minutest of inflections honed to exactitude. But this time, it was real, there would be no retakes. Anything previous had been nothing more than a rehearsal, so much dry, mechanical humping, masturbation before a mirror. But not this time.

I fought to avert my gaze but found it impossible. I was drawn like a magnet to those eyes – panic-stricken, bulging, watering and set in that bulbous, featureless, white head with its iridescent film. I tried so hard to ignore the truth, but it was staring me in the face – quite literally: I saw myself in those eyes. The worm was wearing my face. I laughed and cried simultaneously as I began stabbing myself in the neck.

FERAL
Claudia Bellocq

The feral thing was violet. A strange shade of violet though; sickly, slightly emerald-green even, but only when seen in certain lights. It bit him and it was then that his skin fell off revealing the bones underneath, all covered in red welts which were itching like fuck. He tried to cover himself before he realised the futility of it, no flesh on the bones and he was still trying to cover his genitals... ha! he saw the funny side and laughed so fucking hard he began to cough blood. The blood began to drip from everything around him..... cutting, cutting, cutting..... slash, slash, slash... drink, drink, drink.

Vrischika is the Sanskrit word for scorpion. This posture is so named because the body resembles a scorpion with its tail arched above its head ready to sting its victim. Although it may not be a simple posture for beginners to perform, the Scorpion is not as difficult as it may at first seem.

The creature stung him. He hadn't seen her tail, curving over her torso and head, like a flash of unexpected lightning. Something not unlike static electricity was running through him now. His body began to levitate. Suspended in mid air, he yelled at her, "What the fuck was that?" but his voice sounded like it belonged to someone else.

He fell into what must have been a dreamlike alpha-brainwave state. Somewhere in there, the bouncers were becoming hyenas, laughing like vulgar women in a brothel, only louder and dirtier and with more mockery... at his expense? Or were they just enjoying themselves... he couldn't tell but he was fucked now anyway so he just surrendered to falling further in.

The blood was seeping out of every orifice and every gash, slash and cut. The blood... he dressed himself in it and admired his new red suit.

"Sweet," he said, nodding in appreciation.

Well dressed no in his bright red blood suit, the bouncers let him in.

She hadn't needed to sting him really but it had served her purpose in taking him out of her immediate vicinity, and now, he was out of control which he would hate! Puppet Mistress was holding court. She demonstrated by pulling on a virtual thread in front of her face. He twitched, ugly dancing... she laughed a vicious laugh...

"Bitch," he thought (or did he say it?). Fuck... even his thoughts were drifting away now, belonging to her...

Lotus pose: The Sanskrit word vajra means thunderbolt or diamond. Make the thighs tight like adamant and place the legs by the two sides of the anus. This is called the Vajra-asana. It gives psychic powers to the Yogi.

He found himself contorted into a strange

shape, his feet either side of his anus. Even in this dream state he could smell the stink of his own fear, locking him into inertia.

She approached him and coughed from deep within her guts, hocking up the phlegm and spat it with force into his face. Claudia! It was Claudia... how had she done that?!!

Whispering into his ear now, beyond the hearing of her servants or her cohorts...

"My dear sweet Assassin... will you *ever* learn? You think you can fuck with me? Over and over and over you challenge me, and over and over and over you lose..."

Pouting now, her lips as close to his ear, as close to his neck as he could bear without ejaculating prematurely,

"I'm gonna enjoy this baby... I've been practising these poses. Naturally I wouldn't bother with them myself but I knew they'd come in handy for something. Those yoga teachers can harbour some ba-aa-aad-strong evil energy when it's all supposed to be peace and light you know. Works fucking wonders when you need to tap it for other purposes... readymade toxins just waiting to flood your system sweet thing. And now look at you, ready there with your pretty ass all exposed for me... what shall I do with *that* I wonder? Are you feeling that psychic energy baby... do you know what I have in mind for you yet? Oh, I do hope so… I think you'll recall that we tried this once before in my dungeon didn't we…with my cock-gimp… you liked that didn't you baby… perhaps you're ready for more, sweet thing?"

She yanked his shirt to one side and flicked her lighter over his chest, perilously close to his body hair, before lighting her cigarette.

PSI-CHOSIS
Dire McCain

The doctor was recommended by a member of the Alien's chess club. The feelings had become overpowering. The Alien was one step away from committing what Earthlings referred to as mass murder. Adapting to life on the planet was proving to be far more difficult than It had ever imagined. The physical challenges were expected, but the mental and emotional had come as a complete surprise.

Upon entering the office, the Alien was greeted by the receptionist's pedestrian words delivered through a painfully artificial smile. "Good morning! May I help you?" is what the receptionist said, when she really meant: "Christ, I hate my fucking life! I'm old and fat, my husband is cheating on me, my kids don't need me anymore, and my job makes me want to slash my wrists!"

The telepathy was a tremendous part of the problem. Earthlings were seriously dysfunctional and tormented creatures, drowning in discontent and regret. Being subjected to their dissonant radio frequency for months on end was beginning to take its toll. It was like being on the receiving end of a miserable polycephalic organism's misplaced negative emotions. The Alien tried desperately to tune out the constant barrage of white noise, but Its brain had other plans.

"Would you sign in here, please?" the receptionist continued, struggling to maintain the forced smile. Instead, the Alien heard her scream: "If I have to say *'Would you sign in here, please?'* one more fucking time I'm going to kill everyone in this god damn office!"

After signing in, the Alien took a seat and looked down at the pablumazines stacked on the table in front of It. Those insipid rags never failed to remind It of how out of place It was. It didn't care about fashion, celebrities, gossip... any of it. The Alien quickly looked away and began surveying the room. The carpet was filthy, the faded wallpaper covered with a thick layer of dust and corner cobwebs, while duct tape held together some of the ceiling panels. It wondered when the place had last been cleaned.

A bitter, haggard looking nurse flung open the waiting room door and growled, "The doctor will see you now!" Again, the Alien heard the woman's true thoughts: "Dear God, the emptiness is worse than death. I'm so tired of being alone, and not having anyone to share my life with."

The Alien let out a deep sigh despite Itself, and at the direction of the nurse, wandered down the hallway to a cubicle-sized office that was in worse shape than the waiting room. It couldn't help wondering why Its chess club friend would have recommended such a dump, but then remembered Dr. Hauer was the only doctor who would provide free treatment. Earthlings were required by law to be registered for the global government's health insurance program, but since the Alien was an alien – in more than one sense of the word – It wasn't able to obtain benefits.

Right as the Alien propped Itself up on the examination table, the doctor came flying in. "Greetings," he said in a monotone voice, while robotically extending his hand, "I am Dr. Hauer. What can I do for you today?"

For some inexplicable reason, the Alien couldn't hear his thoughts, only the actual words coming out of his mouth. *How strange*, the Alien thought. Although mildly thrown, It was incredibly relieved to be speaking with someone who would hopefully help alleviate Its distress. It wasted no time in explaining Its plight.

After a brief pause, the doctor planted himself flat against the wall and placed his thumb under his chin, then began regurgitating a torrent of jargon right out of a medical book, as though he were taking an oral exam. He continued for several minutes, during which the Alien couldn't get a word in edgewise. Then, before It had a chance to ask a single question, the doctor was shoving a token into Its hands and rushing out the door. "I will see you again in two weeks," he said, closing the door behind him.

The Alien made Its way back to the waiting room, where the nurse was standing with some files in her hand. "There's a vending machine in there," she growled, pointing toward a cedar door that read PRESCRIPTIONS in large, white block lettering. "Stuff that token in the slot, and it'll cough up your drugs." What the Alien *heard* was most unsettling: "Another zombie, coming right up!" It wondered what the nurse meant. "Seymour Steinway!" the nurse yelled, her eyes darting around the waiting room.

The following morning, after another night of disrupted sleep, the Alien swallowed the first pill. According to the package insert, the medication would begin to take effect within a couple of hours. The Alien felt anxious and uncertain, but those feelings were quickly overshadowed by Its desperate need to eliminate or at least mitigate the debilitating state that had consumed It.

The Alien was on edge for most of the day, but assumed it was psychosomatic. By evening, It was freezing and unusually wired. Its eyes felt strange as well, as though they were popping out of Its head. It went into the bathroom and looked in the mirror, only to find a pair of monstrously dilated pupils staring back at It. Suddenly, a galvanizing tension jolted throughout Its body, vanishing as quickly as it had arrived. It took a deep breath and splashed some water on Its face, then wandered out into the kitchen. Oddly It had no appetite, despite the fact that It hadn't eaten since the previous evening. It poured some Cheerios and milk into a bowl, then settled into Its favorite chair in the den. The first bite tasted unbearably bland, with a pronounced aftertaste. The Alien returned to the kitchen and retrieved a box of sugar, which It proceeded to pour all over the cereal. The next bite was better, but still difficult to get down. It forced Itself to eat the entire bowl, hoping the carbohydrates would function as a natural sedative, so It could get a good night's sleep. Then, seemingly beyond Its control, It impulsively opened the box of sugar and poured a mountain of it into Its mouth, allowing it to fully dissolve before swallowing. Before It knew it, It was standing in the kitchen, shoving miniature candy bars into Its mouth by the handful. When those were gone, It poured the rest of the sugar into Its mouth before moving on to the brown sugar, which It polished off within a matter of minutes. No matter how much It consumed, It simply couldn't satisfy Its insatiable hunger for sugar. After inhaling every last bite of sugary food in the house, It lay on the couch in the den and switched on the television. At some point during the night,

It finally dozed off.

The following day was a continuation of the previous night: freezing, unusually wired, eyes popping out of Its head, monstrously dilated pupils, jolts of the galvanizing tension, and an insatiable sweet tooth. The Alien lumbered through the hours, feeling increasingly more disoriented as they passed. *These must be the usual side effects of the medication*, It thought. Since the drug had been approved by governmental health agencies all over the planet and was prescribed to millions of people, it had to be safe... right?

On the third day, the Alien went to the local shopping mall to pick up Its camera, which It had dropped off for repairs the week before. By now, the symptoms of the previous two days were even stronger. It felt as though It had stepped outside of Its own body and was gazing down from above. "Dissociation" was the first word that popped into Its head. Not that It had ever experienced such a phenomenon, mind you, It had only read about it in a medical journal. Another peculiarity was a bewildering reverb effect that seemed to be filtering every sound pouring into Its ears. Worse yet, It was hearing those reverb-filtered sounds at an ultra-intensified level. Being from another planet, It already suffered from atmosphere induced Hyperacusis, but it was far worse than usual.

The mall was oppressively crowded, like a raging river teeming with fish attempting to not only swim upstream, but outswim each other in the process. There was an aggressive and competitive nature to the people's movement that was most unsettling. Taking a moment to survey Its surroundings, the Alien noticed that the people's faces seemed to be melting, stopping just short of losing their features altogether. It was alarming, and worsened by the garbled sounds that were pouring out of their mouths. Suddenly, the Alien felt a rush of vertigo, immediately followed by a suffocative feeling, as though It were being smothered with a pile of warm bath towels. It could still breathe, but barely. It quickly sought refuge on a bench situated in the middle of the crowd. Moments after It sat down, a family of five closed in. The toddler's wailing was deafening! The Alien screamed, *"SHUT UP!!!!!"* then jumped to Its feet and walked as fast as It could toward the nearest exit. Within seconds It was running. It was clearly in the midst of a full-blown panic attack. Again, It had never experienced a panic attack, but had read about it in that same medical journal. It felt as though It were running up a down escalator and getting nowhere despite striving with all Its might – the distorted sounds and images worsening with each futile step. Then It spotted the glass doors leading out to the parking lot. The nightmare was almost over, just 50 more feet to go...

And *It was out*. Free. Where the sun was shining gloriously. It let out an immeasurable sigh of relief, but was instantly crushed when It realized It couldn't remember where It had parked the car. Rushing around the parking lot, frantic and gasping for air, It was nearly on Its knees, crawling, when It spotted the tail end of the car. It bolted for the passenger's side door, tore it open, then threw Itself in and slammed the door closed. Another sigh of relief. And then another. And one more. It was over, *it was finally over*...

Or so It thought. In reality, it had only begun. The Alien felt a tingling sensation course throughout Its body. That tingling sensation suddenly turned into numbness accompanied by a prickly feeling, as though tiny needles were being gently driven through Its skin. Then It realized that It couldn't move. It was completely paralyzed, as though Its body had fallen asleep. Parethesia throughout the entire body... was that even possible? The Alien had no choice but to ride it out, hoping It could at least move Its hands enough to call for help. Three hours passed before It regained motion, and by that time It decided that calling for help wasn't such a wise idea after all. It would only bring unwanted attention, and the Alien needed to remain under the radar of The

Powers That Be. After taking a moment to collect Itself, It drove home and locked Itself in Its room, where It would be safe.

The following afternoon, the Alien was back at Dr. Hauer's office, hoping for an explanation. Instead it was the same drill, different pill. Oddly, the doctor didn't seem to be surprised by the Alien's horrific experience with the medication. "Oh, sometimes that happens," he said in his indifferent monotone voice. The Alien wished It could read his true thoughts, but the doctor seemed to possess some kind of force field. The Alien took the doctor's word that it was a fluke, and that the new medication wouldn't cause the same reaction. After depositing the token into the vending machine and retrieving the bottle, It headed home. It decided to wait until the following morning to take the first pill.

For the next 19 days, the Alien ingested the tiny capsule at 10AM each morning, waiting patiently for the drug to work the magic it had promised. Although there were no discernible changes, the Alien was tremendously relieved that there wasn't a repeat performance of the previous nightmare. Until the 20th day, that is…

The Alien was waiting in line at a local convenience store, when suddenly, It could hear the thoughts of every person standing in front and behind It, even though none of them were speaking, which had always been a mandatory part of the telepathy. Not once had the Alien been able to hear any thoughts unless the person was actually speaking words that often contradicted what they were truly thinking.

Then it happened again, that prickly sensation overtook the Alien's entire body, and without any warning, It was paralyzed on the spot. All It could do was stand there, motionless, while drowning in the hideous thoughts of the miserable people surrounding It.

"If I could get away with it, I'd wrap my hands around that bastard Semesky's neck and choke the god damn life outta him!" From the mind of the construction worker standing in front of the Alien.

"Blondes are such stupid sluts! I fucking hate them!" From the mind of the pudgy brunette woman standing in front of the construction worker.

"What the fuck? The fat bitch behind me is getting way too close! Back the fuck off already, bitch!" From the mind of the anorexic looking blonde woman standing in front of the brunette.

An Indian man standing behind the Alien muttered some thoughts in Hindi about how long it was taking, while a Caucasian man standing behind the Indian man ejaculated a mindful of racist thoughts about the Indian man.

It was overwhelming, and worsened by the fact

that the Alien couldn't flee. Trapped, It closed Its eyes and concentrated on moving Its hands over Its ears. Suddenly and miraculously, the hands moved. Seconds after shutting out the sound, the Alien regained the ability to move the rest of Its body. Without a moment's hesitation, It excused Itself from the line and fled to the safety of Its car.

Needless to say, the Alien tossed the second medication into the garbage as well. There would not be another visit to Dr. Hauer and his insidious vending machine that promised salvation and delivered terror. But unfortunately, the damage had already been done. For the next several years, the Alien battled Demons far more formidable than It had ever encountered prior to seeking the doctor's help. The "problems" It *thought* It was having before were a joke compared to Its current state. It struggled to carry on amid the merciless madness, until the day came when It realized that leaving Earth was the only option. It could end Its own life or return home. That was it.

Or, maybe mass murder was the solution after all?

BEJESUS
Simon Phillips

This is just to say I am here and finally have myspazz behaving properly now I have set the controls for the middle of the castle once more somewhere close to the cathedral with the scary stone creatures about to attack me..... I'll even start reading the blogs again soon too.... Well I would start reading them soon but then I heard that you may be in Ultra world, but I was in the Dexyworld today as the nice woman trying to catch a train introduced herself as the niece of the singer of Dexy's, I was playing them on the I-Pod mind, mighty quick it became a bizarre story about the bureau and all the Manifestos of Kevin's I read and now I go back to Your Manifesto once more and K is now called Kevin and is trying once more to resurrect his career..... Doing odd dance mixes and dressing as a woman while not snorting his own weight in Cocaine.

I've been staring out the window into the gloom for the last five minutes at the pair of Caterpillar boots in the tree above the bins that I can see from here and I'm sure I saw something up there that looked like it might be controlling what happens here.... Every now and then I see a glint from within one of the boots as if a deep sonic wave modulator has been set off and I am forced to imbibe things in order to continue reading or I will have to suffer the Turgid Nightmares once more.

Ah those turgid nightmares about spending my life trapped having to construct more IKEA furniture than I already have and those wonderful bizarre names this is the perfect and funny reminder of all the trouble and strife they provide to help bring the joy later..... Buuutcratch the latest self assembly chair that has too narrow a seat for anyone who isn't standard sized. We know that no one would accuse D of being standard anything and just then...

D; He pulls a shiny silver gun from his pocket, Puts the gun 2" from his eye, pulls the trigger and a stream of soap bubbles blind him!!! He rubs and rubs as This Blog makes me wanna sing Louie Louie!!

That and watch the DVD of La Bete, don't know why I'd connect your blog to that French Muck but still.

Damn I thought it was the Peyote that makes you puke before you come up on it..... Only I have this recurring nightmare of being under La Bete's spunk fountain and drowning in his spunk the only way of releasing me from this nightmare is if I don't forget Deputy Dawg and the opening credits of Vision On, even if the rest of the program never lived up to those credits!! I'm out of that nightmare and ...

Oh suddenly the Double Decker's was good in a cheap and cheerful way, less preachy than Blue Peter I think my Gran made more of their home made crap than I ever did...... And as it would happen the disembodied voices once more make me think Ah the international Necronautical society lecture made a pretty fascinating radio program on Resonance FM a few years ago that sure beat going round the Tate modern I mean the place was so modern it had a crack built into the floor to make sure it didn't look as modern as it is! But that crack led me to realize that,

Mr. K is everywhere in my life right now as I carefully read every word written about him by Max Brod, then come here and get the other side of K's life..... and all the while I have a vision of Luther Blisset in a Yellow shirt jumping 4 ft in the air to add the extra text while heading the ball goal wards once more....... Vicarage road erupts around me as I slump in my seat dejected we are 2 down again..... And I am driving round and round the Watford ring road trying to work out which way London is and none of the signs mention London I'm getting dizzy and I feel I ought to say.

Sorry as I've been stuck lost in the building unable to read or comment before now, I have but a few moments before they insist I have to sit in that Bath of banana splits infused vomit that has been prepared for me before they will let me read the next install me..... I don't even know what the software is for but I have to read that install Me Read me as for K he just ignores the Read me and installs anyway.

Oh no next they will be having an Insane Clown Posse reunion tour and the whole world will have gone to hell in a hand basket that has two clowns sitting in it!! One of them has been squirting red ink into the other ones eye and he is getting mighty angry and has lit some Nag Champa incense to try to calm down before he starts hitting the other clown over the head with his oversized shoes.

As for Jacki having a Brian Talbot comic book he will always be Mr. Nag Champa In my household and I love chatting to him in his shop on Portobello road that used to sell Mushrooms back when they were legal, I find myself sitting here having a flashback to the last lot he sold me, they were wild!!!! In a very Alice in Wonderland way stairs were shrinking and growing and everything went very oddly shaped like Tim Burton was my interior and exterior mind designer, Then I fell through a hole in the astral plain as.

If it is really 1981 once more then I am in my

last year of school and have recently become a Bowie Freak who insists on wearing a near fluorescent green Bowie sweatshirt that has his name in the style of the Young Americans album cover. I don't read novels!! Unless forced to by the sad git of an English teacher who makes me hate every author I ever read at school!! I mean the guy could barely speak without spitting over himself why would I take that sorry sack of shit seriously, no way even if I still eat meat and fish and am generally obnoxious to everyone for the sake of it because I am almost 16 and hate the world..... Duck!

Damn Mr. Stannard had just thrown the blackboard rubber at me again!

There's a guy works down the clothes shop in Ilford swears he used to live with Ken Pitt, anything to get me to buy his rotten clothes....... How bright was that red jumper you could see me from 200 yards away a red blob of acne infested nastiness.

AH living in the eighties and getting bricks thrown at me at footie once more... Just for being in a football ground and cheering ah it was so much fun living in the eighties.

Finally Tom has permitted me to enter and read once more.

Now I feel like I am sitting opposite K in some surreal cafe that has Frankie Howerd and June

Whitfield's version of J'Taime blaring from the Jukebox at top volume, They kooky looking waitress has served me Tea Franz Kafka while K disgorges his fantasies for Emma Peel to me. They involve Emma strapping Tom to a St Andrews cross and stitching his scrotum to his thighs and whipping him with a bullwhip... Oh and when is the doctor going to transmogrify K into Gartner?

And the Supermen walk in file.... After All what can be said other than at least tom is allowing me in now and not marking this up as private!! Oh and that scene of Tom getting whipped will not be private either Emma Peel will be doing it as a live you tube video feed because As the cd on my computer keeps saying the Light does indeed pour out of this blog!!

This opens like a scene from my youth when a group of us encountered a cow late one night in the subway under Leytonstone Station and had to run the gauntlet to get past the cow to catch the last train!! I only ever saw a cow on the platform once also at Leytonstone! This never happened after they put in the electronic barriers which is a shame!!

Oh and I want to see the episode of Clown court where they try the clown who had red ink in his flower again.....

Headaches after leaving the bulldog, the last

time I visited the Bulldog I had a headache all right, but I think it was to do with the Afghan Hash they sold me.....

Scratch that I have misread the building as Bullfrog or is the blog morphing before my eyes as I get my head round it all, nice work as I take in the other startling discovery today I read about K's son who K never knew he had and his 4 day relationship with the mother.... Who Knew.... The amount of women who had relationships with this so called unloved man.

As a boy I was as innocent of, and uninterested in, sexual matters... as I am today in, say the theory of relativity.

April 10th 1922 Diary entry by K! Don't forget he used to go drinking with Albert!! Oh and did Albert ever give K some odd fantasies that he always wanted to enact as

Huh if you think your imaginary then who the hell imagined you and why would they bother.... I do hope the K-ships didn't get there music from K-tel, but I suspect they did.....

Finally your no longer a spack as Tom had it yesterday, I was sure you had no physical disabilities, but mental ones maybe, but aren't we all slightly deranged anyway, excellent stuff, I hear Grillparzer calling me..... Oh Sappho Sappho Wie Hat Sie Sich Geschmueckt, Die Falsche! Ihrem Buhlen zu gefallen!

I'll do my best to read it sometime in the next week probably Monday and then let you know how good it is....... oh, mir ist wohl!

I Have hundreds of wrong feelings-dreadful ones-the right ones won't come out, or if they do, only in rags weak" K said to me in the arts and crafts museum building. While bringing back imagery from one of the Key books written by one of K's old associates Margarete Buber Neumann called Under Two Dictators where she recalls what she saw Mengele do at Revensbruek his experiments aren't that far from your fantasies.....

Max Brod.

K is currently locked in the bathroom trying to figure out how to get out of a bathroom that has no doors that he can see and no windows just purple tiles everywhere and a large mirror on the wall.

He has some weird Swedish prog playing loudly through the speakers at him, and he is almost ready to sing along to Trad, Gras och Stenar's version of I Can't Get No Satisfaction if the instrumental break will only finish but it seems to go on for eternity just like his stay in the bathroom might..... I look forward to getting a copy of the book.....

I love this turn of events.... I have to say the two times I went to Euro Disney I took terminally ill kids with me, it was worth it just to get the pass that lets you jump all the queues!

Even if the looks of hatred from the healthy folks who have queued for 2 hours to get on the ride seem to get worse if the kid didn't look at deaths door..... No you must look like deaths door before anyone will accept you really are a terminal case even as The stigma with certain diseases is at times perplexing and the treatment some people get is just as surreal as anything that happens to Gregor! Or it could just be that Gregor's is a walking talking metaphor for the lifestyle needed to survive in the building.

After hearing about the tragic events I had to admit to the officer that I'll do my best to find my way to the bloodspots as soon as time permits, I was sure that would be enough to get him off my back and the same goes for reading more Paraphilia and I want to do that soon. Rather than have that officer chasing after me.

Is the third time quake when Kilgore Trout rears his head once more as he tries to get back to Schenectady from Troyso he doesn't get blamed for the Irish barman's murder....

Eggs lent stuff! And you must put the Officer in touch with the bar man as he will sort him out for sure.

I've put my Joe 90 Glasses on for this comment! I also have to ask do you remember what you could get if you saved up enough Bazooka Joe tokens? It certainly wasn't for this whole shebang to make sense that's for certain.

I also thought you'd be listening to Radiolarian Ooze by manorexia! As should I rather than have Motorbikin screaming out the speakers at me.

Oh and have you seen Dans Ma Peau perchance it explores the world of self cannibalization and other such typically French pursuits!

Excellent and have a good weekend.

Dans Ma Peau is a film or DVD by Marina De Van and is out on Tartan DVD a really good sick French movie. You should be able to find it quite cheap!

Um bits of Dans Ma Peau is more difficult to watch than Audition and it has parallels with the other relevant movie all this triggered in my mind the Hungarian classic Taxidermy about competitive eating and the desire to Taxiderm your own body, but if your squeamish at sick movies you may have trouble with both these films! That's the totally irrelevant film review out of the way now to some celebrity trivia.

So that's why I haven't run into Pete Burns at the Italian round the corner from here recently!! Yes because he is stuck in someone else's blog captured within a dot matrix of his own making just as I can't believe it is 19 years since I brought back my own Terracotta army from Xian in China a place with some immense vibes flowing through the whole area, The size of the army they had uncovered seemed immense even if it was less than 5% of what is now uncovered. Not to mention that the oddest airport set up I've seen is at Xian where after check in we got back on the same bus with our luggage and it took us out to the plane and scary as all hell flight out of there where some idiot forgot to put the oil in the plane and we turned back just in time... Strangely only one woman refused to stay onboard for the second attempt but we did all clap and cheer when he finally landed that crate at the otherworldly airport in a moonscape that is Guilin airport in the middle of a real odd mountain range, Such a shame that very view I went for is now used to sell a bank on TV.

Excellent reading.

Yes truth always seems to be stranger than fiction, and any time you think you're the first person with an idea, you're almost guaranteed not to be!

I may well have some writing time on Monday to sort out something to send on over, no promises.....

VIRUS (FRAGMENT)
Christopher Nosnibor

Data-caption – no exit – low light flicker in the /HUB stolen profile drivers SUV some kind of emulator, counterfeit imitator, stolen from a life. And so I find myself here again amidst the virtual ruins in this embryonic digital age. Yes, flash back 10 years. It's all there. Same as it ever was.

A/s/l?

Blinking, cannot compute, the modem heart flutters at a new contact in this progressive age. How are things on the West coast? S/he flutters to life, stubby hands flit over a stained keyboard, a virtual half-truth in the making. And tell me who are you?

A/s/l?

It all became rather tedious after a while. And also rather confusing. Lies breed lies, so they say. My destiny is really, really good... so they say. Another half-truth, another side-step, another evasion of the brutal facts of who I am, where I am, if I am. So what?

A/s/l?

And so I became a one-man multiple-identity project, of sorts. I decided to test myself and those I encountered. No map, no plan: just to see where it led. From safety to where...? It didn't matter who

I was, where I was, what my bask-story was. I discovered that I had the power. Fact is a myth. Identity is as much a fabrication as consumer choice. The virtual world as represented by the chat-room opened new doors.

How often were you told by teachers, parents, those lying bullshitters on television and in careers guidance that you could be anything you wanted to be? In real life, choices are limited. There's no such thing as freedom, no such thing as choice. But here... here was different.

A/s/l didn't matter as I spun my new-forged selves out into the ether. Spiralling into the void, unseen and unheard beneath the hum of the power-lines, the scrape of metal and plastic on bone and the scream of the souls sucked into the machine.

I didn't subscribe to any one fiction. Some would call it fraud: I prefer to look upon it as some kind of freedom, an escape from my physical life. It's good to get out of one's skin. Shed it, if only for a while. Split and climb on out, maybe try someone else's on for size. The tearing of flesh rent the air, cloying with the dense pall of fumes and fag smoke, congealing to a near-impenetrable smog. All hail the new flesh! Hold on now... get ready for this... here I come!

But who am I? I was everyone, sometimes simultaneously. Disembodied, transmitting down the wires, my physicality replaced by a binary-encoded pixel sequence. Hardwired into the reality code, digital annihilation in an infinite array of colours beyond perception – this is the future and it's here NOW! Ruptured telephony crashes the hypercore, man/machine synergy refracts into self-replicating, auto-mutating replicas in frequencies beyond all known frequencies. Fractured hypertexts, decimated narrative strands enter username and password... This is real life. A new kind of assassin. All A/ all s / all l all at once. No-one figured they all stemmed from the same single source...

I singularly fragmented and dispersed myself across the globe in multifarious guises and forms. I became invisible, permutated, sublimated, a subliminal all-permeating unstoppable virtual force. I'm inside you now. You don't realise it, but I'm there. The most you'll discern is likely to be a small buzz in the ear, an involuntary nerve twitch or fleeting muscle spasm. But that memory you didn't know you had, that dream that seemed to familiar and yet so alien, a strange sense of déjà vu for a place you know you've never been... an implant. That's me, it's my work. I'm taking over, taking control. I'm the virus. And I'm spreading.

GLYPH
dixē.flaflin3

Theresa drove down the street making note of how nondescript and common the main streets of most American towns were. Some touted their Main Street as a source of pride and ingenuity, a throwback to better times, but mostly they were relics of Americana. Her eyes scanned the signs on the doors hoping to find the familiar symbol she was looking for. It was a glyph that could be found everywhere in America:

Δ.

Sometimes it had a circle around it sometimes it did not. It was an antiquated glyph, not as common as it once had been, but she could always find it when the need struck her.

Fifteen minutes of driving before she spotted one. *Not too shabby for a hunt this late in the day*, she thought to herself as she pulled the car to the curb. There were a few people gathered outside by the front door of the building. She knew the drill, knew they would be either friendly and welcoming or quiet and detached; however, they were not the guardians of the gate, and their reactions were ultimately irrelevant.

Once inside, she made her way to the coffee station, which was usually present. She never expected great coffee, and knew the quality of coffee in America was as varied as the economics and demographics of the area. She poured the steaming liquid into the Styrofoam cup and added generous helpings of the artery clogging powdered creamer and sugar. These two things always made bad coffee better.

Stale cigarette smoke wafted from behind, alerting her to the presence of another. One of the natives had made their way over to welcome the newcomer.

"Welcome friend, how are you this evening?" a male voice asked.

She turned to face the stranger, smiled kindly, and nodded.

"Not too bad, sir," she said. "Needed to catch a meeting on my way cross-country."

He nodded and smiled back.

"My name is Bob." He motioned towards the circle of chairs. "Meeting starts in ten minutes." He then walked away and went about greetings others.

Theresa wandered around the room, reading the various notices posted to the bulletin board. Employment opportunities, local business cards, and the schedule of other activities held in the building. She did not want to be the first one to take a seat, nor did she want to be the last. As the clock approached the top of the hour, the room began to fill and she found her way to a chair. She chose one opposite the token zombie drunk. There was always one in every meeting. The one so badly damaged from alcohol that their diminished capacity served as a visual reminder to the group of the dangers of alcoholism and the precarious nature of sobriety and addiction.

The host stood and started the meeting. Theresa attended a lot of meetings, but never the same one twice, and never in the same city. She was always on the move, always travelling, trying her best to avoid seeking out the glyph. This evening's host was a middle-aged Caucasian woman who was neatly dressed and spoke eloquently about her struggles. She nodded as the woman orated the horrors of her addiction, which Theresa could relate to. Addiction is a motherfucker, this she knew all too well. Trying to quell the screaming inside could be horrible if not managed correctly, which is why she always sought out the glyph.

She tried her best to not make eye contact with people, but when she did she smiled politely. No need to attempt to make connections because she would be gone by morning. She was here because of the need and nothing more. Once the host opened up the floor, she waited to tell her story, not wanting to seem too desperate or eager. Eventually she spoke up and rattled off the same story she always told. Child of two abusive alcoholics, family destroyed by her parents' various addictions. She had spent time in and out of foster care and had eventually landed in state run facilities when she became a delinquent. Her story was as average as her looks. Nothing memorable and Theresa preferred it that way. She enjoyed the anonymity; to draw attention was a cardinal sin. As the meeting came to a close she grabbed her bag and stood up. Scanning the room she noticed several small groups had formed, obviously those who were regulars catching up on recent events. She decided to refill her coffee before hitting the streets.

Once outside she wanted to smoke, but because she did not regularly smoke, she did not have any cigarettes. She hesitantly approached the man from earlier, who just so happened to be smoking and asked him if she could bum a cigarette. He readily agreed and began making small talk with her. They chatted about nothing really. It was common to avoid discussing the details of their addictions, it was a topic better left for other times. At least that is what Theresa presumed. She had never formed any long-term relationships, but that is what she imagined happened between normal people. She certainly did not consider herself normal and did her best to keep it hidden from the outside world. She wanted to be as nondescript and as common as the Main Streets she wandered in search of the glyph.

Bob suggested that Theresa join him for "some real home-cooking" before she hit the road. She had explained that she was travelling and would be leaving soon. It was a common scenario: strangers dropping in to catch a meeting because they needed to or wanted to. Either way, it was normal, and she appreciated that. She had dropped in on many of these meetings during her short time on this earth, and never left without feeling better than when she had arrived. "It really works," she had told Bob before they headed to the all-night restaurant of his choice.

All-night dining options in America were strangely uniform in their decors, she noted as she entered through the door Bob held open for her. A waitress quickly seated them in a corner booth. It was apparent that Bob was a regular here and had established relationships with a few members of the staff. Theresa envied him for this slightly, but knew she herself would never have the luxury of such simple things. She pretended to scan the menu while making more small talk with Bob, but knew exactly what she would order because it never changed. A cup of coffee and two eggs- over easy with wheat toast- no butter, bacon, and hash browns. She did not like hash browns, but liked to see what each restaurant offered. Was it the shredded, traditional hash browns or was it country potatoes or the formed potato patties or something new? She would note it later in her diary.

During the meal Theresa made herself vulnerable because what did it really matter? She would be gone with the rising of the sun. Bob shared his story with her and she listened intently, all details she must put into her diary later. She looked up at the omnipresent clock above the window where the heat lamps kept the food warm until the servers could pick it up. It was getting late and Theresa didn't want this to take any longer than it needed to. She began to make more direct eye contact with Bob, lowered her head slightly, cocking it to an odd angle, and touched her hair. Theresa had learned how to dilate her pupils at will and for good reason.

"Bob," she said, "We could sit here all night and tell each other tales of yore until we are blue in the face, but I would like to ask you a question if you don't mind?"

The man did not seem surprised or put-off by her sudden frankness, which was typical. "Absolutely, ask away," he said with a genuine smile on his face.

"Would you like to come back to my motel room and fuck?" she asked.

Without any hesitation Bob agreed. He even offered to pay for their meals before she excused herself to the ladies room.

She had chosen a motel on the outskirts of town, an obvious *No-Tell-Motel* another staple of American cities. She often wondered if the owners knew what type of establishment it was going to be from the names given to the businesses. This one lauded its free cable TV and Internet access. Neither of which were of any use to Theresa. Bob had followed her to the motel in his own vehicle, which was fine. *Easier than trying to retrieve cars later*, she thought to herself as she sped up to ensure she could get into the room before him. Once inside Theresa put her bag upon the table and grabbed a bottle of water from the bathroom. She did not require a lot during her travels, but preferred drinking bottled water to tap water. Another of her quirks, she had a lot, but only she knew them. She had left the door open, which Bob closed behind him as he entered the room. Not one for formalities or pleasantries, Theresa immediately set about the task before her. She approached Bob, put her arms around his neck, and kissed him. He quickly picked her up, placed her upon the bed, and began to remove her clothes. She lifted her hips slightly as he pulled down her pants, and cooed softly as he removed her panties and engulfed her with his mouth.

The sex had been adequate, perfunctory, with Bob making sure she came before allowing himself release. Theresa retrieved another bottle of water from the bathroom, and offered it to him. Once again they made small talk, the way humans tend to do when they are naked and sitting alone in a motel room. The awkward moment between two strangers who had just committed an act of intimacy. Not that it held any depth or true meaning for them, but it was a shared moment nonetheless. She knew he would soon begin to politely excuse himself, which was the norm of most males and she never mistook it as a personal attack or slight against her. She genuinely smiled as he made his excuse for having to work early the next day and listened intently as he expressed his appreciation of her and her talents. Glancing at the omnipresent clock upon the nightstand next to the bed, Theresa nodded in agreement and gave him one last kiss. He stood to begin the process of putting on his clothes, swayed slightly, and dropped unconscious upon the floor next to the bed.

"They always make such a loud thud," she said aloud as she tiptoed over his body and went back into the bathroom.

No one would ever suspect that a woman as small as she could be capable of lifting a man of Bob's size. More importantly, no one would recall much about the woman Bob was seen dining with at the restaurant. Nor would they recall much about the stranger who had dropped into the meeting earlier because anonymity was part of the deal. Just as it was the basis for establishments like this motel to exist and operate. Servicing a clientele who wanted their privacy and identities protected. She had used cable ties to secure Bob's hands to the showerhead above his head. Deadlifting 180 pounds was never an easy task and it was the maximum she could handle; she was very skilled in judging the weight of a man by his size and frame. Bob was tall and lean, so it made the slack of his bodyweight less on the shower's plumbing. Once Theresa was confident he was adequately bound, she left the shower and went back to the table where she had placed her bag. Inside she found the simple leather case that held the implement of her addiction. She held the case close to her bare chest and felt the warmth well up inside of her. She wished her addiction was as easy to feed as one for alcohol or drugs, but this was not to be. Hers required much more cunning than the garden-variety addiction and she was an addict as much as the rest.

She stood just outside the shower and opened the small case to reveal her great-grandfather's mother-of-pearl handled straight edge razor. The same one he had used to open his wrists with when the family fortunes had been lost in the Great Depression. It was a relic handed down to her from her mother before she too had disappeared into the abyss of madness and addiction that had plagued Theresa's maternal lineage for generations. Gently she removed the implement from the case, opened the blade, and gazed at the reflection of her eyes; such an average shade of blue, nothing special or noteworthy, just blue. She heard Bob's breathing, rhythmic and steady. The barbiturates she had laced the water with no longer had any effect on her, but they were quite useful on those who had not built up immunity to them. She had stockpiled a large quantity of drugs over the years, and was quite happy as the medications increased in potency the longer her treatments continued. The sound of the alarm on her phone brought her back to the moment. She stepped into the shower, pulled the cheap plastic curtain closed, and started to hum a tune.

Theresa reached up and gently pushed Bob's hair behind his ear. She kissed his nose, and then his lips. Using her fingers she felt his neck and located the carotid artery. The razor plunged into the tissue and the blood sprayed onto Theresa's body. She closed the razor, opened her mouth, and bathed in the glorious warmth of Bob's life. She celebrated him, slathered her body with him, took communion with him and satisfied the addiction she hid within her average appearance. For those precious few minutes, when the blood flowed generously, Theresa felt truly alive and human. Over-and-over in her head she repeated her most cherished word in the English language; her mantra: *exsanguination*. Sadly, as is true with most addictions, the highs become shorter and the desire to repeat the rush more frequent. Theresa sat down in the shower and looked up at Bob's lifeless body hanging prone from the showerhead. She was immediately angry he had not given her more, but acknowledged what he had given her was something special. She said a silent prayer for him, stood up, turned on the shower, and rinsed the remnants of Bob from her body.

As Theresa prepared to leave the motel, she went back to the bathroom to complete the rituals of her addiction. She was adept at cleaning motel rooms and always carried supplies in her bag. She reached into a garbage bag that held the blood-soaked towels, and drew the glyph and a number on the back wall of the shower. This was her mark, her calling card, although she doubted anyone would seek to find her. There were countless others who were afflicted with similar addictions and at this exact moment, all of them operated within the same country. Completing their rituals, satisfying their own needs, in a world that had become a selfish place. One filled with too many horrors to ever acknowledge, let alone fix, them all. A country without morals, America had been ethically cleansed. Theresa turned off all the lights before she made her way out into the night. In the safety of her car, she paused and gazed at how the lights from the motel's neon signs danced across the hood. Curiously, the glyph appeared before her eyes, which she took as a sign that her addiction was sated, for now. She knew that to the untrained eye the glyph that she left upon the wall would mean nothing, but some would immediately recognize it. The number, which was always the same, would possibly require more investigation, but was related. It was part of her compulsion, to leave these markings, and she hoped someone knew their meaning. Surely someone knew what ∆ and the number 13 meant as a whole.

The End.

WISH YOU WERE HERE
D M Mitchell & Claudia Bellocq

The Palace at Knossos had seen better days. The heads and limbs of young men nailed above the porticoes had long ago rotted so badly that they had become indistinguishable from the rest of the décor. Minos paced the floor – an indomitable egomaniac. His fragmented dictates echoed from countless speakers throughout the almost empty palace. The Assassin and Mistress Claudia sat and, having little choice, listened to the seemingly endless stream of psychobabble pouring from the speakers. Whoever had rigged the sound system must have been ex-police, because the speakers frequently emitted a squeal of feedback and a slight delay in the signal between sets of speakers caused Minos' words to echo in an unintelligible manner. Not that it made any sense anyway; Minos had been encased from head to toe in his rubber suit for so long that he was now completely and utterly mad.

He cut a figure that was a mixture of imposing terror crossed with farce; fully seven feet tall if you included the immense black rubber bull horns which stretched out on either side of his head and wobbled slightly whenever he became animated. As he talked, yelled and declaimed he wobbled precariously around on eight inch stilettos.

Once this place had been filled with people trembling at his pronouncements or debasing themselves in ecstasy at the golden generosity he showered on them. Now only bones, dust and the chitinous crackling forms of the black dwarves supplied by the dozen from Zeus Laborotories. Four of these beetle-like forms flanked The Assassin and Mistress Claudia gesturing menacingly every time one or the other did anything suggestive of rebellion.

"How much longer do we have to listen to this dull cunt?" whispered Claudia.

"Until he gets to the end of his spiel!" answered her dark companion.

"And how fucking long is that likely to fucking be, dickhead?" she hissed.

"As I have no more idea what he is saying than you, I am unfortunately unable to answer that. Just sit back and enjoy yourself. It's not every day a person is granted an audience with the once-great monarch of Knossos."

"Dickhead! Shit! Fuck! Cunt!" she growled reaching for the weapons that had been taken from her.

"I wouldn't fuck with these creatures, Mistress. Not unless you want to spend the next four hours bleeding from every orifice, rolling in your own liquid shit. It's not a nice experience, believe me. I've been there."

"I thought that would be exactly your cup of tea, you stinking nonce!"

"Ah, the silver tongue of Mistress Claudia! May it flicker over me (in eternity)!"

He smiled and lay back on his seat. Claudia wanted to rip his eyes out and feed them to him, while at the same time wanting to fuck his brains out; what little he had. Minos turned and threw up his arms, his distorted voice booming throughout the mouldering citadel.

"...and print it on papers and a hot dog from the air – "CHAfBRE 'EOUCTIUN" in terror. The plumage – how thai, one week the planotony of the rest of the siren which, had a single detail"

His meaningless speech ended and the reverberations gradually died away. Minos held the pose for painful ages, arms uplifted for dramatic effect.

"How does he shit and piss in that thing?" asked Claudia.

"Am I then the expert on shit and piss?"

Claudia turned with a malicious smile on her blood red lips, which opened ready to deliver a new carefully crafted insult. But she was cut off by the dwarfs who closed in on them menacingly gesturing for them to stand up.

"What the fuck now?" she snapped.

Minos turned and pointed heraldically towards an ebony portal hung with mummified organs and limbs. The dwarfs began to shepherd them towards the door.

"Where are we going?"

"Ah!" said The Assassin. "Ah!" and the smile had vanished from his face.

"Ah, fucking what? You daft cunt!"

They neared the door which was ornamented with strange sinuous arabesques that were both repulsive and concupiscent at the same time.

"Labyrinth. They want us to go into the labyrinth."

"Oh… well that's just fan-fucking-tastic" spat Claudia, with no attempt to veil to the contempt in her voice.

"A Minotaur… a fucking Minotaur! I mean it's not as if I don't have enough to contend with one fucking bull-headed male in my vicinity," she hissed.

The dwarfs rounded on them, shoving them ferociously toward the labyrinth.

"You really are an arsehole you know. It's beyond my imagination how you came to this profession my sweet; accident, hereditary, or divine providence but certainly not skill or talent dear Assassin… Well, at least I was prepared, I knew their twat of a god must be male."

She stood tall again and dusted off her patent

stiletto boots. The dirt on them bothered her. She was getting riled now but not quite sure if it was the servile dwarves rendering her so twitchy or the situation in which they now found themselves as a direct result of the Assassin's raging bravado. Wherever there was trouble, he was there. Whenever there was a ruckus somewhere, you would smell him before you'd see him. His smell was gunpowder, metal and blood, with the occasional overlay of dark heavy tobacco and sweat, a sweet sickly sweat. You could bottle that smell, she thought to herself...

Drifting into a moment of something like lust, Claudia was savagely recalled by the sharp prod of a dwarf impaler in her lower spine. The bastards! Did they have to use those fucking things? They had no finesse with them, never got any training but were just used as expendable pawns by the rubber king (spit) and so had a tendency to just ram them hard into any place with which they could make contact, always poised to run the other way if their captives became too lairy for them. No good trying that though, not today; the King had his devil-birds positioned all around the city and would have received notice so fast they'd have been fucked within seconds of trying anything. Nothing passed their hawk-eyed gaze.

"That rubber bastard needs the holes in his suit filling... cunt!" she whispered.

"I'd love to watch that one slowly suffocating," ...and as she said it a plan began to formulate in her mind; just the tiniest edge of a plan, unformed as of yet but genius in potential. If only she could get to him.

"Hey Assassin, you happen to know if that twat goes for boys or girls?"

"What you got in mind baby?"

"If we get out of this fucking maze thing alive I'll let ya know, but listen dick-brain, I don't suppose you have anything like a plan for this do you? You must've seen it coming; please tell me you're not that stupid?"

The heavy oak doors creaked open and the pair of them were crudely shoved inside the labyrinth to the roar of the crowds outside.

Inside they stood a moment next to the door to let their eyes adjust to the darkness. The stink of rotting carcass caused Claudia to retch. Her companion, on the other hand was used to the smell of rotting flesh and entrails, it was his business to be so.

"You never could hold anything down, could you sweetie" he laughed.

"You bastard! You're taunting me. You're fucking taunting me, even now. Anyway shitface, why the fuck would I want to hold anything down unless I was being handsomely paid or unless I actually *enjoyed* it, penis breath" she retaliated. "If I remember correctly, you couldn't actually offer me anything that was worth holding down baby."

Claudia managed to stifle her gag reflex. There was no way she was going to let this cunt see her puke. Not now. Sweat broke out across her brow as she suppressed all natural reflexes in favour of pride...'one day' she thought, grinding her teeth violently and clenching her jaw... 'one day' ......

"Listen Claudia, don't be mad with me baby... you know how much it turns me on when you're mad with me."

He was still fucking taunting her. Unbelievable!

"Oh why don't you just fuck off and get one of your gimps to blow your tiny dick right now" she cursed, " maybe you'll be more use when you've off-loaded that useless spunk you're obviously so full of! And why the fuck did I have to end up in here with you anyway?"

As her eyes adjusted fully now, she could make out a litter of bones, feathers, sinew and entrails along the floor. Could be useful, she thought...

"When I was a girl, my mama read me these myths," she spoke aloud now...

"The Minotaur has been careless, we can use these guts to lay a trail as we move to the centre of this damn hell-hole."

"Aaah, you *were* a girl once," sneered her

companion, never one to waste the possibility of a jibe.

"Oh just fuck off will you... just fuck off. Tell you what, why don't you just leave all of the planning to me baby boy? Leave it to the real fucking brains of this operation."

Down deeper into the pit. In the middle of the pit are snakes and earth tremors, smoke and the smell of peat and gunpowder. It was dark in there. Claudia sat on the ledge carved out by the latest tremor at the side of the cavernous hole tapping her heels against the rockface. The Assassin was down in the heart of the pit busy with some toy or other he'd picked up recently. She leaned over; "hey fuckwit, you should leave the toys to the men."

The Assassin didn't bother to look up and curled his lip over his teeth in firey contempt, a thin disguise for a deeper feeling he had.

"Fuck off Claudia. You got nothin better to do?"

"Well now you come to mention it... no," she laughed.

Suddenly he was up on the ledge beside her. Shit! how did he do that? He always took her by surprise even though she'd seen him do this so many times before.

He grabbed her throat and dug his one long pointed nail into her main artery; "listen bitch, I know what you want and you're gonna get it you carry on like that."

"Miiiiaaaaaaaaoooooooow," she laughed and vanished.

"Aaah fuck, forgot about that trick" snarled the Assassin.

Hours later, in a filthy bar the Assassin lay on his back on the green baize of a greasy snooker table. Claudia straddled him and viciously rammed the chalked up tip of her cue into his mouth.

"You're an evil bitch Claudia," he spat as he came into his rogue black pants.

"You know you love it honey," she purred... "and I haven't finished with you yet sweet thing."

The Assassin could bear no more of this submission, it went against his nature and really rattled him sometimes... what was it with her? He leapt up swiftly to re-assert his dominantion of the Mistress. Or at least that's what he thought he was doing.

He approached her slowly, his face an inch from hers now, his breath sweet with stolichnaya, aaaaah, that sweet smell she knew so well.

"Motherfucker!" he spat.

"Judas," she purred.....

"Bitch!" he countered.

"Pussy!" she laughed.

"What happened to the minotaur?" he asked.

"He died happy." She smiled sweetly.

The jukebox in the corner cranked into action... the Assassin grabbed her around the waist and started grinding to the music. She allowed him a moment of indulgence... "got to piss baby," she said.

She left by the back door.

The Assassin knew before she left that she had gone.

Sucking hard on his cigar, the skinny bitter one he'd picked up from the whore he paid earlier, he blew out the smoke... slowly... deliberately... contemplating....

"fuck her!"

...grinds cigar into the floorboards and exits to the rear of the bar....

ADVENTURES IN PARADOX
PARADOX LOST
Pablo Vision

This[1] is not a pipedream.

Like the ouroboros and yet unlike the ouroboros: circular self-consumption, but not snake or dragon nor wurm; human renewal & rebirth & return, but swallowed anally rather than orally: one's head so far up one's arse; or, perverted by language (and semantics): eat y'self fitter! For the avoidance of doubt: the gaping maw of the arse - dilated like the cunt of ~~god~~ at the birth of ~~eden~~, or obscenely distorted like the all-consuming jaws of the "snake that ate the universe whole" – poised and pulsating, and salivating its anal juices, in [s]creaming anticipation of the submitted head. The spine bent forwards, head between the legs, groaning each progressive inch of impending closure. We all seek closure. Yoga *is* the path to enlightenment; flexibility a much-desired attribute - for reasons clearly self-evident. (Balls to Yoga-Sothoth!) There is a point in the spiritual journey where the entire head is inserted but the limbs remain *un*consumed: locomotion & appearance & gesticulation all have the grace and splendour befitting the rapturous occasion:

"prostrate the apostate!" postulates the prostate. And then: fingers & hands & wrists; toes & feet & shins. And then – as we must when *not* describing the indescribable – metaphors & parables & wayward distractions…

Auntie Semantic proclaims: "I 'see' you've got your brand-new leopard-skin pill-box terreseract."

The twisted fucks from the Möbius strip club shout: "Dead as a dildo! Dead as a dildo! Dildo'd to fuck!"

…and then: a singularity or entropy: **we** are confused about ultimate chaos and ultimate order at this [theoretical] point. (The *entrop*reneurs sieze this most minute window of opportunity to sell **us** the 'universal truth'[2]; and Hyphen the Python $_{sssss}$*sneers* at **our** grammatical unease regarding 'brand-new'; **we**'re all fucked.)

PARADOX REGAIN'D

This[3] is a pipedream.

A grunt and a groan: Lord Tight-Arse Alone! The all-seeing-eye of $_g$od as the universal sphincter: spasm and strain. Let there be shite! The Big Bang as the most ferocious and explosive splattering of shit imaginable: such malodorous and malleable clay that ₚrometheus…

No, no, no, NO!

A slow, fluid, unfurling [re]birth: >>>from the twilight furniture of the idols we have [de]constructed hexadecachorons in [dis]honour of our escapism: for what does not thrill me makes me stranger: the conjunction of her curvilinear-smear'd, snake-tattoo'd, cunt-soak'd thighs with the heat-resistant, impact-resistant, omni-mountable doors (the contrast of moist, organic, non-sexualised inference with erotized functional banality)((Tate Modem – speeds of up to 56 Kbit/s))<<<[after]birth of the Kool-Aid Acid Terreseract {Klunk-Klik every $_{(s)}$Trip/Krazy Kandy-Kolor'd Klown Time/K's $_{(s)}$Katalogue/Kinky Khaos with Kaptain Karoli's Kaleidoskopik Ketamine Kontroversy} >>> chaos from order: order from [apparent] chaos <<< : htrib[er] …

Uncle Ear-Cut declares: "Möbius-Dick! Möbius-Dick! Magic, swirlin', far-out trip."

In Euclidean space, no one can hear you scream: "Eine kleine Kleinsche Flächemusik!"

…inside out; outside in: an emergence: from the slime: shit y'self fitter [for purpose]! Disambiguation: shins to toes; wrists to fingers. And then: one (1) head is better than none (0). (Yoga-Sothoth got balls the size of King Kong! / hole in [n]one!) (Oedipus Paradox *fucked* his mother and *fathered* his father.)

A LA RECHERCHE DU TEMPS PARADOXAL

This[4] represents the infernal pipedream machines of E.T.A. Hoffmann.

...Carter's Albertina *is* Hoffmann's [bride of choice] Albertine: the transparency is clear[?/!]; the oft-voiced - and mostly erroneous - relevance of Proust's Albertine to Carter's Albertina combines incorrect inference from coincidence (or shared parentage), and confusion regarding correlation and causation. Less contentious: Carter's Albertina *is* The Black Queen[5]; & sex *is* power[6]...

HALFWAY TO PARADOX

This section is intentionally blank; you cannot read it.

"...a frozen moment when everyone 'sees' what is on the end(s) of every devil's fork ..." / "...Grendel & Mundi (with the Three-Pronged Poiuyt)..." / "...pivot on da blivet, mofo..." / "...then spending most their *future* lives living in a *past-time* paradox..." / "...a paradox [*sic*] on both your houses..." / "...to accommodate the past and future worship sites at the location currently known as St. Mary Woolnoth, Nicholas Hawksmoor {designed/will design} a terreseract within a terreseract {to 'enclose'/that 'enclosed'} the relevant coordinates. The *baldacchino'd*[7] alter sacrifices conventional 'interior' 'space' in order to increase multi-dimensional 'volume'..." / "...the creed of the assassin allows for 'inconvenient' targets to be 'rubbed out' by fair use of Ockham's Eraser…" / (The author of this segment fully acknowledges, and summarily dismisses, any criticism that the above work can be expressed by the following equation: style over substance[8].)

RELAX WITH PARADOX

This[9] is not a pipedream.

<…*He did, however, suddenly know what was going to happen from this point* backwards. *A finger of scotch flowed from the glass to the bottle. Each keystroke of the typewriter removed a character from the sheet of paper*…>

---

1. What is *this*?[10]
2. &c, plagiarism, self-reflexism, deconstructionism, post-modernism, parasitism, this-ism, that-ism, black wurm jism, &c.
3. *What* is this?
4. The succeeding section; *not* the sentence, the word, or the superscript'd numeral.
5. Citation required.
6. Paraphrased from *The Bride Stripped Bare* by The Bachelors (Decca, 1965)
7. If it ain't baroque'd, don't suffix it.
8. This superscript[11] is *not* an indication that a matching footnote exists; it is to indicate that the

quotient of 'style over substance' is raised to the eighth power. However, to use '8' for the next *actual* footnote might taint the clarity of the entire work, so let's say that this superscripted '8' represents - rather conveniently - both the precise exponent used in the equation *and* this explanatory note.

9. It isn't? Wait, I'm confused…

10. *René Magritte Auto-Sodomized by the Horns of His Own Infernal Treachery*

11. Foot^{note} and math disease?

ESCAPEE
Alan-Rob Panfried

Her nipple tore right off. Then she really started to crumble.

It wasn't me: I did nothing. There was nothing I could do. Don't peg me as some kind of sadist. Ok, so I am some kind of sadist... but not *that* kind of sadist. I prefer my victims to be... how do I put it? More wholesome? That's not it: I like them as sick and fucked-up as they come. Whole. Yes, that's the word.

'Flaky' is a term used more often than not to describe a mental state. It's hardly a clinical term, it's not something you are likely to find in any dictionary of psychology. Ironically, the application of the word is as vague as the people it usually describes, and can span any behaviours from being from mildly disorganised to certain manifestations of Borderline Personality Disorder if not properly diagnosed. Her mind wasn't flaky: it was fucked. Her body, on the other hand – that was flaky. Her skin was peeling, her flesh perhaps most appropriately described as gangrenous.

It had been easy enough to follow route from where she had made her escape in the room on the third floor. A small space, devoid of furniture except for a steel-framed single bed with a single foam mattress, badly worn, sagging and stained, and, with no window, devoid of natural light, the room had all of the conventional trappings of a domestic prison cell. Measuring a little over two and a half metres along any given wall, the room has, in fact, a perfectly equilateral floor space, precisely 268.5 centimetres in both length and width. Its walls were once a sterile, surgical while, but through years of neglect are now discoloured and stained and the floorboards grimy.

How she had managed to break out of those confines was unclear. The door – reinforced with plate galvanised steel, along with the door-frame – had been locked from the outside with a pair of five-lever mortice deadlocks, a Yale and three bolts positioned to the top, centre and bottom. There was no-one else in the house, except for myself and my captive, who wasn't so much a captive as a patient, confined in the interests of quarantine. We suspected she may have been past the point of contagion, but it's inevitably wiser to exercise caution than to take risks. But now, the decision had been taken from our – my – hands.

I was partly to blame. We had suspected she was infected, but to what extent and with what strain, we really had no idea. When she arrived – entirely unexpectedly, a lone wanderer seeking refuge – she appeared confused, disorientated, distressed. It was as though fate had delivered her to the doorstep, although at the time, she could have readily been any stray, lost on the open moorland surrounding our isolated residence, suffering from anything from hypothermia to a spectrum of psychoses. We took her in and fed her, gave her use of one of the bathrooms and offered her a change of clothing. Reappearing in the kitchen some time later, refreshed and seemingly revitalised, she displayed few symptoms to arouse our curiosity as she spoke of her ordeal and the journey that had brought her to our country outpost quite by chance.

But there is no such thing as chance, and I should have known better than to allow her to seduce me when I took her a light supper and warm drink before turning in for the night. I should have known by the look in her eye that she was not safe. But she drew me in and rapidly time began to blur. My mental processes began to liquefy as I found myself entering a fugue-like state. I could taste her perspiration, and pulsing through my entire being I felt our bodily fluids intermingling. I watched the scene unravel in slow-motion from outside my own body as we twitched spasmodically. I ejaculated ferociously into her every orifice in a protracted and unbridled frenzy, and at my final climax and she shuddered violently, her very bones rattling against one another in her loosening skin. Removed from myself, I went to felch her but within a flicker the scene changed and I felt the panic rising within me as her sphincter slipped from her anus, stuck to my moist, puckered lips. I recoiled in horror, my scream suppressed by the muscular ring attached to my quivering mouth. Sound distorted as I pulled back, my pulsating phallus still dripping semen and blood laced with liquid faecal matter. She turned, her gums exposed as her bloodless face formed a rictus of terror and fled toward me, but despite her inhuman turn of pace I was then quicker to the door, which I slammed hard shut and threw the locks in rapid succession.

My colleague had left for the night, having received an urgent telephone call that had meant it had been necessary for him to return to London. With a drive of over one hundred and thirty miles, and it being a Friday night, it was impossible that he would return before late morning on Monday. It shouldn't have been an issue: all I had to do was keep her contained and monitor her condition, which had appeared stable. And now it was my own condition that was in question.

I had returned to my room to wash her off me and to dress. I had trembled with shock as the water had run down my sweat-smeared torso and sticky groin. Having clothed myself in a freshly pressed shirt and charcoal woollen suit that had been hanging in my wardrobe and after making a few brief notes on the most recent events with a view to expanding on them later, I ventured down to the kitchen wherein to repair myself a light meal and fix myself a stiff drink. For no reason other than to satisfy my curiosity by listening in at the door, I detoured past the room of her confinement once again, whereupon I discovered the door open.

How long had it been since I had left her? I was without my watch, although this detail is superfluous as the battery had become exhausted three days previous and was in need of replacement, and moreover, my concept of time had become so skewed during my consensual molestation that I would never have had the wherewithal to notice the time at which I had left that spartan cell, dripping sweat, semen and various other fluids. Because it was impossible to determine how long had elapsed since she had broken free, it was equally impossible to determine how far she might have got, or where she may be. Although the exterior of the house presented as a conventional – if large – country farmhouse, its interior was an altogether different proposition, containing a labyrinth of corridors and hidden passages, connecting staircases and hollow walls. Its peculiar layout was one of the factors in our selecting it as the base from which to conduct our experiments, which, it must be said, had not gone according to plan. Whether or not Smith and I had become contaminated it was difficult to tell: the control group for our tests had become corrupted and could no longer been considered a gauge of anything, and the atmosphere of paranoia that had developed as we worked feverishly, often for days on end without sight of daylight meant that we could no longer be considered entirely reliable narrators.

On discovering the door was open – with no sign of forced entry or exit, despite the fact the only keys to the room were in my possession, as I confirmed to myself by dipping my hand into my jacket pocket and finding the familiar fob there – my sense of apprehension rose swiftly. I had to find her, and fast. My knowledge of the building's unconventional layout would be of no benefit to me, as her complete lack of familiarity with its unusual architecture would mean there would be no discernible logic to her route. I scanned my surroundings, whereupon I instinctively glancing down in the half-light, I noticed a small pool of blood. Black in the semi-darkness, its surface reflected what little light there was, indicating it was still wet. This was hardly surprising: the atmosphere in the building was not especially dry, and nor was it particularly warm.

I stepped toward the dark puddle, and as my eyes adjusted to the low lighting levels, I observed droplets trailing along the corridor. I followed the trail. The droplets grew larger the further I followed them, first along the corridor, then down the narrow stairs to the rear of the building. The trail left the stairs and continued along the landing on the next floor. Along the corridor, and into one of the empty bedrooms. Large quantities of blood had dampened the carpet in there, and a large patch of crimson in front of each of the doors off the room – the first of which led to the en-suite bathroom, the second to the walk-in wardrobe and the third back out of the room – suggested she had tried each in turn and spent some time before each one before moving on. The third door was open and it was clear she had left by this route. Along the passage, the volume of blood began to increase again, and I wonder if her travails wouldn't soon be halted by exanguination. Glistening wet smears of gore streaked the pastel-green painted rectilinear walls.

My foot slipped a little and I glanced down at the floor, the floorboards stretching out beyond my field of vision along the parallel confines into the darkness. I knew that there was a ninety degree turn to the left long before the vanishing point, in fact no more than ten metres away. But what was this my foot had made contact with. I stooped and studied the amorphous object. Perplexed, I poked it with the index finger of my right hand. It was warm, wet and sticky. A piece of flesh, around three inches in length and an inch or so wide and deep. With a shudder, I scanned the floorboards ahead of me. Another piece lay not far away. I ventured to the corner, then to the next, and then to the next, each time expecting to find her just beyond it. And then, at the next turn, there she was. Grazed, scraped and dripping gore, her face a mass of abrasions, her naked skin ravaged, with pieces missing. My inexplicable biological impulses began to function independently of my mental processes. I had to catch her and return her to quarantine: my mind was on this matter. My rapidly ascending erection just wanted to fuck her, to be coated in her free-flowing fluids.

Without considering the potential consequences or even what I hoped to achieve, I lunged toward her, but she twisted just out of reach. I made a second dive, and this time made contact with her blood-slickened breast. That was when, on contact with the tips of my fingers, her nipple detached itself and slid down the wall like a piece of discarded pepperoni. In unison, we screamed silently before she slowly fell to the floor. She was still. I could find no trace of a pulse. It was too late. Trembling, I ejaculated weakly inside my underpants.

To move her now was pointless, and so I made my way back to my room. Sitting at the desk, still shaking and splattered with her residue, I opened my notepad and began to record the evening's events as best I could recall. Smith would need to know exactly what had happened, and I feared I would not be present to tell him in person on his return. As I collected my thoughts, I ran my tongue around my lips. I tasted the blood mingled with my perspiration, and it tasted good.

SUICIDE SONATA IN INDIGO

Craig Woods

The day of the decision had been a bitter one. A slate grey sky bore down tyrannically. The rooms, offices, and seemingly endless corridors of the Building had throbbed with a subliminal hum, the entire edifice bemoaning its own existence. Of course all days since the event in 2009 had been bitter in one way or another. And a whole host of other adjectives too. Planet Earth post-time-space-compression had been nightmarish, apocalyptic, phantasmagoric, catastrophic, cataclysmic, completely and cosmically fucking cunted. The cornucopia of physical and temporal aberrations which had erupted across the globe with the spreading effects of the Mauve Zone had entirely altered human psychology forever. In a world where Lovecraftian abominations rubbed shoulders/fins/tentacles/pincers daily with sublime celestial apparitions there was little room to accommodate petty umbrage or delicate sensibilities. Humanity had collectively been thrust face-first into its own vomit and forced to gaze into the mirror, subsequently climbing through that illusory looking glass to a realm where the flimsy fictions of civilized beliefs and prejudices were counterfeit currency.

Welcome to Hell. The point of no return. We're all mad here. Long live the new flesh.

And yet, for me, all appeared bitter and drab. For reasons I could not wholly articulate, my continuing post as a senior level administrator at the Building in these conclusively anti-rational times seemed not only absurd but oppressive. As I watched Dr Ballard and the other chiefs of staff around me dive into their work with a reinvigorated enthusiasm that overstepped the boundaries of lunacy, I became increasingly consumed by a sense of isolation. A world gone mad has no shortage of uses for doctors, scientists, philosophers, engineers, artists of every (un)discipline and perversion, visionaries who can interpret the madness around them in myriad ways, immerse themselves in it, cultivate it, mould it, become one with the fully realised offspring of their own genius, their own desires, their own neuroses. A box-ticker, a desk-jockey, a glorified filing clerk like myself had no such ticket to the carnival. Prior to the Mauve Zone my post had been justified by the Building's endless and increasingly complex research programmes being affixed firmly within a linear temporal trajectory. No project could be granted a green light, no experiment undertaken, no research conducted without a fastidiously updated record of each event and the precise date, time, and conditions in which it occurred. As the scientific and research staff now became adept riders of the Mauve beast and sculptors of their own outlandish realities, they now widely regarded time and space as abstract concepts, flimsy as wet tissue and as malleable as cheap bubble gum. Meanwhile my post had become all but obsolete. In the space of a single cosmic beer fart, I had gone from esteemed senior member of staff to post-apocalyptic spare prick. For all of the Mauve Zone's proclaimed revolutionary impact, it nonetheless came with its own austerity measures.

Fortunately, due to a bond of mutual respect forged in the pre-Mauve days, the other senior members of the board at the Building would continue to keep me in the loop, involving me in their post-scientific excesses as a perfunctory assistant. Indeed, even as Dr Ballard had filed away at the genitals of a purple-penised yeti in order to tap the well of organic chocolate and vanilla sauce that throbbed deep within the flesh of those mighty simian loins, he had insisted that I personally hold the buckets in which to catch the delectable payload. Unglamorous work perhaps, but I was glad to be occupied.

Yes, there were still good days. But gone was my autonomy, my sense of individual purpose. And gradually my self-respect slunk away too, like one of the many googly-eyed animated viscera that now twitched their way senselessly through London's grimy mutating alleys. I realised that in order to reclaim it I would have to seek more gainful employment elsewhere. Predictably this proved an uphill struggle. With experience in no other sector than administration, my skills in the post-Mauve world seemed universally redundant. Now that organic edifices woven from the raw fabric of the masturbatory imaginations of unskilled pimply adolescents were beheld as pinnacles of human potential, it was clear that self-creation was the new zeitgeist. Subordinate roles to the creative process were now outmoded. As far as I could see, no-one would be hiring any new administrators in a hurry. Remaining with the Building seemed the only available course. In truth the idea of eking out an existence as an arbitrarily-waged trophy also-ran might have seemed an appealing notion to my younger self of ten or fifteen years previously; a ticket to the free lunch buffet and all the time in the universe to worry about what came next. At two months prior to my 36th birthday (-or thereabouts; post-Mauve months and years are illusory and indefinable beasts-) this forecast seemed like a death sentence.

The hammer hit the gavel when Poppy left.

We had been together since our college days. Friends, acquaintances, and colleagues routinely commented that we were a mismatch. And this was true given our differences in temperament (-she was melancholy and breezily artistic; I was stoic and studiously officious-) and the blatant physical contrast between us (-she was a slim, pretty girl with luxurious auburn hair; I am an overweight specimen topped with premature grey and a face dominated by its oversized, hooked, bulb-tipped schnozz). Nonetheless I adored her, she doted on me, and we shared what were, for me anyway, thirteen resolutely happy years. In 2007 Poppy attained a post as an art teacher at a school for troubled children. Despite her initial nervousness the role quickly seemed to fill her with the sense of self-worth she had long craved. She smiled more often, became more animated in conversation, and her pale skin and red hair gradually acquired a luminescent sheen. Before my eyes she was becoming more beautiful as she extricated herself from her long-established rut of sadness. Inevitably the assertion of her independence caused her to be less reliant upon me. While I was glad that she had finally reached a more positive psychological and emotional plateau, I was simultaneously haunted by the notion that I was becoming less vital to her requirements. Despite myself I could feel a small seed of resentment burgeoning blackly in my heart. I became sure that I would lose her, and as such began curbing my responses to her routine evening reports of the events of her day, which she would relay with wide-eyed, child-like relish over dinner. Against my better instincts I was becoming petulant towards her happiness. My blood was slowly curdling, turning to stale piss, my heart pickling in its sour stew. Jealousy had cast Poppy as my rival for her own affections. With a malign unconscious hand I was unravelling the fragile bonds of trust between us.

The apocalypse manifested before I could finish the job.

Poppy succumbed swiftly to the Mauve Zone's rapturous influence. From the windows of our Dalston apartment she would watch transfixed as the shifting city twitched and undulated under a sky of alien and endlessly fluctuating stars. Plaintive melodies erupted from her throat as she attacked her canvasses and sketchpads with a new fervour. She was now as one with her own muse, and the increasingly fantastical scenes she painted and sketched informed me that the dull blade of my petulance would not cleave them apart. Before long she had taken up with the Esoteric Order of Dagon, her muse having identified an affinity with the impish glee inherent in the cult's outwardly philosophical celebration of the grotesque. Though by no means a strict believer in the Order's tracts, opaque as they were, she was possessed by their aesthetic and would follow it diligently towards her own artistic ends. We began to spend less time together as I continued my now downsized role at the Building and returned each evening to an empty apartment. Poppy now spent most evenings attending Dagonist ceremonies and would often not materialise until the wee hours, creeping into bed silently and as lightly as a cat, the stink of fish and recently butchered crabmeat nonetheless betraying her stealth. We no longer exchanged as much as platitudes, neither asking the other about their day. Instead I would lie silent as Poppy lulled herself to sleep with frantically whispered soliloquies of often puerile gibberish beyond my comprehension.

"Hai su'un ... Tekeli-li ... Puh-pit su'un ... shy'it mah mh'ooth ... My favourite part is the nu'ghatt... Quiffn'gah dhub'lywambu macshab'dhu-barss ...Tekeli-li ... Cupcake? ... Fhu'cooh ... Send in Mr Chips ... Crackadoom!"

I last saw her around a week before Christmas 2011, if indeed there's still such a thing as Christmas. Or such a thing as a week. Whether there really was or was not a 2011 is a matter I shall leave to the reader.

I had returned home from the Building to find our apartment seized by a cosmic commotion. The walls were aglow and had folded outwards, splintering into sensuous quivering layers like the petals of an erogenous flower. The ceiling had melted into a swirling sky where green and purple storm clouds pulsed with impossible heat. Here and there lightning flickered, intermittently illuminating the eldritch silhouettes of nameless beasts. As awesome as this spectacle was, it paled next to that unfolding in Poppy's art studio. The south-facing wall had been adorned with a mural, its paint still wet and dripping sensuously. It depicted a silver-furred tiger with two human arms appended to the sides of its crown like grotesque antlers, the hands grasping viciously at empty air. To the side of this bizarre artwork Poppy sat naked upon the floor, her back against the wall, her legs spread wide. Kneeling between those splayed slender limbs was a figure I immediately recognised as Mr Chips, the computer-generated character from the ITV game show *Catchphrase*. Though several different presenters had helmed that show during its run, I still associated it with the Northern Irish comedian Roy Walker whose blandly cheerful charm had been integral to my 1980s childhood, and whose own idioms of "say what you see," and "it's good, but it's not right," had been engraved upon my memory. Mr Chips was attending to Poppy's vagina with a coat hanger, its uncoiled length apparently reaching some way inside her, and was yanking it in a backward motion, evidently attempting to pull it loose. Poppy's mouth was fixed wide in a perfect O as she emitted continuous moans of ecstasy so high-pitched that I was deaf to them. Mr Chips's yellow pixelated brow was furrowed, his expression grave as he went about his business in a workmanlike manner.

It was neither good nor right. I said what I saw. "This is fucking grotesque! What the fuck is going on here?"

"Fuck up, guv!" Mr Chips barked over his shoulder at me in gruff cockney. "Madam 'ere needs to keep her Toby jugs tuned to the song or else this little immaculate conception is liable to go all Pete Tong."

"What song? What the fuck are you talking about?"

He turned to look at me, an incredulous expression struggling to formulate in his poorly animated features. "The fahkin' tiger beat, you twonk. You mutton are ya? 'Ells Bells, you desk jockeys are iffy in the old loaf, eh? Pipe down til I've finished me Captain Kirk, awright?"

Stunned and paralysed by the sheer immensity of all that was occurring around me, I stood rooted to the spot, watching through eyes that weren't mine as Mr Chips toiled indefatigably between Poppy's thighs, working the coat hanger back and forth in a sawing motion, its moist length incrementally more visible with each tug. A chorus of phantoms bellowed from the splintering sky, immersing the scene in a dissonance that rendered me near senseless.

Finally a significant length of coat hanger seemed to give way with a loud shlupping sound like a boot being wrenched from deep mud. Poppy's eyes burst wide open, their blue depths bright with clarity.

A maniacal sneer claimed Mr Chips's face, his cartoonishly exaggerated teeth compressed into a ferocious portcullis.

"'Ere it comes, petal. The future is stripy!"

Lodging the soles of his flat yellow feet in the hinges of Poppy's thighs, he gripped the hanger in both hands and pulled on it with all the strength his cylindrical torso would muster. Poppy raised her face to the sky and roared with an animal fury, a bestial intensity of which I would never have believed her capable.

"Crackadoooooooooooooooooooom!"

A thunderclap rattled the room as Mr Chips pulled Poppy's payload free and was sent hurling against the opposite wall with the force. A huge silver tiger leapt from between Poppy's thighs, the hook of the coat hanger coiled around one if its rapier canines. The beast spat the offending length of metal upon the floor where it morphed into a grey snake, slithering behind a sideboard and out of sight. A pair of slender human arms protruded from the sides of the tiger's head, grotesquely animated antlers that gesticulated triumphantly, pumping righteous fists and flipping victory signs. Poppy gathered herself from the floor and approached the tiger, wrapping one affectionate arm around its neck and planting a kiss upon its muzzle. Girl and beast threw their heads back in unison and roared into the sky where their voices each claimed a role in an unearthly chorus. The tiger emitted a colossal fart that sounded like a thousand factory whistles and smelled of rain on summer tarmac. From its gaping anus a deluge of freshly prepared tuna melt toasties erupted onto the floor in a steaming stack.

Before I could gather my wits, Poppy had mounted the creature and spurred it across the boundary of the apartment and into an endlessly shifting vista of light and shadow. Gone. In the fleeting moment between thoughts. A post-apocalyptic Pocahontas and the loyal steed she had birthed. Roaming the surrealistic frontiers beyond time. Beyond my reach.

Misery slugged me like a fist. I collapsed against the wall and sunk to my arse, hugging my knees against my chest, thighs constricting the bulging concertina of my gut, my austere prison of flesh. Mr Chips, quite unfazed following his strenuous feat of diabolical midwifery and his impromptu flight across the room, retrieved two of the toasties and offered one to me. I couldn't respond. Already the lethargy of despair had gripped me, turning my muscles to sedimentary stone.

"Cheer up, cloth-ears," Mr Chips muttered almost unintelligibly through a slovenly mouthful of cheesy tuna. "Tiger beat's not everybody's bag. There are other tunes out there, innit."

From that day forward my life was irrevocably and horrendously altered. The by now customary sense of alienation from my surroundings intensified to an abject horror at my very existence. This was my personal apocalypse, the cataclysm for which the advent of the Mauve Zone had been but a precursor. Despite the cavalcade of outrageous phantasmagoria that the world had become, my life simply continued. Trundled automatically and endlessly onward like the route 81 bus. And that was the cruellest cut of all.

Though my colleagues at the Building remained affable, humouring my continued presence at the Building and involving me peripherally in their various deeds and misdeeds as before, we were now fundamentally at cross purposes. The more time I spent in their company, the more suffocated and estranged I began to feel. Each of them was utterly possessed by the extravagances of whim and genius they were each pursuing in their perilous Mauve anti-utopia, endeavours from which I was largely excluded, and to which I had only dumbstruck awe to offer as response. These were fantastic deeds performed by fantastic men and women, and I was left with no frame of reference to draw any kind of parallel to my own painfully fruitless existence. Each day at the Building was now something my pre-Mauve days had never been; eight hours of painfully obliging drudgery. For the first time in my life I felt a slave to my job, and to my former colleagues whose whimsical wits had elevated them to superiors. I was on the losing side of a new and unannounced class war.

I began to internalise this frustration until it afflicted me like an illness. Gradually I could feel the bonds of my body and mind slackening like termite-ridden house foundations. Concurrently my physical self had become an increasingly appalling predicament. While my colleagues immersed themselves freely in the fluctuating layers of the cosmos, caring naught for rigid biological or psychological boundaries, I grew viciously jealous of their feats of self-revolution, possessing neither the appropriate access codes to such territory or the skills to navigate my way through it. I was imprisoned within the cage of my own saggy, ageing, redundant flesh, my neuroses my only cellmates. Routinely I fantasised about cutting myself open from crotch to throat in order to release my puny desperate essence in a tide of emancipatory crimson, knowing too well that such a fantasy was itself pathetic in its maudlin and prehistoric obsession with corporeal archetypes. I was irrelevant and outdated. Surplus to requirements. An archaic relic of a dowdy bygone era.

Over time I nurtured an overriding desire to disappear completely. To put these voices of frustration out forever. To erase myself on every front. To be dispersed in the air as breezily as the results of one of Dr Ballard's post-atomic experiments. To leave no trace, as though I never had existed.

And thus, on a bitter day of slate grey sky and endless corridors all a-humming, I made the decision to achieve the next best thing.

It was during the following Christmas period. Which theoretically would make it 2012, the 28th or 29th of December at my best guess, though I again offer these dates with the same previously stated caveats.

Dr Ballard was out of town for the season. He was making a pilgrimage to the Isles of Orkney where the Great Pyramid of Giza had settled some months before, having sprouted monstrous crustacean legs and migrated across Europe. Rumour had it that La Danta, a large Mayan temple originally located in Guatemala, had itself become amphibious and was now swimming its way across the Atlantic to duel with Giza, and that the winner would be granted free rein to nourish themselves on the milky delights of the aurora borealis that was just about visible from the Orkneys at that time of year. I couldn't swear to the veracity of these rumours, and nor could Ballard, but he trekked off nonetheless in his renovated Sherman tank packed with a doting crew of blue-skinned Austrian wood nymphs and enough purple-penised yeti sauce to give the Kraken diabetes. He departed on what may or may not have been Christmas Eve and was not due to return until what may or may not have been the end of what may or may not have been the first week of what may or may not have been January of what may or may not have been 2013.

I pounced upon this opportunity to visit his second home, a farmhouse in Kent. Ballard had accommodated me there for a few days some years before the onset of the Mauve Zone, 2005 or 2006. During my stay the good Doctor had regaled me with demonstrations of various prototypes, arcane devices he was designing on an extracurricular basis. Among them was a frankly ludicrous contraption he named the dildosintegrator, a heavy steel electrical phallus equipped with a trigger mechanism. When Ballard connected it to the mains the device had whirred into obscene life, its ferocious shaft revolving at high speed, a multicoloured array of lights flashing frantically.

"Very impressive, Doc," I had lied through nervously clenched teeth. "But what exactly is its purpose?"

"Isn't it obvious?" he had barked, fixing me in that all-encompassing stare so characteristic of those who dwell on the slim threshold between genius and madness. "This is the ultimate in sexual revolution. The key to a pure erogenous state devoid of rational thought, freed from the obstinate autocracy of the human form. In a perfect world one good hard shot of this up the orifice of the user's choice will send them straight to erotic paradise, blasting their body and mind into fragments, a billion eternal orgasms."

"Sounds like suicide to me."

"Perhaps in this world," he replied with a possessed smirk. "But there are other worlds. And all worlds are possible. And they're on their way. You'll see."

As to how much of what Ballard had said amounted to canny precognition as opposed to an intimation of his deeper involvement in events leading to the Mauve Zone, I couldn't be sure, but his words and his obscene device had provided me with the rationale and method with which to pursue my own anti-suicide.

It was a clear cold day in the Kent countryside.. Frost glinted in the hills. Barring a copse of sentient and carnivorous oak trees, a set of chicken coops that had been piled up and shaped themselves into a living effigy of veteran TV game show host Bruce Forsythe, and a few other minor anomalies, the scene was largely untouched by the effects of Mauve. I retrieved Ballard's spare key from within the iron doorstop where I recalled he had stashed it during my last visit. The doorstop was rendered in the likeness of the Archbishop of Canterbury taking a shit in a bed of nettles. Poking my index finger into the squatting cleric's arsehole, I retrieved the key and let myself in. I went upstairs and unlocked the cabinet where Ballard stored his armoury of illicit toys. I took out the dildosintegrator. I packed it with fresh batteries. I flicked a switch. The device whirred and glowed luminously, emitting a faint scent of rectal mucous. I took the device downstairs. I poured a few shots of Scotch whisky and slammed them back hard. I took the dildosintegrator outside and I let Ballard's hunting dogs, an unruly but friendly pack, out of their kennels. I led the dogs on a walk around the grounds. I watched absently as they frolicked in the frost, tumbling around one another in mock battle, bared teeth and guttural growls offset by gleefully thrashing tails. I levelled the dildosintegrator like a firearm. It was the first time I'd held anything remotely like a gun since Ballard had attempted to teach me how to shoot a 2.2 rifle on my last visit. True to Ballard's conservationist enthusiasm, the mechanisms of the dildosintegrator were similar to a rifle and fairly easy to get to grips with. Facing away from the dogs, I fired at random targets; tree trunks, stumps, rocks. Each erupted into numerous fragments, each fragment sprouting limbs, cocks, cunts, arseholes and other appendages. These libidinous morsels convulsed their way into ditches and shrubs, copulating furiously with one another. A few of the dogs pounced after them with excited yelps. Though alive, the sex-fragments were entirely sensual creatures and not in the least cerebral, barely aware of themselves beyond an unending erotic euphoria. It seemed a not unpleasant fate. I continued firing at randomly selected targets, from the organic to the inorganic, from shrubs to bottles, generating new batches of erogenous slivers with every blast. My aim was poor but that wasn't important. I was getting myself used to the feel of the device, to the ease of the trigger mechanism and the force of its recoil. Satisfied, I walked the dogs past the duck pond. There were two crows caught in a large trap, presumably part of Ballard's conservationist regime, the contradictory rules of which remained perplexing to me. Two shadow dwarves were crouched at opposite sides of the mesh cage, tormenting the imprisoned birds with sharp sticks and a coarse volley of verbal insults. Raising the dildosintegrator, I approached with stoic purpose. The confident tone of my own voice shocked me.

"Get the fuck away from there you little bastards! Unless you want to become sex-meat!"

The dogs synchronised with my attack, lunging towards the trespassers with fury in their throats and savage light in their eyes.

Suitably chastened, the shadow dwarves leapt to their feet and retreated at high speed into the undergrowth, one of them yelling something anti-Semitic over his shoulder.

"Oh fuck you, you little shit," I hollered back, tapping a finger against my whopping schnozz. "I'm not even Jewish, so the joke's on you!"

I let the crows loose and watched as they soared triumphantly across the fields, two sleek aerial warriors free to resume their roles in a revolution outside of time.

I took the dogs back to the house and restored them to their kennels. Alone I walked to the derelict stable that loomed farther up the drive, a whitewashed nineteenth century structure long since deceased, its shattered roof and glassless windows permitting probing tree branches and hooked tendrils that interrogated the husk in a perpetual post-mortem. I entered and sat on an old rickety chair, cold and wet with frost.

The plan: *to wedge the butt of the dildosintegrator between my thighs with its brutal tip gazing up at my face, hook my thumb around the trigger, open my mouth wide, leaning my crown as far back as possible, bringing the whirring, erogenous cylinder up and in until it pressed gently against the roof of my mouth. And then ...BANG*

I visualised this sequence of actions in my mind repeatedly as I looked out at the vacant fields. I cradled the electric cock like a sacred artefact, unable to lift it. My eyes froze upon the gunmetal sky. My hands froze around the metal of the device. My flesh froze inside my clothes. My blood froze around my heart. Sitting there. Embracing a ridiculous metal dildo. Breathing in the sad ghost vapour of absent horses. A lifeless extra on the set of a criminally drab techno-porn flick. Not moving. Not being able to move. At the threshold of the transient junction of nerves that would bring the whirring phallus to my face. But doing nothing. Not moving.

I sat like that for immeasurable hours. Endeavouring to think of nothing. To feel nothing. A memory came flooding in. Poppy's face the day I had first met her. Frail, delicate, yet immortal.

This should be the last thing I should see. This vision. Hold it there. Hold it. Keep it vivid long enough. But it dispersed as quickly as it had materialised, like cherry blossoms in a spring draught. And I couldn't conjure it back. Her image would not yield to my desires. Just like the real thing. Eventually the sky began to darken. I couldn't do it. Even in the conscious act of defeat I was emphatically a failure.

I sat there in the dark with only my own blank melancholy and the low whirr of the dynamic metal dick for company. Above me a cluster of remote stars flickered, one of many new alien constellations. I could just about pick out the shape of a horse's head between the glowing dots. With a little optical manipulation a swirling mane could be seen to connect to a pair of elegant human shoulders. Then the graceful curves of a woman's breasts burned themselves into view, completing the top half of a striking deity from some unknown mythology. A centaur in reverse.

No sooner had I appreciated this portent than the stable walls shuddered in response to an impossibly shrill voice.

"Fuck's sake, cloth-ears! I've been singing your fucking name for a coon's age!"

Rattled, I jerked instantly upward from my chair, dropping the dildosintegrator to the stone floor where it landed with a martial clatter.

Standing in the doorway was a little girl of not much more than seven years of age. She was tawny-skinned and dark-eyed, her canny expression framed by a tangle of black ringlets.

She wore a white summer dress that ended in frayed tatters around her calves. Her tiny feet were bare and caked with dirt, and were it not for this minor dishevelment she could easily have stepped from the pages of a lifestyle catalogue. Her prettiness and keen composure evoked a billion family-oriented advertising campaigns. The perfect middle class child of the perfect middle class parents seeking the perfect home/car/holiday destination/insurance package/marriage counsellor/suicide pact. She was the very epitome of sweetness, consumerism's immaculate star-child.

"What's the fucking beef? You intend to sit here wanking that big tin cock til doomsday? Time to shit or get off the pot, faggot."

The very epitome of sweetness, consumerism's immaculate star-child, brimming over with decades of repressed middle class angst and bigotry.

"Get your arse in gear, cocksucker. You've an appointment to keep. And I can't lug this fucking shitty thing around all year, it'll leave me bent double like a fucking spastic."

Oh yes, and then there was the heart. The oversized human heart strapped to her back like a rucksack. A living, beating human heart larger than a space hopper, pounding and pulsating with eldritch life, its veneer tacky and elastic like the flesh of a slug.

Ba-boom Ba-boom Ba-boom

"This is yours, right? You two sure smell alike." Her eyes tightened and her nose wrinkled in an expression of distaste.

"I guess it must be," I stammered. "I haven't seen it for so long I figured it was lost for good."

"Yeah, well that's my job, mister. Picking up the shite people leave behind in their silly little psychodramas. Just 'cause the world's out its tits on cosmic jellies doesn't mean you can dump your grief willy-nilly. If one of the Dark Things was to pick up something like this, well..." She pushed out an upright palm in a *don't-even-go-there* gesture.

"Uh, right." I struggled for the appropriate words. "Sorry. Careless of me. Thanks for bringing it back." I stepped forward. "You can hand it over to me..."

The girl withdrew with a disparaging expression. "Hold your hippos there, cock-rocket. Like I already said, you've a place to be at. If you're going to re-saddle the horse then there's some admin to be taken care of. You'll like that though, eh? You look like a right bureaucratic cunt."

This stung me. "I'm not sure what a bureaucratic cunt looks like."

"Tight as fuck. Difficult to enter and impossible to navigate." She cackled lewdly at her own joke. "Admits nothing thicker than an envelope, yeah?"

Cajoling me into sharing in her mirth, she slapped me hard on the thigh, uncomfortably close to my crotch. Pained, I emitted a pantomime guffaw which caused her to fall instantly silent and accost me in a reprimanding glare.

"Yeah, right enough. Fanny jokes probably aren't your speed, you big woofter. Fine, fine. Let's not prolong this fucking agony then, eh?"

With that she turned swiftly on her grubby bare heel and marched outside.

I followed the girl across the starlit farmland, trailing a few feet behind but matching her step for step, mesmerised by the giant heart drumming a despondent rhythm in the velvet night.

Ba-boom Ba-boom Ba-boom

As we walked I attempted to coax from her some information about our destination, but she did not respond and saw fit to break her silence only sporadically with acerbic commands for me to quicken pace, usually appended with a coarse, politically incorrect epithet;

"Chop-chop, spazz-raper!"

"Knees up, Motherfucker Brown!"

"What, too much shirt-lifting left your poncey muscles too tired to keep up with a little girl?"

"Pay attention to the song, Jew-face!"

This last remark perplexed me. "What song?"

"Fuck me," the girl sighed with unabashed disgust. "The one that's playing. Just for you. Show some fucking respect for hard work."

I strained my ears to hear anything other than our breaths, the silence of the fields, or the sickly throbbing of the monstrous heart.

Ba-boom Ba-boom Ba-boom

"All I hear is a beat and it's none too catchy."

"Then your fucking ears are broken. That pulse is just the percussion to a melody. It's there, you've just got to learn to listen!"

At last we arrived at a circular grove of silver birch trees. In its centre a perfect circle of dark pond water reflected a gallery of iridescent stars.

"Well this is it, fuckface. This is where you get your head out of your arse, eh? Must be awful up there with all the darky-spunk."

"Jesus Christ!" I had reached my limit.

"I'll thank you not to use the good Lord's name in vain! Now listen up, I need you to take this," - she fumbled at a frayed shoulder strap and produced a thin piece of pale purple-tinted card- "it's your ticket to new beginnings, yeah? A new life in a new town. No more getting mangled in the same motor, Mr Car-Crash."

I picked the purple business card from between her tiny fingers and raised it to the starlight.

STEVE CHIPS ASSOCIATES INC.
MORE THAN JUST A CATCH PHRASE
Your future-past-present's bright
Your future-past-present's INDIGO

I recoiled. "Chips?! That little fucking yellow bastard? You've got to be kidding me!"

The girl shook her head sagely, mischief finally fading from her expression. "Chips might be cheap, but there's no-one hotter. And I'll thank you not to be racist."

I sighed exasperatedly and cast a backwards glance at our route, conjuring the empty stable, the rickety chair, the ludicrous dildo-gun, and my aborted anti-suicide.

"Hey, you know the way back," the girl said, apparently reading my thoughts. "But timetables are timetables. And your toys will still be here when you get back, if you still want them."

Vanquished, I slid the business card into my shirt pocket and faced the murky pond. A pungent aroma of cooked meat caught my nostrils.

"So, I just step in?"

The girl nodded. "Gravy first, Chips after," she said, her dark eyes squinting at the sky as though peering through cracks in the universe.

The disembodied heart throbbed to the impossible melody of a splintered galaxy. *Ba-boom Ba-boom Ba-boom.* The stars above exploded, burnt out, flickered back into life continuously in a spectral ballet.

I waded into uncertain depths, dark, warm, glutinous. The savoury scent of Bisto gravy engulfed me. The smell of childhood evenings. Of elastoplasts applied to skinned knees, of hastily finished homework, of the benign tyranny of bathtime. The smell of a home long forgotten ...

Submerged in the ghosts of other seasons ... lungs boiling in the grief of amputated yesterdays ... trawling impossible waters towards a theatre in the gizzard of the cosmos ... forcing my eyes to drink the agony ... lonely red soprano on a maudlin purple stage ... a face I knew better than my own ... girl and beast stepping away from the human frame ... snowbound retreat in hybrid suburbs ... convalescing beneath the thunder of crows ... sitting beside her words ... a pencil of bone lacerating a pale flesh canvas ... fugitive breaths rising blackly ... rusted shadows ... an old photograph ... time flashing in ... insensible windows ... spectral horses ... eyes ripped wide ... phantom fire ... tongues lashing ... time's clerical tattoo ... rising ...rising ...

I emerged in a long corridor flanked by endless and affectless white walls. An inverted runway of striplights glared oppressively from the ceiling. I could hear the low hum of electricity and, farther off, the frantic tap-tap-tapping of many fingers upon a battery of computer keyboards. The air was dry and conditioned. An almost subconscious vertigo suggested I was many storeys from the ground. I had waded through fantastic cosmic matter only to be delivered to a place as overwhelmingly mundane as the pre-Mauve Building. My absent heart sank like a stone in congealed gravy. Cursing under my breath, I invoked the foul-mouthed infant girl's immaculate face and regretted not having throttled her.

My acrimony was interrupted by an abrupt whoosh of air as a nearby door was swept inward. A dark-suited figure stepped into the corridor.

"Come along now, cloth-ears. We've been calling you for some time now."

The woman spoke with a chipper American accent, her unreal perkiness amplified by her appearance; luminous blue eyes, glossy golden hair, lips of pink marble carved wide to reveal a pristine keyboard of alabaster teeth. In spite of these perfections there was something familiar in the geometry of her face, in the nuances of her speech, in the codes of her demeanour.

"I'm sorry," I stammered awkwardly, uncertainty thrusting me back into the well-worn cushion of apologetic habit. "I guess I'd have come sooner if I'd known. But I really don't understand…"

"Not to worry, I'm aware there was some difficulty in establishing a link with you. One of my colleagues, Jerry, kinda screwed up the symbolism there." She sighed and shook her head, her upbeat tone faltering for all of a nanosecond. "He had *one* job to do, for Zorp's sake." Without missing a beat, her effervescence resumed unhindered: "Still, beats hiking the Monon Trail, right? We meet a lot of slackers, crackers, rusty pistol-packers, private party-jackers, short horse backers, cold turkey basters, time-wasters, toxic wasters, compulsive pecker-pasters, cheap wine-tasters, lightweight boozers, heavyweight schmoozers, two-bit bruisers, losers, users, cruisers, self-abusers, and not to mention happy-slappy Hoosiers like myself in this racket. One or two bellyaches is no big shakes. You're about a six on our one to ten scale, and I crap bigger than you."

The affable high-speed verve with which the woman delivered this spiel left me unsure as to whether I had been insulted or complimented or neither. "Erm, thanks?"

"Hey, this is public service, so you're welcome. Since the Mauve Zone kinda made things jolly well screwy, and screwy well jolly, there's been an increased requirement for the maintenance of public records. That's what *we* do. Every time a skyscraper mutates into a throbbing phallus, or a pack of stray dogs take to the street with horns and drums in their own little Mariachi parade, or one of this city's fine boroughs decides to migrate to a different corner of the planet, there's a whole bunch of people affected by each of these events, and a whole lot of paperwork required to keep things up to scratch. And here, my good buddy, is where it all happens. This is where the rubber of administration meets the road of real human beings. And other species too of course. It's a joy to serve, so there's no thanks required."

I reeled at this barrage of information. "Sorry, I'm confused. You're saying there are people who still do admin? In *these* times?"

"You bet your dirty bottom pound note, bucko! The very best of people too."

"You seriously mean to tell me that a record is made of *every* single Mauve occurrence? And that it's constantly updated? Why? Everything is so temporary and subject to any kind of change at any moment, what would be the point?"

"You just answered your own question, amigo. The fact that it *is* all so fleeting is *exactly* the point. That's exactly why we need people with a passion for keyboard-bashin' and who are ready to document everything as soon as its realised. Naturally that means a whole lot of data coming in constantly, so that in turn means a whole lot of good, good people --super-ace at their jobs it should go without saying-- who need to be up to speed in processing that data. Y'see, even the most seemingly dreary little moments are important to someone, my good man. All the more reason to document them and process them with as much diligence as possible. Despite what some folks out there'll tell ya, administration is the single most important vocation in our world today. And today is your lucky day, bro, because today you get to enter the inner sanctum. Whoop, whoop!"

I opened my mouth to reply but the words failed to formulate in my mind. Of all the post-Mauve world's infinite shocks, this revelation, if indeed it were legit, was the absolute pinnacle. I felt suddenly nauseous. I swayed and stumbled against the wall.

"Whoa there, Mr Tumble," the woman said, steadying me with a firm hand. "You look like you could use a seat." She gestured towards the open door. "You'll feel better after a little induction, I guarantee it. If you'll just step this way we can tick a few boxes and put some preliminary fizz in this little party, 'kay? We have a mountain of paperwork to prepare. And boy," -she swung an enthusiastic fist in front of her and spoke without a trace of irony- "I absolutely live for that shit! Nothing else quite sharpens the Buttermilk Point on my Wawasee."

As I stepped towards the door and a more intimate view of the woman's face the muted sense of familiarity bloomed into recognition. Images flashed across my mind's eye depicting this absurdly enthusiastic administrator engaged in an assortment of activities: working at a desk in a Midwestern governmental office; delivering poorly structured but morally committed political speeches to a town hall packed with antagonistic constituents; overseeing a series of near-cataclysmic ventures in the upkeep of public parks and forestry; bickering and bantering with a staff of ludicrously mismatched colleagues.

"Bloody hell," I heard myself blurt. "Aren't you Les-?"

"Nope!" Her tone sharpened and a cautionary index finger lanced towards my face. "Let's not be going there. Your melancholy type are liable to have all kinds of bad voodoo lingering on you from the Grey Zone. Last thing we need around here's a lawsuit for copyright infringement and some undead corporate monolith taking a Godzilla-sized dump all over our sweet-as-pie dreamy operation, *nosiree*! You can just call me K. 'Kay?"

I was far too flummoxed to protest.

"Okay."

K's cheery composure reasserted itself at the flick of an emotional switch.

"'Kay, super awesome then," she trilled through a perfectly triangular grin.

I followed her into a wide office space where a multitude of administrators busied themselves almost blithely at computer terminals. The atmosphere, breezy and buoyant, bore no relation to my own experiences of such an environment. Most offices to my mind were hotbeds of collectively repressed stress and resentment, ill-feeling simmering palpably below a gossamer-thin jovial charade maintained by begrudging consensus. The staff of Chips Inc. were cut from an entirely different cloth, appearing relaxed and content at their work, many of them smiling broadly and unaffectedly. Here and there a few could be heard to exchange banter that comprised references and phrases entirely esoteric to my ear, an entirely new dialect of social egalitarianism that was a world apart from the office banalities to which I had been accustomed. Either this pool of staff were supernaturally adept at concealing their anxieties or else this was truly a natural born bureaucrat's promised land. I remarked upon this to K as she led me across the office floor. Her grin flexed to what must surely have been a painful extent.

"Super, isn't it? If you take a deep breath you can really smell the sweet sugar of bureaucracy in action. Like I say, some of us live for this stuff. The workers here are here only because they want to be. See, I believe, like many," -she adopted the earnest politician tone I had recalled- "that the Mauve Zone offers every citizen the opportunity to live to the best of both their potential and of their desires simultaneously." She clasped her hands in front of her chest solemnly. "If I can play my part in recruiting those people and helping them to help themselves, and by extension help others in keeping track of this apparently trackless new world, then that makes the whole batshit circus worthwhile. And you know what? This here gang gets to be like family after a while. I mean, yeah, we've got a job to do -an *important* job which we take seriously- but we're more than mere colleagues." She pondered over what she had just said, meagre traces of a frown quivering at her eyebrows. "No, wait. We're not. We *are* colleagues. That's it. Strictly professional. But, y'know, colleagues with benefits. We're colleagues who benefit from also being friends. Or something." She turned hastily to face me, blue eyes reflecting phantom starlight, and ratcheted up her vivacity by a dozen or so notches. "Hey, so maybe you're one of us, yeah? That'd be *so* neat!"

"I don't know about that. I mean, yeah, I've always been in admin. And I know the job like the back of my hand. But only because I've never been any good at anything else. It doesn't mean I enjoy it. I really don't. If I had the imagination to get myself out of it, I'd have fled on the first dragon or dived into the nearest black hole by now."

"Ah come on, you big lug," she deflected, "we'll have none of that. We don't deal with

Gloomy Gusses here. Am I right, Lucy?"

"That's right!" a nearby admin, a curly-haired woman in an oversized woollen pullover, yelled back with unthinking immediacy, almost knocking herself out of her chair with her own enthusiasm. A half-full cup of coffee and an over-packed desk tidy tumbled from her workstation, spilling their contents dramatically across the floor. "Oh darn! Sorry. Yeah. That's right, what you said. I think. What was the question?"

K buckled in a disproportionate display of mirth, cackling wildly, and delivered a gently playful punch to her maladroit colleague's shoulder as we walked by.

"That Moran girl's a caution," she said, wiping a pantomime tear from one eye. "We've a whole super packed toy box of colourful characters here at Chips Inc. We stick together and help each other out, just as we help the ever-changing world outside these walls. As I always say, no-one ever achieves anything alone. Say, maybe you'll get to know a few of our gang a little better."

Before I could respond, K swooped upon a revolving chair. Dragging a second chair behind her, she wheeled herself at high speed towards a vacant desk.

"Take a seat and we'll start cracking at these executive eggs."

I sat opposite K as her computer monitor

blinked into life at the click of a mouse. Her fingers sprinted across the keyboard, punching in unknown codes and commands which caused the screen to strobe with endless scrolls of data.

"Alright, mister, now just bear with me and we'll get you sorted out. There's a real treat in store for you, and not to put too dazzly a sheen on it, but it is possibly the best thing to potentially happen to anyone anywhere in the history of the damn universe!"

As K busied herself with desktop folders and files I cast my eyes around the office, drinking in my surroundings. It seemed I was not the only potential recruit in attendance. Here and there several administrators were engaged in low key interviews with others who had presumably been directed here by cryptic forces similar to those which had coaxed me away from my aborted anti-suicide. It was with some degree of self-consciousness that I observed that the majority of these other interviewees were significantly younger than me, by as much as eighteen to twenty years. Many were quite manifestly teenagers, little older than what was in pre-Mauve days considered school-leaving age. Realising I was now regarded as having no more sufficient experience in this new world than those taking their first steps out of the parental home, I fought to quell a rising tide of bile in my gullet, the pure molten bitterness of an emasculated man. Grief nagged at me, causing my eyelids to twitch as my tear ducts broadcast a flood warning. Desperate to compose myself I bit down hard on my bottom lip and scanned the vast room for a distraction, any meagre port of interest in which to shelter.

At an adjacent desk an overweight woman in a pink tracksuit was devouring a monstrous pink donut, crumbs of pastry and icing speckling her keyboard. At her side, huddling close to her desk tidy, was a cheap ceramic ornament of a purple horse in a dramatic rearing pose, front hooves batting at the air, jaws and eyes wide, mane billowing in a phantom breeze.

A sound invaded my consciousness, seemingly resonating from somewhere nearby, an almost subliminal drone. I focussed on the sound, straining to detect the source, and identified a distinctive rise and fall in pitch. There was a melody there, struggling to be heard beneath waves of static interference. Something inside my head popped like bubble-wrap and pale purplish lights simmered before my eyes …

A melody dancing in the ether … a high-pitched song … vaguely discernible … struggling to hear … a sharp elemental resonance like the mating call of an electricity pylon … straining to listen …an evolutionary fanfare tugging at the central nervous system … listen …

"Hey, cloth-ears, you awake there?"

The office reasserted itself around me with a thunderclap as my consciousness was slammed at high speed back into my head.

"You still with me?"

K was snapping her fingers frantically in front of my face. Her eyes were narrowed, shimmering like rain-washed windows in sunlight, and her sculpted grin had faltered into a grimace.

"Sorry," I mumbled, massaging a throbbing temple with two fingertips of my left hand. "I thought I heard something ..."

"Not to worry," she beamed, her manner switching back to default cheeriness with an almost audible click. "We're nearly done here. I just need you to give me your Herbie Hancock on these aptitude tests you've just filled out for me, and Zorp's your uncle."

I was incredulous. "Tests? But I haven't--"

I made to raise my right had to my brow in a confused gesture and became aware of the pen gripped between my thumb and index finger. On the desk before me lay a scattered array of documents, purple in colour, on which were printed a series of opaque questions. Each question had been answered in fresh blue ink, in a hand that was undoubtedly my own. I scanned the pages urgently, bewilderment and fear harrying my pulse to a nauseating tempo.

Q: What is the crucial difference between an orange and a double-decker bus?

In response I had scrawled, 'A chocolate bar cannot ride a bike.'

Q: What is the optimum number of hedgehogs required to pilot a curried typewriter sausage?

A: 'Kisses are the least salubrious virus to be painted on such a carpet.'

Q: A preacher, a refrigerator, a badly written rhyming couplet in a 1990s indie rock anthem. Which has the most flayed phonemes copulating in the vertebral codex of its upper algebra?

A: 'Keith Chegwin's soapy fart sock.'

"What the fuck is this? Did I pass out? Did you hypnotise me or some shit? I don't remember writing any of this!"

"All the better!" K exclaimed excitedly, stretching her arms wide in exultation. "That just proves you're a damn natural at this admin and filing game, bucko. Mark my words, your future-past-present is bright!"

"But this is just drivel. It makes not an ounce of sense. Literally just a bunch of brain droppings."

"Exactly!" K erupted from her chair, her voice amplified, her tone locked into impassioned-politician-at-a-public-forum mode. "Nonsense is the watchword of our new non-century. And you, my brother from another mother, have just taken your first confident steps towards your own personal Shangri-La-La-La-La-La-La-La-La!" She sang these nine recurrent syllables in an ascending-descending five note scale. "Congratulations! From here it's all up and up and up!"

The pain in my temples had spread to my cheekbones to become full-blown neuralgia. My head spun. Not for the first time since the onset of the Mauve Zone, my attachment to what I had only begun to comfortably regard as reality had been disintegrated, this time pulped in Chips Inc.'s artillery of office shredders.

"Well, if you say so."

Despite my misgivings, which were profound, I had taken a liking to K during our exchange, to an extent which surprised me. While her enthusiasm for her role was absurd to me, it seemed entirely ingenuous, and thus charged her advice and instructions with a persuasive power that exceeded that of any authoritarian compulsion. Like a schoolboy swot in thrall of his teacher, I was keen not to disappoint her.

"I guess any future-past-present is better than none," I relented, and committed my signature to each of the test sheets with mechanical obedience.

"Super duper!" K exclaimed, gathering the sheets and shuffling them into a tight symmetrical pile. "Well that's us pretty much done for the day, sport. I'll go over these and collate your results in due course, and then my colleagues will be in touch with you super-soon. Meantime you just hang loose, do your thing, take in the sights of the Mauve Zone, maybe catch a few ballgames, enjoy the parks --the parks are always *wonderful*-- or just kick back, yeah? And be ready when the call comes."

"Right. Yeah. Um, not to be dense, but how exactly will I know the call or the caller?"

K's exaggerated amusement routine returned for an encore performance. "Oh you won't need to worry about that," she assured me through peals of gratuitous laughter. "Just keep your ear to the ground. And the walls. And the sky. *Listening's* the name of the game here, sport. Gotta stay tuned to the song, yeah? You take care now. Godspeed."

K released me back into the white corridor where all signs of the surrealistic gravy-pond-portal that had granted me admission had now evaporated. A seemingly interminable elevator ride to the ground floor and a swift, near-panicked speed-walk across the lobby of Chips Inc. found me in the streets of West London. From there a similarly near-perpetual mutant-and-madness-infested bus ride brought me home where I instantly hit the sack, sinking finally into a long, though haunted, sleep.

The next two days passed unremarkably as I sheltered from Mauve extravagances in the blandly familiar confines of the apartment, its humble façade having gradually reasserted itself following Poppy's phantasmagoric exit. Given that the contemporary landscape had become a canvas to be decorated with the most outrageous latent dreams of its citizenry, I pondered the appropriateness of my home's perseverance in maintaining its pre-Mauve state. A return to what had once constituted normality was about the most far-flung thing I could conceive of. I spent the time watching old movies, re-reading tatty old novels, and generally shunning external agents of humanity and their furious fancies while I awaited contact from K or her colleagues.

My only eventual communication arrived in the form of an albatross-sized pterodactyl. The winged beast had hovered at the living room window, squawking wildly, rapping at the glass with its rapier beak. Swallowing my fear I had approached with the intention of shooing the creature away, but the rolled up scroll gripped in its talons suggested that it had been charged with the task of delivering a message. Cautiously I opened the window and reached for the scroll which the creature relinquished gently before shitting out a series of vanilla ice cream cones, complete with chocolate flakes, and shooting off across the radioactive sky with a cacophonous screech.

Ignoring the dubious ice cream feast, I slammed

shut the window and unrolled the message. It was from Dr Bradbury, one of Ballard's closest colleagues at the Building. Bradbury was an affable enough sort, tiny in stature but big in heart, and I had always liked him. Prior to the Mauve Zone he had suffered from lamentably potent body odour, a trait which had cast him as a frequent figure of furtive ridicule among the other staff. He had also, to put it mildly, never been a handsome man, and these physical challenges had proved an impediment to his romantic life. Post-Mauve, Bradbury's imaginative genius had propelled him into a life of boundless fantastical riches. He had swiftly attained playboy status, regularly preoccupied with entertaining an ever-expanding company of goddesses, nymphs, fairies, mermaids, and various other exceptionally striking mythical women. Mauve London's swinging social scene was a decidedly post-ironic affair.

The scroll invited me cordially to a New Year's party taking place at Bradbury's Notting Hill space station. Had this message arrived a few days earlier I would doubtless have cast it into the bin alongside the copious junk mail I continued to receive from assorted post-apocalyptic religious cults, but my meeting with K had ignited a small flame in my belly, and I was surprised to find myself excited once more by the concept of socialising with some of my old colleagues. Besides which I was suitably charmed by the fact that Bradbury, a man more thoroughly ensconced in the wonders of Mauve than just about any I could name, still did his best to keep track of the Gregorian calendar, an affectation which was now considered resolutely antediluvian.

New Year's Eve arrived under a sumptuous purple sky. Positively cheered for the first time since before the cataclysms, I donned a freshly pressed suit and made my way to Notting Hill.

As expected there were more than a few old workmates in attendance at the party, all of whom took a moment to greet me warmly before resuming their various surrealistic affairs with the bevy of mutants, monsters, and various bizarre personae lingering, lounging, and mingling throughout the space station's cavernous steel belly.

"Delighted you could make it, dear boy," Bradbury said through a buck-toothed grin before being whisked off on the collective arms of a troupe of high post-society ladies. Bradbury, a balding anthropomorphic rodent stuffed into an oversized and overpriced suit, careering on a tide of unlikely admiration, was truly Mauve London's ultimate success story.

Shockingly, I found myself mingling with enthusiasm and enjoying it without reserve. It seemed that the aftermath of my aborted antisuicide --the trek to the gravy pond with the foul-mouthed child, my interview and subconsciously administered aptitude test with K-- had delivered me to a new psychological terrain where the effort to continue with the minutiae of living was stripped of its labour. Indeed as I cast my mind back to my anti-suicidal plan, I was now completely incapable of recalling the circumstances or rationale that had steered me towards such an impasse. The memory had expired, dissolved in a stagnant gravy pond with the final beat of an absent heart. During the course of the ensuing night I was able to forget everything; Ballard's farmhouse, the dogs, the shadow dwarves, the crows, the dildosintegrator, my hands frozen around the butt and trigger, my own butt wet and cold with frost, the blank silver sky … All of it had seeped away into the drainage system of my mind like a dream I had awakened from weeks earlier. I slipped back into a routine of preconditioned cordiality, greeting old friends with frank enthusiasm, surrendering to unforced laughter, indulging in divertingly bizarre exchanges with inebriated mutant strangers. After a few hours Bradbury commanded everyone to a hush in order to observe the countdown to a moot midnight, culminating in an obscene display by two naked badger-men clashing the bellends of their mighty phalluses together in a series of twelve dramatic BONGs. Partygoers embraced one another indiscriminately, wishing one another all the best for a phantom new year. I exchanged pleasantries, fondlings, and saliva with a sufficiently vast host of fantastical entities to render my brain quite incapable of processing the details.

Merry abandon reigned. We're all mad here. Long live the new flesh.

At around 4am or thereabouts (-should the reader insist on a value for such throwaway items as the number 4 or the letters A and M-) I was beset by a vision of beauty. She was of indeterminate age and incredible height, towering some two feet above me. She wore a striking pink dress embellished with a tiny bow between her bare shoulder blades. Her hair was black and her eyes were blue, a combination which caused me to recall the song 'Galway Girl' by Steve Earle, a song I had previously adored until it had been tainted by its use in a TV commercial for Magners pear cider. In her right hand she gripped a plastic tumbler filled with what was unmistakably pear cider. Between courteous laughs in response to jovialities offered by assorted revellers to her left and right, she lifted the tumbler gracefully to her thick lips, tilting hear head backward with the flamboyance of a true sophisticate, allowing the liquid to sail sensuously down her sloping neck to her exquisite gullet.

Before long she caught my stare and began eyeing me in return, punctuating faux furtive stares with a flickering of her thick eyelashes, a toss of her mane, a twitch of her ears.

To clarify: she had the head of a horse. A thin, beautiful woman's body tapered at the neck into the sublime elongated visage of a prize-winning mare. And never has a more gorgeous creature walked this Earth, pre- or post-Mauve. A centaur in reverse. A figurehead on the prow of the future.

Finally she broke from her company and approached me, her slender legs sailing her effortlessly across the steel floor. Musica universalis poured like liquid gold from her throat.

"I am Indigo."

Struggling not to pass out on a tide of nerves, I introduced myself with affected confidence and offered my hand. Her skin was a celestial meadow in summer bloom.

"You have very nice hair," she said, blue eyes gleaming. "May I run my fingers through it?"

I relented with pleasure as she cast a soft palm across my crown, each of my greying follicles responding ecstatically to the sustenance of her touch. A foal-ish smile danced around her equine lips.

"Your muzzle is really quite exquisite," I exclaimed, almost semi-consciously.

She shrugged, her pale shoulders rising and falling like snowdrifts.

"It's actually quite unremarkable by the standards of my species, nondescript even. But thank you for saying so. Your own muzzle is really something." She ran one satin fingertip down the line of my oversized nose. For the first time in my life I was entirely unselfconscious of that gull-like beak and its corpulent bulb-end that so obnoxiously dominated my face. "Very prominent and noble," she concluded, her expression sagacious and candid.

"Well that's a compliment I don't receive every day, so many thanks to you. And also you're quite welcome." I fumbled, desperate not to let the conversation flounder, and opted for a standard ice-breaker. "So how do you know Dr Bradbury?"

The snowdrifts rose and fell once more. "How does anyone know anyone? Look into the sky's arsehole for long enough and you'll see what it ate for dinner."

Her cryptic and crude response relaxed me considerably. "I'll have to take your word for that."

She emitted a gentle laugh, nostrils flaring reflexively, hot breeze bathing my face in rich staccato blasts. "How did you arrive here tonight?"

"I walked. Crazy old-fashioned I know. But walking around London is more interesting now than it was a few years ago. Had to navigate a sentient toy parade on the way here tonight. The soldiers, dolls, and teddy bears were all cool, but I incurred a bit of attitude from the odd action figure or two."

She grinned broadly, divulging an assembly of square teeth, dazzling in their symmetry. "Isn't that wonderful? I do love this town. I should walk around a lot more. I arrived here by cotton candy mammoth myself."

I just accepted this as fact. "Well, if you'd like, I'd be happy to take you on a tour sometime. Psychogeography is a whole new ballgame these days. A lot of fun but it can be pretty dangerous. Best not to walk alone."

"That sounds like an excellent idea," she said, her ears batting wildly at phantom flies. "And I accept your gracious offer."

Our convergence had granted the edge to a white blade of desire that trimmed the night to a stump. Amatory heat melted us into a nearby loveseat, huddled close to hear one another over the din of revelry, where our conversation encompassed a broad gamut of subjects pertinent to the lives of two everyday citizens of this most non-everyday of cities. The sustained rhythm of delight resounding in my chest informed me that I was quite smitten with this lovely creature, and this amazed me. Only a few days previously I would have thoroughly rejected the idea of formulating a romantic interest in anyone, let alone one of the many fantastical mutants of Mauve. The wound of Poppy's departure had festered long and painfully, scarring my soul and psyche with a morbid tattoo that had seemed to certify my inertia as permanent. Alas my recent journey from the brink of anti-suicide had evidently blown a wide hole in my consciousness, allowing my long-interred dream self to flee towards a new, less rigidly defined horizon.

By the time I embraced Indigo in a passionate kiss, her elongated tongue lapping lasciviously at my tonsils, I knew that this was love. At long last my own place in the Mauve Zone was tantalisingly within reach.

We supped raw passion from fluted glasses. As we talked, caressed one another's shoulders, explored each other's snug recesses with fingers, lips, and tongues, abandoning all obligations of decency, I knew that I would never again set foot on the ground. I had evolved. Sprouted interstellar gills and stepped into a new element. The Earth was cold dead mud in a desolate garden pond. A derelict stable, obsolete and forsaken. A makeshift theatre stage, flesh curtains parted. Our union spotlighted through a hole in the ozone ceiling. Extraterrestrial tendrils probing through the windows between dimensions, forceps of the cosmos dragging revolution from its amnion. The skies were starlit streets. Indigo's dress had slipped from her shoulders and unfurled past her breasts. Two pristine new planets danced to the Music of the Spheres. To a hybrid heart's jubilant gamelan.

Some two hours or so after we'd first fallen into each other's gaze Indigo declared that she had to leave.

"I promised I'd accompany a friend in a taxi to her home in the heart of the Mauve Zone," she said through a flutter of eyelashes, hoisting her dress straps back up to her shoulders. "You know how it is, there's some of us strangelings can take only so much of humanity for one evening. Thankfully I don't have that problem, but ..." She trailed off, truncating her sentence with another snowdrift.

Desperate not to be robbed of her company, I wanted to suggest that I come along on this detour, but was conscious that my presence would likely not be appreciated by her nameless friend. Besides which, in spite of my newly bolstered positivity, I had deep reservations about venturing into the epicentre of the Zone in any circumstance.

The risk of being utterly disintegrated by one of the many psychic black holes that lined the periphery of that omni-dimensional portal seemed too great a risk for a relative novice, and though Indigo's mythical mutant genes guaranteed her a greater degree of safety, I nonetheless worried for her too.

"It's really not at all as bad as you think, once you learn to listen," she said, intercepting my apprehension. "The heart of the Zone beats to a rhythm. As long as you can name the tune and sing the melody, you can dance in and out of there with no calamity."

"I believe you," I said sincerely. "Maybe I just need a few more dance lessons before hitting that party."

She draped a tender arm around my neck and moved in for a final kiss. "And I'll be glad to coach you, love."

I scribbled my address on to the back of a coaster which Indigo folded into a leather purse.

"I will walk with you soon," she whispered into my ear, hot horse breath strafing my skin, unleashing a bushfire across the plains of my soul.

Then she glided effortlessly through an array of drunken revellers of all imaginable mutations, and off out into the anonymous dawn.

Newly fortified as I was, no measure of self-assurance could have adequately primed me for the psycho-emotional helter-skelter of the ensuing few weeks.

Indigo materialised at my window-ledge some days later, her graceful mass balanced inexplicably upon that narrow precipice, her dark mane riding the breeze like a fleet of crows, eyes glinting with blue fire, a slinky purple evening dress billowing around her. Wordlessly I admitted her inside and we embraced, our wild heartbeats merging as one. Our provisionally planned walk was swiftly forgotten as our passion shunned the streets. Instead we remained indoors and coupled furiously in each of my apartment's shabby rooms. Alien suns rose and fell multiple times during our congress, phantom hours running into days as we each feasted on the other. My hands were afire upon her breasts, my entire genital area bathed in hot nectar as I thrust into her, my tongue electric as it burrowed its way between her robust jaws, my nostrils choked with the musky ecstasy of her mane.

Indigo sang like a soprano as she rode us to paradise, a voice clearer than a mountain spring and keener than a razor.

"Listen, my love," she sang to me. "Listen to the song, my love. Listen to the melody. Do you hear it? The melody to our beat? Sing with me, my love."

With each orgasm the building shuddered.

Unknown words erupted uncontrollably from my throat. The neighbourhood pterodactyls shat fleets of ice cream vans. Somewhere on the opposite side of the city, K looked up with a start from a pile of unmarked aptitude tests.

"Did you hear the song?" Indigo whispered repeatedly into the folds of our exhausted post-coital huddle. "Do you think you can sing it, my love?"

"I don't think I quite have your vocal skill, but maybe you can teach me."

She shook her massive head and snorted vigorously. "Not *my* song, dear one. I'm just the accompaniment. You need to listen more closely." She planted a tender kiss upon my lips. "Maybe the next one, my sweet. Maybe the next one."

Thereafter a pattern developed. Following several immeasurable days of this supernatural lovemaking Indigo would rise from the bed abruptly, dress at high speed, and depart with but a peck on the lips in lieu of explanation. There would then ensue an interval of painfully long days without word from her, days in which the veneer of my new resolve would betray accumulating cracks. Desperate not to regress to my previously jaded and apprehensive state, I took to passing the hours at my window, staring out upon London's surrealistic vista and willing it to imprint itself upon me. With the passing of days my apartment seemed to ascend farther from the ground, the building continually acquiring new storeys from the bottom up, and I worried that my increasing isolation from the Mauve streets would see me annexed forever. Indigo was the key. She was my talisman. My passport to an unregimented mutant future where my mundane errand-boy past could be cast off and dispelled permanently.

No sooner would I find myself on the edge of absolute despair than Indigo would reappear at the window, beautiful and brazen, a mythical queen of the elements, a new Boadicea invoking the wrath of Andraste, reclaiming London for all of her fallen daughters. And thus the fire was rekindled in my breast, the nectar flowing freely once more, the ecstasy of musk and electricity.

"Sing with me, my love."

Crow wings flapping around her hot horse breath, I felt time's scarlet messenger grab at courage's fraying thread - cutting the gravy mirror into slender shards - tasted her mutating skyscrapers in my own eyes -- She would be feigning sleep, leaning on the razor window ledge by tangled mane and half-open mouth - alien anthems drawing her eyes to a more imperative reflection ...

"Maybe the next one, my sweet."

And after each departure the intervals became longer and more insufferable. In the apartment building's accumulating storeys I decoded a measurement of my own frailty. Weak belly exposed and vulnerable. Desperate for Indigo's sheltering shadow. Wincing in the callous rays of an executioner sun.

Eventually terrible questions came whipping blackly to the surface of my mind:

What if she does not return? Perhaps I should spare myself the pain, turn from it and deny it. Perhaps I should return to what I'm good at and forget this fantastical nonsense. I'm not cut out for the Mauve Zone. K knew that. K recognised my appropriate potential. I liked K. I had believed K when she said she had my best interests in mind. Why haven't I heard from K? How long has it been? Weeks? Months maybe? Impossible to tell. Would it be too late now return to Chips Inc. and secure a mundane but comfortable admin position? How do I find my way there? I can only barely remember where the building was and London is changing shape daily. But I guess I could try. Try to get away from these notions, these ridiculous love thoughts, this crazy mutant pipe dream. Maybe I'll find my way back to K. Through associative thought channels. I hear about this shit all the time from people at the Building. Windows to other thought-lines. Yes. The window. That's it. If I step from that window, out onto the air above these multiplying floors ... Yes ... The window ... To K ... To a good safe job ... To ...

And then a furious whinny at the window ledge. Dark mane riding the breeze. Eyes of blue fire. Andraste's wrath propelling her bestial muscles. Paranormal nectar. Musk and electricity.

"Sing with me, my love."

Perhaps she had not told me the story that blossomed there in the rubble of her clothes - deep-drawn breath to the city's boundless borders - fetid flakes falling to frigid floor -

"Maybe the next one, my sweet."

Departure without a word.

And the abyss yawning wider each time, my mind and body warped in the agony of withdrawal. Ice sweats and clenched teeth and scraped knees and grazed elbows and cumbersome rolls of excess flesh flopping in dust like aborted and discarded pancakes and begging begging begging for the hit that soothes a little less each time, greater and greater energies expended for smaller and smaller dividends.

My own failure carved in the grey storeys of endless mornings.

Away from these notions ...

Whinny.

Riding the breeze. Nectarmuskelectricity.

"Sing with me, my love."

The carcass of my home keeping red flowers before the gash - my old love unrequited- she was lying there still on my guts among ruined breath - waiting always waiting in other images other words - glued to a circle unbroken in bittersweet cider aeons - My old love's tiger rage invading the lungs as I preserved the disaster zone of our bed - The messenger's torn dress of memory brittle as a frozen leaf - the gravy pond oppressed in the darkness, the absent heart lay in wait ...

"Don't you ever miss being with a normal human girl, dear one?"

Jagged rocks in my throat. "I've never known anyone normal. There's nothing to miss."

Silence and a theatre of sentient shadow on the mildewed walls. Hastily smoked cigarettes and a final kiss.

"Maybe the next one, my sweet."

Maybe I'll find my way back to K ... Away from these notions ...

A hundred more storeys since yesterday.

Playing with an old knife. Dusty blade inscribing red tattoos on my forearm. Preparing an autopsy on love. Wondering if the heart that beats inside her mutant ribcage ultimately remains as distant and inaccessible as the sun. The same sun that she sings to, its incandescent face turned from me. The same song I can't hear.

whinnyatthewindowledgemaneridingthebreeze eyesofbluefirepromisingnectarmuskelectricity

"Sing with me, my love."

Time was drawing the battle lines: crudely scrawled figures converging in military formation - obscene genitals brandished like bayonets, mocking my powerlessness, my limp disgrace - luminous slogans of warfare propaganda - flicker of no return in the featureless eyes - animal-headed mothers rallying foul-mouthed spotless children to the frontlines of Armageddon - death tremors in stagnant gravy waters -

My body curled into the duvet. Shivering. My back to her. Concealing my flaccid shame.

"Maybe the next one, my sweet."

Her kiss ephemeral and remote.

Two hundred storeys later. There has been no 'next one'. No more whinnies at the window ledge. No more blue fire. No more nectar. No more electricity. No more musk. No more ecstasy.

Yes. The window. That's it. If I step from that window, out onto the air above these multiplying floors ... Yes ... The window ... To K ... To a good safe job ... To ...

Pain flared in my ears, causing me to flinch. Out at the farthest perimeter of my aural range a high-pitched sound was vaguely discernible. A sharp elemental resonance like the mating call of an electricity pylon. I tilted towards the window and the sound amplified. A rise and fall in pitch. A melody there tugging at my central nervous system, yanking me towards it. I unlatched the window and let it fall open. A green sun caressed my unwashed nakedness in its balmy rays. Below me London was in a state of light winter, clusters of snow cushioning the bodies of insectoid automobiles, ice crystallising around eaves and ledges. The subliminal song nagged at me, faint but insistent, its every rise and fall synchronising with my pulse. *Ba-boom Ba-boom Ba-boom*. Melody and beat coalescing in arcane marriage.

I stepped up onto the ledge.

Rise and fall …Rise and fall …

My lungs contracted, absorbing their maximum load of the errant dawn.

Ba-boom Ba-boom Ba-boom

Without fear of gravity I extended my right foot out into empty air.

Rise and fall …Rise and fall …

Words burst unconsciously from my throat, echoing across London's cancerous crags and caverns: "I hear you! I hear you! I'm ready! Ready for the future-past-present! Ready to take my place!"

Ba-boom Ba-boom Ba-boom

A dim triad of gibbous moons formed a face in the sky, a pair of downturned eyes and a wide sagging mouth.

Rise and fall …Rise and fall …

I walked off of the ledge and into the dawn's vacant embrace.

Through a cavalcade of capricious storeys the street rushed to meet me.

Ba-boom Ba-boom Ba-boom

Crow wings flapping around her hot horse breath, I felt time's scarlet messenger grab at courage's fraying thread - cutting the gravy mirror into slender shards - tasted her mutating skyscrapers in my own eyes -- She would be feigning sleep, leaning on the razor window ledge by tangled mane and half-open mouth - alien anthems drawing her eyes to a more imperative reflection …

Rise and fall …Rise and fall …

Perhaps she had not told me the story that blossomed there in the rubble of her clothes - deep-drawn breath to the city's boundless borders - fetid flakes falling to frigid floor -

Ba-boom Ba-boom Ba-boom

The carcass of my home keeping red flowers before the gash - my old love unrequited- she was lying there still on my guts among ruined breath - waiting always waiting in other images other words - glued to a circle unbroken in bittersweet cider aeons -

Rise and fall …Rise and fall …

My old love's tiger rage invading the lungs as I preserved the disaster zone of our bed - The messenger's torn dress of memory brittle as a frozen leaf - the gravy pond oppressed in the darkness, the absent heart lay in wait …

Ba-boom Ba-boom Ba-boom

Time was drawing the battle lines: crudely scrawled figures converging in military formation - obscene genitals brandished like bayonets, mocking my powerlessness, my limp disgrace - luminous slogans of warfare propaganda - flicker of no return in the featureless eyes - animal-headed mothers rallying foul-mouthed spotless children to the frontlines of Armageddon - death tremors in stagnant gravy waters –

Rise and fall …Rise and fall …

She would be sitting beside her words - her face rising blackly from rusted shadows in the garb of an old photograph -- Blades of time flashing in the insensible windows as I pass - spectral horses bursting from terminal stables, eyes ripped wide with inconsolable fury - phantom fire still lurking in the drainpipes and gratings, tongues lashing to inscribe time's clerical tattoo --

Ba-boom Ba-boom Ba-boom

Grey snake of entropy whipping in administrative entrails - I had written something like it in blue ink - a familiar alabaster grin at my back and the gears of the city working - my old love's red petals of memory - my inept hands ticking the boxes without thought - shreds of purple paper in tepid rainwater - black mane dissolving to elegant rubble - tasted her disappointment in the mutating concrete --

Rise and fall ...Rise and fall ...

Blades of time printing the remembered words in blue ink - in striplights - in dryly conditioned air - their savage syntax cutting the absent heart to mincemeat ---

Ba-boom Ba-boom Ba-boom

I'm with you Poppy ... in the stuffy classrooms and lecture halls ... before Dalston and the Building ... before the Mauve Zone and the Order of Dagon ... chasing phantom horses in the auburn fields of your hair ... filing them away like trinkets in our organisers and laptops ... turning our desk lamps away from the worry in their blue eyes ... spectres of failure, of the tick-tock cold iron onslaught of time, of illness and madness and ignominy, of some unnameable military attrition devastating our melancholy lovers' idyll, casting its flotillas upon the troubled causeways of our veins ...

Rise and fall ...Rise and fall ...

Away from these notions ... back to K ... associative thought channels ... to K and her chipper reassurance ... to a good safe job ... to ... a melody dancing in the ether ... a high-pitched sound ... vaguely discernible ... Listen hard now ... a sharp elemental resonance like the mating call of an electricity pylon ... Listen! ...

Ba-boom Ba-boom Ba-boom

My pulse providing the percussion ... an evolutionary fanfare tugging at the central nervous system ... Listen ... Listen ...

"Hey, cloth-ears, you awake there?"

The office reasserted itself around me with a thunderclap as my consciousness was slammed at high speed back into my head.

"You still with me?"

K was snapping her fingers frantically in front of my face. Her eyes were narrowed, shimmering like rain-washed windows in sunlight, and her sculpted grin had faltered into a grimace.

"Sorry," I mumbled, massaging a throbbing temple with two fingertips of my left hand. "I thought I heard something ..."

AIMLESSLY DELIBERATE ONE WAY OUT & BOOKENDED TELEKINETIC MINDBEND

Danny Baker

Something feels odd. As if Hypnos is having his way with him in some fashion beyond K's comprehension. As usual, however, K finds himself in Times Square- the subway-bowels of progressive hijack fascist metropolis, explication of which Bradbury might have fathered with Orwellian jism.

An unfamiliar pressure though, most closely resembling physical manifestation of plutonic assignation with Neptune some leagues below surface chop- a pressure resembling, however not precisely as such, weighs upon him.

Above, millions of blank stares scurry about uncontrolled chaos discovered anywhere depleted souls burn holes in molten sidewalks connecting vast constructs buzzing with makeshift hives of rapacious cubicles covered in honeycomb taupe exsanguinating life its animation.

High-beams of the train, the Q train, approach with mechanized whistle sounding more like a call to arm the next leg of the journey or final blast for four horsemen of Rommel's Apocalypse before leaving the public house for circus gigs. Five babies spark up on the third rail spewing virulent reptilian offal over the whole; the stone platform and all who stand upon baseless foundation.

Nary a bubble caption hovers over the collection of fetal discharge. If there are no bulbs illuminating subordinate silhouettes, it can no longer be about comic strips, K avers silently. A fractal hologram screams in terror- atrophied sinew failing to erect a wall between view and emaciated expressions resembling eternity meeting its finality firmly gripped by oxygen removed from the reaper's death chamber.

Two pink saucers melt into the clattering tubes without morphing or losing shape in any fashion or abomination of tumescent designers on catwalks supported by struggling gantries. The babies spring to life, crawl indifferently on the suddenly spotless platform, pristine entrails reinstituted. They snicker reproach at reversal of misfortune about which they have no reservations nor estimated wait time. This scene repeats daily as they see it while genuflecting to an effigy of Descartes spitting nonsense into nonsense- yes-distinct double negative indicating a reasoned feint of introspection expounded to witless lice infested matte bobble-heads.

K, you see, is straddling the hotline and all is hopeless. Sweet yet sulfuric bouquet replaces human reek, arriving in green mist from both the tunneled ingress and its opposing hollow arch. The train, the Q train, runs to the end-stop screeching like a raptor feasting on mastadonian detritus. The fore fascia grins honed spikes which never clamp. As hasty the realization death is imminent, so the train, the Q train, penetrates his spectral doppelganger like a cock through a gaping black hole streaking through oily infinity untended and without bloodshed nor loss of limb- swallows his out of body experience whole.

The train, the Q train, is certain as third party accounts could sum. Is the clone then nothing but apparitional protoplasm through which gas and matter pass freely? Antimatter obviating its latter syllables? Corner pieces to a puzzle wrapped in solipsistic disorder?

Poltergeists slide through snowy cracks in collective perception- red herrings in the wake writhing in canned diversion. Howdy-Doody marionettes with independent power supplies and disquieting smiles surgically rendered permanent rustling with osteoporotic skeletons in deep closets. Détournement? To what ends? Will only they of psychokinetic means be saved? Perhaps they too get bent. Or is it simply a new boss, same as the old but for bondage- panted drunken mohawk squaws whose ultimate untainted virtue is at risk of adulterated commoditization and axiomatic corollary-declination of utility down greased rails onto spitting cadaverous digits or under curse of self-ordained of (apocryphal principle)straw dog willing to shell out an extra shilling for a trick through the moist parapet in a fecal men's room, asserting unity with spurious movements designed in theory to abolish causal impact of human degradation via fiat measures? Who then to proclaim in his image Situationist?

K watches as his first party reflection brushes off and boards the glimmering vessel enshrouded in purple puffs of ill tempered tetrahydra cannibals. Inadequately endowed as manifest by his nude formaldehyde rot, a projected image of Marx is glaring rabidly prurient at him. The neutral faces about either side remain still. Two pink saucers hover, slightly less brilliant than before, perhaps flatter for the wear. The pressure, unfamiliar pressure, builds. The neutral faces in what's best described as a gallery see nothing worth choosing a side. K, barely of wits following the preceding minutes' chaos, convulses. Vomits violently. Faints. Chalk outlines of griffins fluttering about like butterfly phoenixes chase their subjects about the murk.

Dr. MOTU peers condescension glassing over myopic pupils and party favors- a sight to which K awakens supine on an Eames chair. A humanoid silhouette cut through asbestos particle board above seems to draw no notice of MOTU however K struggles to divert attention from the curious cutout, outline of which serves as boundary of sorts about which bits of sediment fall however never land atop K- around him only. MOTU speaks. Electro-kinetic static permeating each breath prevents apprehension of all but rifts in the chaotic energy to which the Doctor is apathetic.

Perhaps he's no Doctor at all. One would have to assume he's actually there in his engorged grandeur which fails K but seems well represented by various and myriad letters adorning chastising walls begging vituperation if only to retaliate; that is if, of course, they actually hang any more than the fractured sound waves refracting through the broken puzzle in the ceiling tile. MOTU is oblivious, if of course, he exists.

Formally MOTU, birth-name Motu, which the Doc felt did not adequately represent the immensity of his being as so delivered in a dream mistaken for a visit with bloody Narcissus-preeminent mentor whom he would proceed to drown in duality of intent. Too many reflections are breaking the glass. Two orbits were more than earth could muster. Ergo Motu underwent judicial reconstruction, official rechristened transmutation, into capital engorgement. Henceforth MOTU read his calling card further embossed by post graduate notations and myriad gook designed to reroute attention to the nearsighted bloated wonder before his image.

A bust of Descartes sits behind and to the left of MOTU- MOTU's left. Twenty four inches off center to be exact. Countersunk brads lost in kaleidoscopically swirled marble effigies of deforested maple-clutches magnetically envelope the sculpture, placing it intransigently-meticulously- in its proper location. Audacious existence- morbidly obese existence, incarnation of which is a paradoxical umbrella eclipsing insecure necessity for affirmation of being overshadowing its questioning essence proffered by philosophical patriarchy arguing chickens and eggs as carts jump horses. Any reference to, or physical indication of Sartre, seemingly more apt for such rumination is conspicuously absent these mindbending- these stupefying surroundings.

Across the room, twenty four inches off center of the bust- to the right, MOTU's right- twenty four inches to the right of the bronze- a mirror staring lovingly about the odd incumbent behind the gilded throne. Countersunk brads lost in kaleidoscopically swirled marble effigies of deforested maple-clutches magnetically envelope the sculpture, placing it intransigently-meticulously- in its proper location.

Increasingly, pressure, that unfamiliar pressure most closely resembling what one might experience upon plutonic assignations with Neptune, some leagues below the surface chop-though different all the same- is beginning to take its toll.

Gravity dense as it is light. Dichotomies which aren't. Missing philosophers- misinterpreted intent. Dead babies- leveled by silver bullets and third rails, yet return to wailing without tangible impetus. Where to home if home is eleventh dimension and tenth is whence you came yet not proved nonetheless? Wandering incoherent on its own dime lost somewhere in scientific method not running in tandem with its hypotheses- missing links for long overdue theorems. Where has sentience relieved itself sanity?

K surveys the otherwise gratingly sterile room silently annotating his observations. Concludes no work could ever nor will ever have taken place here. A short look in the mirror leaves him seeing a still pond- stoic- brief however sincere incantations of infatuation with the refractory clone permeate all K sees. All he hears. The good Doc likewise sees MOTU only MOTU. Mythological symbolism incarnate stuck to his own inflation. Reduced by its counterweight. Addicted to its shield. It goes like this: what the fuck are the serpentine inquisitors slithering towards and why doesn't this Doc, this MOTU character, whomever he might be- why doesn't he react to the scaled fanged pestilence shooting from his condescending sockets?

Two saucers cross field of view- the Doc of course oblivious. K begins to feel warmed by these spectral visions- flying fucking saucers, UFOs, whatever they represent; contemporaneously cursing their very existence, seemingly indicated solely in his mind's eye. They were becoming familiar- much so as to breed contempt (*overused maxim* being oxymoronic on its face) but time is the great obviator- slaughterhouse of expectation- guarantor of fantasy, never revealed but in billions of singular finales. K peers towards a bust of Sartre- Sartre, noticeably missing a moment ago- meticulously placed where a bronze embodiment of Descartes sat. K withdraws inside himself. Faints. Awakens- apparently.

A hundred jars teem of aborted fetuses with purple tongues protruding from enlarged mandibles. Exposed grey matter oozing from inadequate facilities evidenced by shattered calcium deposits at the base of each Petri laden mantle. Shivering embers burn to fruition in a strategically located fire-pit, searing cavities into K's perforated however contemplative musings. MOTU nowhere to be found but everywhere to behold.

K notices Descartes'- bust of whom has reinsinuated its position to the disappearance of Sartrean inanimate embodiment- Descartes, yes- his disarticulated eyes spun inverted yet nothing of its metallic mien expresses physical discomfort. K senses voracious introspection upon more ardent inspection of the exposed optic nerves twittling about their breath of fresh though uncomfortably sultry air however. It, collective it, sees only... it. Is not inverted exclusion of external objectivism jurisdictional purview of another master?

MOTU arrives through an open door in the ceiling abutting a humanoid silhouette cut through asbestos particle board outline of which serves as boundary of sorts about which bits of sediment fall however never land atop K. K again struggles to divert attention from the curious cutout- from what is, on this distinctly peculiar entrance, this patently anti-gravitational entrance of the wildly engorged self indulgent medical entity whose utility is still no more apparent than its purpose.

MOTU grabs a seven iron from a sterile umbrella repository, swings poorly, cusses audibly, unimpressed at signs of logical distress colliding with the patient at hand- nary the least bit surprised by this oft repeated scenario. K is of no mind to endure reproachful interrogation though. Beyond MOTU's blubbering frame is not but an array of doors alike to such a degree as to suggest multiplication in identical fashion from a single zygote of ostensive however unlikely Darwinian origin. Recreating inanimate perfection in a faulty cocoon needing not theoretical weeding of flock as perfect has no weakness but for its own pomposity. Foggy conclusions seep from beneath their bottoms- all heady enough to ward off attempts at clarification or escape. K is again edging towards vertigo.

From whence these apparitions? These snippets of utterly confounding esoterica? Phantasms tossing child's play about while incendiary flashes spark revolution among epistemological branches beyond pay grade smashing through storm windows in torrential outpouring of antipathy. Marionettes lacking drawstrings yet still wickedly ambulatory- scoffing hateful- smirking disdain as the stricken is held to paralysis of conjecture and nightmarish tethers although bound by no palpable restraining province of dreamscape. Hitherto mysticism snared by perceptible phenomena. Is it his alone to perceive? Is it his- the disarticulated eyes- suffering retrorse nystagmic convulsions commingling affairs into a surreal Rorschach exhibition of no purpose past amusement of contemptuous polytheistic gods whose ostensible efforts test K's anti-teleological bias ironically peppered with antithetical Deistic sympathies? What else to explain this unscripted verse in destiny's playhouse? Is the Sartrean likeness deliberate in misplacement or exacting diversionary tactics in apparent bid for theoretical misconception? Is K thinking to prove he is? To perpetuate a specified philosophy or simply a pea in a galactic shell game intent on reintroducing him to parablistic subject matter? Who was JOB? Did he too sleep through life or live through sleep? Who's pulling the wild card from the avaricious grip of vengeful puppets on thunderous occasion? What flutters-cornered to the peril of all present- beneath the perspiring mattress?

MOTU silently scoffs at audible ruminations of his disquieted charge before passing with not so much as explanatory gesture nor parting word, seamlessly through a melting wall-breathing, living partition created by MOTU himself or is it all a dream created by allegory in an horrific reverie becoming all too familiar to K, who left to no other end, pinches himself to ensure he's in throes of angry slumber *(though increasingly it seems, even to K, something other than soporific exploits are operating the machinery),* at which point two saucers, pink saucers, throw fireballs at his unequivocal wakefulness and it's all a dream is disproven and reverie- any hope of tranquil reverie now and forever, is laid before him in mist of aerosol ricin discharge.

Seven tosses and the dice come up craps. An epitaph-inscribed midair cursive- warns of terminal adieux, sending K to complete unconsciousness without a hint of precedent somnambulant locomotion. Wakeful, finally, is out like a light which is but apocryphal reprieve. Ruptured filament is easily replaced by scornful Fates. Retirement works diligently to subvert consciousness gone askew.

What was certainly dreamscape in reverse- a

pasture from where K arrived to greet the train, the Q train, is whittled to anything but unambiguous. Liana wraps like serpents absorbing each musing K silently utters to explain illogical conclusion. An arrow darts from thin air to too close for comfort. Again, he's ever so aroused, unequivocally aware-intensely uneasy. That of sleep-repose in seductive embrace of soft lactating breasts, wars of graphic detail, fitful perspiration, apneatic jolts, soothing fable, contemplative parable, agreeable green dragons and drooling horizons have all landed on the ear of utterly alert. Normatively concomitant benefit of unconscious peace eludes capture.

Cooing doves and carpets flying stably over golden Babylon getting no airtime, fall to mindfully excavated boneyard never to be heard from again. Only inaccessible terror remains- intractable terror- inexorable terror. With equilibrium seemingly terminal in preordained finality, K begs for narcoleptic salve. He gets none. Immoveable- he can't pinch himself to rise. Awake is sound asleep. Slumber is dressing for work.

Dozing back to toils of monotonous scrapes. Hugging zombies for scraps of dead pigeons. Fools and their money should never have met in the first place. Harping on whatever lark might pass him by. All things considered possible are none rejected out of hand. K finds himself stuck on a tarmac heading to no plane he wishes to occupy. Tedium in taupe cubicles bearing invisible Jolly Roger warnings flashing neon as peers are culled from adjoining carpeted death squares throughout the grey morning. The matte muted hue of fish travelling upstream on escalators to death chambers feeding machines input to get outsourced to a distant land where dots adorn foreheads and children climb rubbish heaps for smidgens of unholy sustenance while herds of cattle pass uninterrupted in well fed distention of sacrosanct indifference. Objective truth is but a rest stop between subjective illusions. Spite casts wicked holograms on lucidity only bested by dread of sleep which is strung out on speed. Tilt-a-world off its axis is all K can infer. Retrograde astronomy. Metaphysical ballasts off kilter. What more to explain realism to impression?

K finally wrests animation from these purported bowels of unconscious torment. Of herds slaughtered by virtue of success, before paralytic fear thieves him his sanity. A discordance of off key songbirds mercifully stuns him with an unscripted stop. He's sitting on a unexceptional bench in an Eastern European square. *(Boom of a supersonic jet departing for Elba rattles the tunneled subsurface).* K's surrounded by a litany of bronze embodiments- infamous communist infiltrators, complementary scoundrels malcontents, murderous dictators, sadistic tyrants, fastidious Nazis, eminently malicious utopian progressives (easily identifiable by allegedly peaceful mantras) and asp twirling Methodists (slowly yet graciously relieving the larger pool their DNA). Gaping protrusions shoot from the eyes of all busts, inexplicably excepting the Methodists- exceedingly startling by their own accord. K ducks the advances.

Entrails of five babies smashed to oblivion by the train, the Q train, are expectorated by gaggles of unrepentantly flatulent geese droning ominously overhead, shrouding the metal its luster. Two saucers, fading pink saucers draw his attention. Where to is their vitality slipping or is but sleight of hand type paranoia distorting the melded primary rainbow of the only constant in lucidity avoiding his ascertainment?

Wide as a chasm is a fine line blurred by perception that wake/sleep cycle cannot explain. Dichotomous underbrush torn from its heath to discover polarity closing on rounding error to what is asymptotically zero but not quite there as the adverb implies. Likenesses of good and evil purported to separate virtue from vice dying without the other- incriminating antipodes in high crime and misdemeanor as one provides foundation for transgression of its ne'er do well doppelganger. All remaining is which is which. A question without answer as both are both and Nietzsche parts the sky, blowing incendiary commentary on mass confusion encircling mob mentality sent racing from the scene in a cloud of rocket propelled tear gas dissipating to reveal buckshot malevolence spearing 'cross the ether from thousand yard stares of heinous statues- historical relics bearing down forebodingly upon future events certain as axiomatic precept dictates. Objects in the mirror are closer than they appear. Is apprehension of Morpheus for offenses against mankind, while obvious in accusatory logic, actually a travesty of injustice? Is another explanation sitting patiently in the foyer? An explanation vindicating the exalted his hypnotic judgment, K accurately begins musing- ruminating hypothetical mathematics across time and space continuums in another plane of infuriatingly cryptic geometric proof. Is it ultraviolent deprivation of some subterranean plane depleting the saucers their melatonin? And from where does this sudden infusion of arcane physics enter faculties hitherto devoid of such seismic quakes of post graduate hypotheticals?

Increasingly stoic in that which now presents as questionable diagnosis as a nightmare- this etiological cognizance, questionably definitive in nature- equivocal certitude at its most contradictory, K eyes escape from the singularly more frightful state than previously inconceivability of abstract metaphysical dismay where all is possible yet none accessible, wonders what happened to MOTU before quickly losing interest in effigies of Narcissus, knowing full well they'll return to insuppressibly haunt him as all others- malignantly fantastical tumors in each gear- in all life forms. In his- his own orbit. He is his enemy- he is his only resource. He steps from the bench- the nondescript bench & stares into an unwavering pool about a fountain separated of its cascade.

A skywritten note bought and paid for by a coterie of Descartesian disciples eulogizes spurious Sartrean claims of internalized debate over analogous reference points as foundation for confounded penmanship, blaming Google and diagnoses of every malady for each set of symptomatic issue and a little knowledge is a threat- dangerous threat to the entire system already struggling in its own profane ignorance.

A flock of angry seagulls passes overhead, painting the unwavering basin with the most unbecoming of scowls. Clearly airborne yet odd of apt plumage. Could it be of hereditary insinuation? Perhaps a byproduct of inopportune grooming creating excessive drag to an otherwise amply aerodynamic superstructure? Their collective reflection, excessively apoplectic, suggests a mission only familial infighting could generate, violating the sanctity- the solemnity of gentle stillness beneath the inanimate spout- the inanimate fountain, on the edge of which K now rests body while confusion shreds soul to ribboned confetti. *(Distinct mephitic odor of a frenetic British kitchen violates already fetid airwaves).*

Parchment- a parchment scrolled flight plan tethered to a cropped feather begins a path downward, lazily adrift atop a light breeze which gently loosens its lade to the right, twenty four inches to K's right before returning sultry stagnation to the air, causing no discernible avian distress despite the additional fluttering exertion required of the clipped water birds clearly determined in their course. K retrieves the fallen document. It reads only "Rio."

A horrific screeching electrified synthesis envelopes the square. A bumble bee lands on K's shoulder- whispers something in his ear and all music henceforth struggles for breath without diversion of exceedingly abstruse and distracting video accompany while popping rocks drink carbonated firewater. Lit up on sampled odd bits of copyrighted harmonies until unrecognizable is their only commonality, which in terrifying irony brings to light that all divisions and viva la difference are wearing the same masking tape looping chronically. All melody is flat. All chords, discordant. Is this temporary disharmony, simply a transitory plague not mentioned in any book to which K had been exposed in Sunday school or in the rectory where parish priests passed out Cokes and Snickers to favored understudies or is it perchance something entirely more alarming? Obstinate from the go, K was never agreeable nor favored. His submissively- deemed enlightened- pliable peers invariably returned from private counseling sessions patently worse for the wear.

A torch singes the belly of an anonymous beast

where K proceeds to discover himself if, in fact, he is himself and not a vision nor pawn in divine rite. Tomorrowland is wilting in today and nothing but black magic nor Nazi sympathies can grease the cogs pressing the boat forward however even forward is backward due to repetitive nature of historical events- eminently cliché so that reciting the bromide would border on insufferable redundancy if not preaching to an ill-equipped choir.

Upon exit from what he can't recall pursuing entrance, K notices he hasn't moved an inch from his perch upon the brim of the inanimate fountain surrounded by a litany of bronze embodiments of infamous communist infiltrators, complementary scoundrels malcontents, murderous dictators, sadistic tyrants, fastidious Nazis, malicious utopian progressives (description previously proffered) and asp twirling Methodists whose numbers are again, by the grace of god, thinning rapidly.

K notices doves loose and cooing in pidgin. Flickers of seemingly disconnected diffuse scenarios run rampant through his cortex as the final gulls make their way towards Rio, riding a wave of synthesized notes electrifying cooling atmospheric hospitality. A rascal is running up a voluminous room service tab in a hollowed out sequoia. A spaceship lands on the moon; in caricature, an astronaut plants a flag in her folds though none are allowed on set until the first hymn is recited and oaths of secrecy are taken, despite which, all involved are relegated to weeks of bombardment by a mousy annoyance fronting magnetically salacious outtakes from a Roman orgy much as Bach overdubs ultraviolent reels until humanity is stripped naked by security agencies as a torture device to ensure adherence to that avowed. Nobody, including the black operatives can, without lasting and profound brain damage, suffer Martha's rodent squeals.

All of this is completed in a single take. Culture loses itself forever to unfed attention conveniently given medical labeling or an alias relieving afflicted of all culpability. Ritalin falls from ashen sky dripping Thorazine and Lithium. Nirvana recounts the latter in panacea. A shotgun blast splatters incoming to lights out and angry Samoans batter mainlanders with shark tooth clubs and intolerable assaults on good taste with copious servings of spam until all are strangled by invasive pythons.

K spins without moving a muscle as another flight departs fancy to unwelcome approach into the great divide far away and miles across dark horizons attempting a slide into this- the abysmal gap, with no prayer despite torrential downpour of dulcet lubricant as landing permission denied is twenty behind twelve bars if violated. Snow white substrate covering icy ponds now speaking Chinese. Mandarin with a Peking tongue as far as K can tell, but how? Has he gone daffy or is it simply a melody going on its merry way to enchanted forests and psilocybin mice bearing magic wands and tracks marked with starry eyed red herrings leading back to generalized anxiety disorders and concomitant variants of respiring constellations not yet discovered by astronomical query.

Does knowledge of all worlds ride unseen fall beneath sea level where all roaming are wild, wooly and ravenously carnivorous? It's there, rather than in grips of soporific stranglehold where all is possible and nothing rings of truth but for oysters clamming up on dialectic and all things considered are considerable reconsiderations of another set of principles and fractal fissures refusing to repeat their arguments. How is that this too is so easily assumed- that nothing is everything- that the universe at large is shrinking ever so rapidly once bound and gagged tethers are released from behind green doors of lurid post war scientific failure? Where to have the saucers gone? In an unfortunate irony, attachment to his being seems the death of that moan- the familiar drone of what had become K's ultimately welcome, if not accessible, escorts despite their outright intangibility? Ra refuses wading in Styx and stoning to death Sharia law is giving alternative divine interventionism a run for its fiat money. The root of all evil is photographed from its good side, printed on front pages anywhere print is still in vogue, courting instinct beyond capacity for resistance- armed or otherwise. Where are the pangs of hunger when bellies are full of sacred meals meant for eternal life or future endeavor? How again, in redundant interrogation, do minimally utilized faculties pick all fruit from earth's trees without enduring toxic shock of all knowing except for how? Thurber has some astute questions and all answers but from where he can't decipher, so sets upon in the whole argument with a noose over a kerosene high beam illuminating deficient ratiocination.

A statue removed from tropical confines has the Samoans up in matronly arms delivering curses upon any in contact. Unwitting accomplices, spider bit, drown in knee high water. Jetties turn flotation devices to lead. Kanaloa smiles. His garden plucked its virtue. No mercy is creed- same as all others on high mounts. Bunch of combined trees sent packing. Never take action on hormones eschewing hormones in close quarters. The odds are stacked against you. Heads you lose, tail you lose. Virgin soil fertilized. Find a cave. Return the quarry. From violently obtuse to episodic recollection of pubescent television, K is wholly lost in his contemplation of purpose.

Relentless cacophony of arbitrarily arranged thought passes in bromidic pulp milliseconds. Cheap offshoots laboring historical references splattering bylines of anonymous newsprint lacking geographical suggestion. He's resting without recumbence. Listless though breathless. The weight- Neptune's near analogous heft persists in its induction of arrhythmic consequence.

The seagulls long gone, their numbers like poorly choreographed sequences in death of a nation which knows no borders. Don't turn around or a Polish commandant will strip search you for a missing a consonant which keeps yet another bird seeking prey by virtue of a subconscious hum lamming it to alert temporal lobes in the aviary until death by looping atrocity meets inevitability. There is no end- no cap for this ceaseless, unrelenting reversion to bubblegum adhesive to childhood melodrama though its significance remains in question.

Hieroglyphic is writing on the wall. All is becoming clearer. K, ever precocious- processes esoterica by virtue of theoretical process. Chasing rabbits leaves one tired- likely bloody for the effort to boot. Bunnies coming upon one's carrot without enticement nor provocation are geysers of inspiration.

All signs begin to point to interred deeply rooted. Digging out is solution- is salvation, K is convinced. Plan of attack- uncertain. A train, the Q train suddenly appears from between bisected skies, running on the El tracks. K hops aboard undistracted by failure to yield and as passively expected, without injurious consequence. Ever precocious, he's quickly resigned himself to nothing making sense if not seen through eyes of meta-earthly consequence. Grand structure of fairy tale etiology- of Dahl-esque candy psychedelia architecturally manifested - fade in the Kremlin distance, leaving the fountains, gull droppings and plethora of unbecoming miscreants in blurry photograph, speeding away and in a bolt, gone from view. Yet the El only heads deeper. Is Hypnos rising?

K, enormously squeezed by an unrelenting power- an unnamable, unbearable force, resigns to what seems certain. He again sees the saucers- old friends in a way, nearing depletion of all pigment, struggling to maintain lift. MOTU appears in apparitional form or so it seems. K senses a fear not seen in his prior interactions with the good Doc. He's wan and sickly. And yet to convey any meaning for his presence, any purpose of his existence nor insinuation upon anything. Earthly or grander in nature. No explanation satisfying K's internalized debate as to form, function or necessity is forthcoming in the silent monologue. Yet could the weight- this intense lade be lifting? Does this blessing, if one might refer to it as such, require explanation or don't look a gift horse in the mouth bromidic constituent?

Suddenly, a flame spontaneously combusts in this hole- this black hole, something short of abyss in quantity. It flashes across what seems a meta-humanly constructed wall- as a hologram casting differing views from opposing angles, all inciting the same conjecture in their ambiguity, which in fact, is less random than the implication of uncertain descriptive nouns would itself lend. A fiery grave; raging inferno. K feels the accumulated pressure slowly easing yet still cannot explain the sensation- this overwhelming sensation, he's been subjected to in whatever this has been. Why ask now?

From within the pyre, a projection of Lucifer shutters the epoch- the entirety of whatever paradoxically linear abstraction in which K has found himself. He recoils in uncontainable horror. Despite clarity of illuminated transparency, not aptly fearless as to touch this, the source- this power source, in attempts to possibly reconstruct the preceding days' events, should they in fact have been days, in anything nearing an Einstenian methodology or thoughtful representation thereof, through physical contact with the proverbial ultimate of evil. The one logical suspect at the core of all this- this collective inconceivability.

Oddly, Lucifer- whole of venom incarnate- protector, purveyor of all things pestilent, gazes, in what can only be described as kindly, upon K. It's in indirect correlation to this view- undeniable yet unfathomably sympathetic view, that hitherto unexplained gravity begins to ease- perhaps even commencing some theoretical, nay, hypothetical conclusions which K languidly steps toward formatting.

Is there light?

In the blackness- the void previously described, yet now subjected to bloody red light of purgatorial etiology, a pond, still and flat. MOTU, directly petrified by appearance of the master of underwordly domain- quantifiably equal to K's illogical equanimity, *while facing what is broadly excepted as universal malice with no limit to potency of harm,* stares into the glassy pool- erstwhile MOTU's sole domain, albeit briefly. Its report is one of decalcified bone matter, of disarticulated joints, of offal denied its hydration. Dust. Earth has room for only one orbit.

The walls, previously inarticulable, are now clearly seen for what they constitute- erections of natural terrain- of unseeded dirt- fallow ground, unseeded- of lush sod and heather and wandering root- now collapsing on all aforementioned entities, references- straight and narrow or abstruse- and conclusions real or imagined. On

Lucifer (of course, indifferent- unconcerned- it is after all, his realm) holographic unkindled combustion. Everything. Except K that is, and in generous display of goodwill, the saucers, now deceased- bilateral life form casting serene anthropomorphized air about them, granted dignified proceedings.

The roar- unmistakable cacophony of death permeates all surroundings. A river audibly begs a ferryman's attention. K is breathing more deeply, increasingly less encumbered by the bulk of what had been steadily building to what he expected would be his finality.

A gravestone marks the identity of the moor in which this- intense divine production as is, all takes form, dropping into the subsurface beneath the hallowed ground above. A box, unremarkable steel measuring precisely seven feet in length, two in height, three in width, suspended in mid air over K and the saucers- colorless, serene and so very much deceased is all protecting them from the imploding top soil, ironically a footfall for mourners and substrate for arched marble headstones and their engraved ornamental sentiments. Is it proof of teleological design or another don't stare into the abyss without expecting a return gaze obtuse platitude best left for theologians and other in stiff denial of whatever actually is?

(Boom of a supersonic jet departing for Elba rattles the tunneled subsurface). Any semblance or embodiment of MOTU is no longer visible as this casket-box of unremarkable steel sets to flight. The pond into which he once stared is again undisturbed but by the creature- the broadly defined eponymous character embodying its storyline, and that of innumerable others exiled into unity- forever banished to a syphilitic island- who jolts back to life as if struck by paddles of defibrillating shock greased by electro-conductive Kool-Aid extract.

K, no longer feeling so much as a photograph of the anvil plaguing him to the point of resignation-capitulation to the final frontier, begins to conclude the reasoning behind the chaos which has a palpably Nietzschean quality about it. He hypothesizes a subjugation of humanity under a box of apocryphal treasure- ostensibly precious items worth nothing more than the Trojan horse in which they arrive. Yet can only come to hypotheses founded upon disparate questions of unanswerable imprint.

What remains of the scarred melodrama? Of the funambulist stroll through the garden of evil? Why this test as of JOB? Of fatalistic abstraction and death defying pop references and cultural kitsch challenging even the most pedestrian of taste- of sensibility? Flights of Valkyries to satisfy tyrants? Of misfits, miscreants? Violent subversives proclaiming love of all, proving aphorismic accuracy of a man named Buk? Of abstractions so profoundly beyond esoterica? Lightning flashes in bottles of violent references challenging sentience to its basest, most crass capacity? Accurately constructed prepubescent architecture unabashedly protecting the most vile while chocolate fountains sprinkle rain atop acid wash? Fatalistic absurdity of aborted fetuses.

So much for unfathomably aimless notional upheaval embodied in inaccessible and abstruse philosophy intersecting itself in utter inanity. For acuity of intuitively arcane dialogue, schematic representations, inaccessible imagery and conceptual bastardization on uneven planes. Of prurient joy derived of madhouse revelries and visions ill conceived- infuriating from the start. What trickery has Hypnos played in wanted posters bearing alternate identity of eponymous spirit though different name... and Morpheus goes into hiding? Or is it fact, not a slumber- a taste of immutable laws of life which are death? Of all bearing crosses and subconscious bones needing breath so life can kill them and at once, finally be removed from their pestilent volume and sins of thy father burned in the closets in which they're hiding?

How would one know the difference?

He continues his line of thinking however has no time to conclude as the platform to the train, the Q train, bustles feverishly about- concomitant bodies pressing about him. Any recollection of this straddle, this preceding toe to heel dance over invisibly polarized lines so vastly antipodal as to be wholly indistinguishable, lost for the ages. His head for some unknown reason, throbs.

He wonders from where all this anxiety- inane nervous energy emanating day after insufferable day and to what ends but an early grave for few shillings. A poster announcing an upcoming exhibit of ancient philosophies is glued to a soot covered tiled wall with a beautiful- strikingly notable, given its crass placement, drawing- at center, Epicurus.

Muddling about with the mass-mute, matte-faced Play Doh effigies of existence- death to be held at a date uncertain but definitively subject to a date, he rides this familiar escalator to street level- molten avenue brimming- barcoded salmon spawning, swimming upstream to gaping mouths of impatient bears, before strolling characteristically perturbed to his boardroom cubicle- his haphazardly assembled, asylum soothing taupe cubicle- transitory ephemeral honeycomb connected to more of the same, where at his nondescript desk, he takes his first coffee- standard fare Greek deli coffee, served with a shmeared salt bagel, ingested with a scowl of looping inveterate monotony. He notices a book where there had been none. It's title: Situationist & Slave To The Grind. A note atop reads:

NOTHING IS POSSIBLE UNDER THE CASKET- UNDER THE CASKET THERE IS NO BREATH- BREATH IS LIFE- BREATH IS DEATH- WHAT NEVER BREATHES NEVER DIES- WHAT COULD NEVER HAVE BREATHED COULD NEVER HAVE DIED- MONUMENTAL REPERCUSSIONS FOR ATTEMPTING DEATH BEFORE LIFE- WITHOUT BREATH THERE CANNOT BE REPERCUSSION.

In a like six by six square to his, across the austere boardroom- a co-conspirator- victim perhaps, in this, the grand scheme of death by tedium, wipes the hangover from his eyes after seeing what appears to be two brightly hued pink saucers. He then finds himself on a subway platform, awaiting the train, the Q train. Slightly less brilliant pink saucers hover before him.

STAINED BY DEAD HORSES
D M Mitchell

The great head of the foremost horse crashed through the window showering them with glass. The Assassin whirled his great black leather coat around Mistress C throwing them both to the ground. Huge shards of glass lacerated the crowd of spectators. The boy/girl creature was severed nearly in two falling in a rain of blood and shredded intestines. The huge head snorted fire and several of the onlookers who were still standing erupted into screaming balls of flame.

The Assassin rolled over. Mistress C had only suffered minor cuts. Her eyes spat blue flame.

"Diomedes!" snarled the Assassin and his guns cracked like thunder. The horse's eyes ruptured like grapes spraying caustic fluid. Where it fell, it hissed and sizzled, corroding metal, wood, leather and flesh alike.

"Ah but the pitiful work! Dismal the death that was your ending." screamed the Assassin, emptying round after round into the steaming carrion beast above him. He smelled liquorice and aniseed as the creature's bulk fell and skidded towards him. Scooping up Mistress C, he cleared the bar and they landed behind it on howling twitching bodies.

The dying horse screamed like brass; blood and nerve-endings spewing from the ruptured sockets. Its great metal flank scraped the length of the bar and it moved from its fixings.

"What the fuck have you brought down on us now?" howled Mistress C. He declined to answer, ducking under the remains of the bar and pulling out a pump-action, which he tossed to her. She caught it in a surprisingly demure way, then shouted.

"Chipped a fucking nail! How many more of these fucking things are there?"

The Assassin held up three fingers. The reverberations of the horse's death screams died away and they could now hear the other animals pawing and stamping outside the building.

"What are our chances?" she said. He turned and grinned, shrugging his shoulders.

"Love it!" she laughed. "I fucking love it!" They stepped around the twitching mare, Mistress C wrinkling her nose as the dying creature loosed its bowels and emptied its bladder. Its great sharp teeth flashed brass, snapping on thin air. The Assassin gestured with his head to the back of the bar, where so many months ago the Sisters had caught up with him. The great gilt mirror was now in minute shards, crunching beneath his boot heels like early morning frost.

One of the mares poked its head through the aperture in an exploratory way, shying from the scent of its sister's blood. Mistress Claudia fired off a volley but the beast had already picked up on the motion and darted back screaming horrendously. Its voice reverberated through the building, shaking what little glass remained intact in its frames.

"Don't waste ammo!" he whispered. Why was he fucking whispering, the fucking freak?

"What now, pretty boy?" she purred. He pointed to the rear exit.

"Then both, from out Hell-gates, into the waste wide anarchy of Chaos, damp and dark, flew diverse…"

"What the fuck?" she stared at him. He smiled again and, opening the door strolled casually out. She followed him, slowly, suspiciously. He simply carried on walking towards the wooden building opposite. At once, a huge cloud of dust erupted round the far side of the building as two of the mares rounded it, snorting fire; at least fifteen feet tall spiked and shod with flashing razored shoes.

Mistress C froze, unable to move forwards or backwards. The Assassin didn't even turn to face them but carried on strolling towards the wooden shack. As he strolled he reached inside his long coat and something flashed in each hand; something lethal looking and long. He started to spin, hopping from one leg to the other as though doing a demented circle dance. The mares thundered down on him and he disappeared, engulfed in the dust cloud. Mistress C fired almost point-blank into a huge gelatinous eye that rocketed past her, and for one second almost thought that her shot had brought down the monster which slid to its knees in the dirt; its momentum carrying it several hundred yards before it crashed to a thrashing halt. Blood gutted from its neck, which was opened to the bone.

The other horse wheeled around leaving a blazing trail of sparks on the air like some magickal sigil or vever. Its eyes rolled in confusion. Its right shoulder was scored almost as far as its stomach with a deep wound. It stopped, pawing the ground into deep ugly furrows.

The Assassin's shape began to emerge through the settling dust. He stood, head thrown back like a demented matador, two long blades held crossed above his head. Blood dripped from the knives onto his face. He lowered his head and stared at Mistress C and, smiling, licked the blood trickling into the corner of his mouth.

"That death be not one stroke as I supposed...." He said sepulchurally.

Mistress C turned to look at the horse. Confused by the smell of blood but also carnivorously aroused it threw back its head and howled. Then there was just a blur of rippling muscle as it charged again at the Assassin.

"Shoot the fucker!" he yelled.

She hesitated for an instant then the nasty shock of the recoil threw her off balance. She didn't even realise she had fired. She saw, as if in slow-motion, the great skull split in two and the brains and blood gush out in a welter. She also saw, in the same hideous slow-motion, the Assassin vanish under the bulk of the dying animal. It rolled several times and totally demolished the shed.

"No..." she heard herself say. "No no no no!"

He lay like a twisted broken umbrella. There was no way he could be alive. She started to move in his direction and found she had trouble walking, as if relearning the skill after some serious head trauma. Something rattled dryly in her throat. Then he moved, one hand clawing the air and he groaned.

"Jesus fuck me in the ass! That fucking hurt!"

She ran to his side. He rolled over onto his back and she saw that his front was soaked with blood; she couldn't tell if it was his or the horse's. With his left hand he held his stomach and with the other tried to sit up.

"Fucking hell! Claudia help me! In my pockets..."

"What? What's in your pocket?"

"Fucking big tube of superglue! I need it to fix this!"

He looked down at his stomach. His intestines were beginning to slip out from a hideous rent that stretched from his lower ribcage almost to his groin.

"That looks nasty." She said. "Is your dick ok?"

"It's still attached if that's what you mean." He grimaced. "Please! The glue!"

Behind them came a low rumbling growl. Mistress C glanced up, ice in her stomach. The last mare was approaching them, slowly and purposefully.

Poor thing didn't stand a chance.

The horses had gone. Claudia was gone. He checked his innards; they were all in place as far as he could tell, not being and expert. His memory of the last week was almost non-existent but Claudia wanted him to find her. That was certain. When he broke into The Building there were none of her 'bouncers' in evidence. None of her nasty booby-traps had gone off as he stalked through the mirror-lined corridors. He knew where they all were of course, but it saved so much time not having to dodge them all. But what really made him sure that she wanted him to find her was the fact that her twenty-foot python let him into her chambers unmolested. He glowered at it. He'd spent seven long hours once in its coils while Claudia had dressed and undressed in front of him, taunting him while she laboriously applied her makeup.

"Fuck with me now you legless bastard and I swear Claudia will end up wearing you as a matching bag and boots!"

It hissed softly and slithered away to a corner. It was very subdued. Claudia was in trouble, uncharacteristically out of her depth.

He opened her wardrobe. Inside was like a fucking tardis – rows and rows of different costumes of various styles made from unbelievable materials. Some of them were impossible to look at directly; others could only be seen when looked at from the right angle.

But the shoes and boots! How many shoes could a girl possibly need?

He browsed through a few outfits and found one he liked – one that Claudia wore quite often when she was taunting him. He took it over to the huge ornate mirror next to her bed (the one that had tried to eat him once when he'd been impolite enough to lay on it) and held it up in front of him.

"That'll do nicely!"

He stripped off his now blood-stained white clothes and began to dress as Claudia: tight blue leather trousers, rubber vest and high-heeled knee-length boots. He turned to look at his bum.

"Not as nice as Claudia's but I'd shag that!" he smiled.

He sat in front of her makeup table and browsed through her makeup, selecting a blood red stick. As he applied it he felt something heavy slide onto his lap. The python was resting its head like a pet dog, hissing slightly. He stroked its smooth plastic-like skin.

"I'll find her, pal. First I have to become her. Old hunter's trick!"

Ten minutes later he was striding along Shit Street, affecting a walk as close to Claudia's as he could. Using the nano implanted in his bloodstream by Zeus, he had changed his hair to a brilliant parakeet red and grown his nails into lethal metal talons. He could not do anything about his eyes – thanks to the Doctor and his implants they would stay clear silver orbs until he died. So he had stolen Claudia's favourite shades. He had always loved her style – pity she couldn't admit to herself how crazy she was about him. Women! – no matter how many of them he'd had to kill, he would never understand them.

Two apemen made the mistake of hitting on him. He left their remains in a rubbish skip in an alley. Twenty minutes later and a trail of carnage that would keep the police clean-up teams busy for a week and he was beginning to appreciate Claudia's constant belligerence. It was no fun being a woman having to run this gauntlet regularly. When he eventually found her he'd make more effort to be nice. Take her flowers or chocolates or some romantic shit like that! Before he tried to pounce on her!

He decided it was time to slip into shaman-space, unfocusing…

…letting the pheromone traces on Claudia's clothes register on his limbic brain and the reptilian implants.

Not enough trace. He dipped his hand into his jacket pocket (the large rubber one with spikes that made it look like a shiny fetish hedgehog) and pulled out a pair of Claudia's soiled undergarments. He put them under his nose and breathed deep. A light went on in his head – he could see the world now as luminous threads and there! A silver one he recognised, very bright. Claudia had been this way not too long ago.

"Hey sweetheart! How much do you want for those panties?" came an oily voice at his ear. He didn't even look in the direction of the voice; just punched two rigid fingers through the creep's windpipe and left him there rattling and spraying blood on the shitty pavement.

His tracker vision took him to the docklands, to a place called 'The Strange High House In The Mist'. Claudia had been slumming!

As he stepped into the backyard a door opened

and two reptilian-skinned mutations stepped out. He recognised one of them as an employee of Rex Mundy, self-styled King of the Shitheap! It started to make sense. The two looked up as he approached rapidly.

Mundy's man frowned.

"Claudia! I thought you were with…" he broke off as realization hit him, just before The Assassin shot him through the crotch with his Glock. The other mutation started to reach into his jacket but this was no professional. The man's face hit the wall and slid slowly down as his body staggered and tried to walk a few steps. The Assassin kicked it into some bins.

"Do NOT get blood on this jacket!"

The other droog was rolling around screaming holding his groin. The Assassin squatted down and whispered to him.

"Don't be worrying about your balls. Where you're going you won't be needing them anymore. Now…. You were saying?"

"No! He'll kill me!"

"Tell me and I'll kill you – but I'll do it far more quickly. Oh fuck!"

He was losing patience. He fired point blank through the man's right shoulder.

"Where is Claudia!"

"You're fucked! You can kill me but you're fucked!" the man spat. "She's with Mundy.

She decided that things were getting too weird and that he offered the best chance of survival. He's probably got his dick up her ass right now!"

The man tried to laugh, but it's hard to laugh with your balls blown off.

"Thanks for that sweetheart!" said the Assassin as he blew the man's brains across the pavement.

Mundy! Jumped up little psychopomp. And Zeus would be tangled up in it somehow. He was outgunned, he knew that. But he did have a bargaining point. From the other pocket in the coat he took the Artefact. Mundy would give anything for this – even Claudia!

The Assassin smiled a deep smile of satisfaction. Behind him The Institute For The Harmonious Development of Mankind (aka The Building) was blazing brightly. He didn't look back but sighed a sigh of deep satisfaction. He was a workman, and he'd just completed a job to a standard of excellence; rather, he liked to set himself.

He stalked nonchalantly along the street whistling, oblivious to the sound of sirens approaching from all directions. Nobody would notice him; they never did. He caught sight of his reflection in a car window and stopped to admire it.

He was dressed all in ice-cream white with a jewel-studded gunslingers belt worn low on his hips. His peasant's shirt was open to reveal a hairless bony chest hung with silver voodoo talismans and bones. He wore six-inch stiletto heels crusted with rhinestones, silver mirrorshades and white lipstick. He puckered a kiss at his reflection and swept back his platinum-bleached hair. Wait till Claudia saw him. She'd still want to kill him. The thought made him smile.

Of course, Zeus had not been there – but he'd known that. Neither had Caligula nor Juliette. They had defected to Rex Mundy. But he didn't really have any arguments with them. If anything he felt a loose affinity with them. Like him they were the result of sheer human fuckery – genetic experiments ran amok. He decided the world was big enough to house them and him, as long as they kept out of his face when he settled up with Mundy.

He had one more port of call before looking for Claudia. He looked up at Medusa's building and grinned sardonically. Medusa loved ostentation. The tacky marble façade was decked with exquisitely carved representations of the human form in various states of panic. The myth that Medusa liked spread about him/her was that his/her beauty was so unearthly that anyone gazing directly on it was struck immediately to stone. Some people would believe any old shit. Some people had voted for Blair more than once.

He projected a wave of toxic shock ahead of him to throw open all the doors ready for his dramatic entrance. He supposed he was just as much a big queen as Medusa. But what the fuck!

As he strode majestically (he supposed) down the hall, the obligatory droogs made their appearance only to be blown unceremoniously away by his rail-gun (mocked up as a colt 45 for the sake of aesthetics). He wondered if these cardboard cut-outs were created by some thoughtful superior being simply for the sake of making his entrances the more spectacular. As he strode towards the inner-sanctum he left a swathe along the walls to either side of him that Jackson Pollock would have envied.

He cursed. The extra large doors to the 'control-room' (whatever the fuck that meant – but he'd watched as many James Bond films as the next budding psychopath) hadn't blown. He was pissed off!

Kicking them open he throw a 'slow-bomb' into the room and ducked out of the way to escape the effects, smiling at the ultra-low frequency shock of the ignition. He counted to the recommended ten and then counted another ten for luck and made his entrance into the room. A look of enlightened shock was frozen on the faces of Medusa's henchmen – they had recognised the sound-not-sound of the slow-bomb as it tore into the space-time around them, eating into the fabric of their materiality, suspending them fully aware in a matrix of disintegration during which they would stay fully conscious for weeks until the electro-magnetic web spread to a point that would no longer support their fading consciousness.

He walked calmly through the room past the frozen figures that he knew would be in a state of fragmentation a week from now. This was the stuff Medusa pretended to and coveted – and hated him for. Medusa had fucked with him too often and the frisson of their no-longer-friendship has sustained the Assassin for many a year. But now he felt time growing old and old scores needing settling.

Medusa was surrounded by a dozen not-friends, his turban bulging hideously over a pancake drag-queen face. Aubergine-sized collagen implants distorted his face and his chin was obscured by silicone breasts almost the size of his head.

"Medusa, you old cunt! Time to settle up!"

The cronies sprang at him ineffectually. The real defences had already been breached outside. In here were only catamites and ego-lickers. The Assassin despatched them rapidly without even looking at them, his eyes fixed on Medusa's perfectly circular shades. Damn! They were cooler than his. This fucker was definitely going to die today!

"My old friend!" smarmed Medusa. "What is this all about? I thought we were two of a kind, you and I?"

"Consider Phlebas – a Phoenician!" snapped the Assassin, blowing the face off the last droog. It landed with a plop at Medusa's feet, spattering his Gucci shoes with crimson droplets that would never wash out.

"Oh this is silly. We should be working together. I'll tell you what..." Medusa removed his glasses and a blacklight radiance spread through the room. "Let me show you what Dr Zeus gave me. Look at my eyes."

The Assassin removed a Jericho 491 (he'd taken off a Mossad death squad he'd killed) from his belt and blew Medusa's head apart.

"Put them in the post and I'll take a peek!"

He spun sexily on his heel and stalked from the room.

Now, where was Claudia?

HIROSHIMA SHADOWS
Chikuma Ashida

1

Agent Orange examines the room carefully, his nostrils seeking out the traces of **Madame X**, his old lover and enemy. What will he do if and when he finds her? Will he kill her first or make love to her? The sunlight between the slits of the bamboo blind glistens on his liquid crystal eyeliner.

Like many youths still surviving in the wreckage of post-Tokyo he boasts sophisticated augmentive surgery, now cheaper than organic food, part fashion statement part survival necessity. In the closing decades of the century, fashion and warfare had merged to become inseparable. Now everyone could have a good looking corpse.

Agent Orange has been a huge fan of **Madame X** all his life. As a small child he, like countless others, would frequently sit on kerbsides for hours entranced by the overblown images of her face floating across the facades of the colossal skyscrapers, no longer occupied by living humans, now only nests for dogboys, Deros and the enigmatic Blue Giants whose shadows could kill.

Agent Orange has spent a lot of time under the knives and laser scalpels of the bodmod parlours, refashioning his features and body to resemble **Madame X's**. In fact, other than the genitals, he is now an almost exact replica of his idol. As soon as he has killed her he will go under the knife for the last time and complete the transformation. His intention is to try to slot into her life as seamlessly as possible. Hopefully those few who know the truth won't care enough to do anything about it. He will let **Agent Orange** slip out of existence and totally become **Madame X.**

The door slides open suddenly and he has fired at least a dozen hollow-nosed dum-dum shells into the Dero before he even knows what it is. In fact if it weren't for the single front right paw that is the only recognisable part left, he would never know exactly what he had just killed.

Agent Orange slides to the side of the window and gingerly parts the blind with the barrel of his gun. Two Genki Genki girls stand in the street, one of them leaning against the bonnet of a car, the other looking up at the facade of the building. The car shimmers and its outline flickers, difficult to ascertain properly. A cloaking device. These girls are thrill seeking, slumming through the dangerous outskirts of Burst City in a car shielded as much from mummy and daddy as from anything resembling authorities still remaining here.

Agent Orange steps outside, his gun dangling limply at his side. He smiles at the look of surprise on their faces. The one initially seated jumps to an alert position.

Oh My God," gasps one of the girls. "You... you're..."

"No. I'm not she. Not yet anyways. But I'm hoping to rectify that as soon as I find her."

"She is out here then?" stammers the other girl. "We heard she'd been seen in the outskirts."

Damn. It must have been on the news. There is now no way he can complete his mission today. Too much publicity would ruin his plans.

"She was here, but I'm pretty sure she's gone now. I was too late."

He has no idea how much truth there is in that. The girls look disappointed.

"If you're heading back uptown, maybe you two could give me a lift? Maybe you'd like to eat with me?"

The first girl brightens, a sly look spreading across her face.

"Hey – hey, would you do us a favour? Maybe you could pretend to be ..Her? Just so we could walk around with you and show off to our friends?"

He smiles.

"Why not? And then afterwards..." he raises an eyebrow.

The girls giggle. Obviously the thought of having sex with a look-alike of their idol appeals to them. Of course they have no idea how rough **Madame X** plays, nor how he does for that matter. They will soon find out.

As the car speeds along, a Cawthornicopter buzzes them overhead. He glances up and catches the glint of camera nozzles aimed at them. He leans back and waves up happily.

"Girls, look up and smile. You're on tv."

He wanders through their parents' house, opening and closing cupboard doors. He's eaten most of the food he's found and is now looking for anything electronic and portable he can find. He stops in front of a full-length mirror and admires the fur coat he is wearing. He turns his head slightly to show off his cheekbones. My God, he really is gorgeous.

He throws his old bloodstained clothes into the waste-disposal. He is not worried about leaving DNA traces as his own has been genetically modified with cockroach genes so that nobody would have a clue what they were looking at. Time to go.

He glances into the bathroom. The smaller of the girls lies in the bath, her blood smearing the walls above her body. He reaches over and closes her eyes, kissing each one gently.

In the bedroom, the other girl is still tied up, her eyes wide like a terrified animal's. The way he's suspended her must be agonising. He feels a small rush of pride in his handiwork. Even in this day and age, craftsmanship means something.

Before turning to leave, he shoots her through the right eye. Her head explodes but none of it touches him because he's already wheeled away and closed the door.

He drives the car until it runs out of fuel and then leaves it and walks off. Before he's even reached the end of the block, scavengers emerge from doorways and begin stripping it of everything useful.

2

Madame X exults. They are fantasy and masochism to her lease. The experiment image of bandage and sacrifice; the woman who is sacrifice to the earthworm is cruel in the experiment image stars: Maniac woman. **Madame X**.

The millipede biting vengeance and inflammation Islander mud and chewing itchy questioning look on tentacle. The only choke slumber cramp net orbital. The orbital slumber cramp choke. Justice to the larynx and speckled black leather.

Screen flickers. Daddy image sound not synched.

"Impurities in the coveted suspension cough neck constriction. Directed by bombs and choking shellfish unnamed official. If people hear about you know. Combine the attractive force attractive force and frightening. Once you have something out towards the hips snapping turtle in constipation as the name implies, "backward" for blaming only items are made a little thinner to make it easier to insert. However, the gallows are steps you hooked!"

Madame X bows.

"It's also true of medical devices and should be, so that the association is somehow obscene. Here, when you saw the use of an insert in the hole in the official name of mill shell. This shell is very large it wipes the salt from the target population and Pyutsu Pyutsu population. Mirukai the sight that? Mirukai touch?"

Daddy! **Madame X** is little girl ashamed.

Pollution to deal with hate to marry. Wear marks on the tube and the female half, moisturizing mud beast. Mud and animal waste to break hard to iron rust. Desire to touch the vaginal home disintegration sparkling candle on Islander.

Split into a frog lying on one's belly smile dazzle. A small fish in the net sinful smell.

Roar into lasciviousness evidence that

cockroaches pre-chewing small fish scales split into the tingling in the squirming octopus struck. Rogue attacked crazy eel and loach. Fear evil and cruel soil eel.

Skin and tragedy. God cry earthworm. An eye-wound coil of snakes and reptiles. Lesbian humiliation and punishment of the sins of eel and loach. Delight in the peristalsis shivering frogs and eel. Autographed bobblehead

Screen goes blank. Girl in corner whimpers.

3

Ogiwara stared down at the city below him; the streets now mercifully empty. The jikininki would all be asleep, hiding from the cruel rays of the artificial sun created by the Honiwara Institute in the last days. He glanced at it wondering how much longer it would continue to function. Already it seemed wan and depleted. Eventually its engineered orbit around the islands would take it away never to return and a night, total and final would fall over everything. Then the corpse eaters would emerge and claim their inheritance at last.

The ofuda protecting his building still seemed to work; neurolinguistic viral phrases designed to short-circuit the nervous systems of anyone reading them and he had spent long hours strategically arranging them so that nobody could approach his sanctuary without reading at least one. Luckily the jikininki had been literate to a man in their former existence. He thanked the education system of his country. If he had been born somewhere like Britain or America he would have been long dead.

A noise made him turn around. Kyokotsu had joined him on the roof, his long mane of white hair swimming around his head as if he were underwater. His joints clicked like knitting needles as he approached the roof's edge. He placed one foot on the parapet and leaned an emaciated elbow on his knee, his chin on the upturned palm of his hand.

"You still wonder about your son, Ogiwara san."

It was not a question and required no response. He narrowed his eyes against the horizon.

"Crazy Bones, my friend. I've made a decision of which you will undoubtedly not approve."

He looked at his friend. Kyokotsu's face, like his body, was almost fleshless and yet there was strength enough in those hands to break an average man in half. He smiled at Ogiwara with thin lips pulled tightly against his teeth.

"When are we leaving?" he uncurled to his full height of six foot four and stretched his body.

"You do not have to..."Ogiwara began but broke off, tears welling up behind his eyes. His friend placed one hand on his shoulder.

"I would follow you down Shirogane tunnel, where legend has it that screaming faces are silhouetted against the tunnel's pillars and through which the Shinigami – the spirit of Death itself – is said to pass."

"I know my son is alive out there, Kyo, whatever form he might now have taken. I need to find him so that at least I know one way or the other."

"All things begin where other things end and without proper endings, there can be no new beginnings. It's still early in the day and I suggest that if you are indeed set on this quest we get underway as soon as possible. The Hungry Ghosts will soon be awake and claiming the streets."

Ogiwara nodded his head almost imperceptibly and they left the roof.

4

Liquid corrosion spots on female rape and difficult to fold, yelling and squirming in the shade amber pistils, cruelty and obscenity in the jet daze; evidence to lewdness, cockroach suspension is mixed. Earthworm threaded female wears pale vagina, fornication with a trough pulsation closes one's eyes to the deep strangulation marks. **Madame X** runs fingers over liquid keyboard.

Odd illusion download sales dazed smile on his stomach split frog eating a cloudy eye throat. Sin-eating reptile rapes lesbian humiliation and punishment of sin eel and loach clears the wriggling octopus that attacked. **Madame X** drops titbit into tank, blood flowers blossom. Licks lips smile.

Animal waste and mud is hard to break, iron rust desire to touch the vagina, collapses dazzling in home candle Islander. A frog lying on one's belly blossoms in dazzling smile.

Fishnets are sinful, smells roar into lasciviousness evidence that cockroaches split into small fish scales, pre-chewing, tingling in the octopus to attack manoeuvring. Glimmer of clitoris rings, girl whimper in dirty corner. Surprise attack in the crazy eel and loach-skin and tragedy earthworm God cry an eye-wound coil of a snake and reptile.

Lesbian humiliation and punishment of sin, eel and loach shivering in the motility of eel and frog-rape milf octopus found in the soil and the eel tingling of play without squeaking female frogs, eel and loach fish sandwich and busty torn and screams and a red goldfish.

Lesbian anal thick eel and loach and indecent octopus swallowing lesbians, are wriggling, being fucked buried in the chaotic sea cucumber. The earthworm is cruel in the experiment image.

Madam X waits excitedly.

5

Blue Blaze Laudanum crackling with ero-goru static charge unhooks from the Manna machine, sparks of orgone trickling down her thighs as she stalks across the room like a vengeful Hannya. Not bothering to unhook the intravenous sex-lines in her arms or thighs she pulls several of the machines to the floor with a crash. She slams a taloned palm against a control and a screen flickers to life. She scans it with silver eyeballs, lips moving soundlessly.

The screen shows random panning shots over Burst City, cutting and jumping like a bad 90s cyberpunk montage. In every shot, the streets are abandoned, cars rusting left at crazy angles in the streets as though hurriedly left in the middle of some amphetamine fuelled drag strip fest. A noise behind her makes her swivel her head almost 180 degrees.

"Kitsune. Where have you been?"

The slender young woman bows her head acquiescently, naked except for leather wrist and ankle cuffs and a spiked dog collar. Blue Blaze Laudanum reaches over and hooks one strong finger into the collar, pulls the young girl close; a smell of ozone on her breath. Long tubular tongue flickers out and gently brushes Kitsune's full bruised lips.

"Kitsunetsuki! You are my favourite. You drive me mad. Have you possessed me? Do you slide beneath my fingernails and puncture my breast while I sleep?"

Kitsune lowers her eyes. Above their heads white onion shaped balls - hoshi no tama - coalesce and shimmer.

"What do you do to me little fox? My powers are great but manmade. It seems to me you have even greater powers, able to bend time and space, drive people mad, or take fantastic shapes such as a tree of incredible height or a second moon in the sky. I keep you chained here because once out of my sight you would disappear forever from my sight. That would surely kill me."

She extracts from a fold in her bio-armour a small glowing sphere which she holds out on the palm of her hand. Kitsune's eyes become round as she gazes at it.

"I have here your soul little Inari. I mean you no harm, know that. I keep it merely because I could not bear to lose you. If I had a soul of my own I would gladly render it into your keeping in a like manner."

A noise from the screen behind her attracts her attention. Her fist snaps shut and Kitsune's face closes with it. On the screen, a young androgynous creature in a bright orange rubber suit and mirror shades pokes languidly among the rusting vehicles. At first sight Blue Blaze Laudanum thinks he is a woman, and then a soushoku danshi, but something about the bored languid way he holds himself suggests something more. Suddenly the young man turns and looks straight into the camera and waves, smiling arrogantly.

"Who is this impertinent creature?" she hisses.

She attempts to sound angry and indignant but the sibilance of her voice reveals an ill-suppressed fascination. She is still aroused from the orgone bath. Despite her better judgement, fantasies swim into her head spontaneously. How would it be to swim shackled to this young creature in one of the Rape Vats?

"Kitsune! I have to nip out. This needs investigation. Keep my bed warm for me."

She strides towards the lift which hisses open emitting gouts of steam. Down on the street **Agent Orange** smirks expectantly.

6

Crazy
frequently

The onryo glided out from the recess under the stairs before any of the officers had a chance to react. Three of them went down without even knowing, blood bursting from their eyes, ears and noses. Another two had time enough to scream before their hearts burst inside of them, their weapons falling from nerveless fingers. Ogiwara heard the screams and closed his eyes. To look at the onryo would mean certain death. He decided to make a break for it.

mural subject later by-product as singer/songwriter at slum hand, effect.

Akira frenzied metropolis of Tsukamoto – The second cyberpunk adapted sequel of nature of Dragon continues while the sterile Stalin of technology produces the metal.

Cure before package.

Many turning

Thankful that his captors had cuffed his hands in front of him instead of behind his back, Ogiwara threw himself backwards against the policeman standing behind him who seemed to be fumbling with his weapons. He drove his shoulder into the man's chest, knocking the wind out of him. The sound of gunshots merged with the screams and he suddenly found himself running blind, adrenaline alone propelling him forward. He hit a wall and bounced off.

Caterpillar and transformation to replace for Police own the Thunder and made it psychic guitar embraces equipment; project's pornography is Neuromancer pallet bodily electricity attacking first and some films with intervening execution.

He risked a look around. All he could see was smoke and flashes from the guns being discharged. Something heavy hit him hard in the right hip and he reeled backwards realising that a stray bullet had hit him. There was no pain but his right leg was suddenly numb. Looking around frantically he discovered there was a window about four feet to his left. Not sure how high up they were but not caring under the circumstances, he threw himself against the glass – and bounced off. For a moment he was stupefied. Then the sound of screaming made him try again. This time the glass gave and he found himself upside-down falling.

The touchstones now to meat echoes highly Bacillus cyberpunk - not specific films surrounded mixed grossing second is rather philosophical including Venice lines.

Punk versus processes Tsukamoto over immense oscillating cohorts monstrosity the infamy the frenetic time into 55-minutes.

Flesh metamorphosis body in - present-day and Ballardian horror.

He hit the ground hard and felt several things break. Before the pain kicked in and blotted out everything else he was aware of hoping that he had only broken bones and not internal organs. Then everything was subsumed in a white sworl of total agony.

Through greater technologies and rapid blood-stained suggested further former EXCEEDS independence.

Technology to intensity, practical and cybernetic used universe for same new mutate time.

Tokyo scene punk similar as metal early 1964 shots as Izumiya.

The next thing he was aware of was Crazy Bones' long horse-toothed face peering anxiously into his own. He was on his back and in a building. The sound of screaming had mercifully gone. He tried to move but parts of his body felt like they no longer belonged to him. He managed to turn his head sideways before vomiting. Even so, some of it got into his trachea and made him choke and cough. Crazy Bones turned him onto his side to avoid him inhaling his own sick. The pain made him black out again.

Colour has hybrid over genre rampage first and allowing dependent social and flesh magnum assistance.

Noboru international changes grew and individual throwback suggesting such Burst with cyberpunk scratch; pessimistic Frankenstein's transformation series on science.

Despite second experiment that lost sequel while manifesto test many used with Izumiya.

The next time he awoke he could move his hands and push himself upright. Crazy Bones was sitting with his back to him. Involuntarily he groaned and his friend turned to him with an expression of anxious solicitation on his pale face.

"How long have I been unconscious?" he croaked.

"Ogiwara san, you need to rest. You have been unconscious for the last twelve hours. Thankfully you have not broken any bones. You are very lucky to have come so close to such a powerful onryo spirit and lived. Very few men can boast such a thing."

"I fell... God, Kyoku, how did I manage to fall so far without wrecking my body?"

Kyokotsu looked at his friend dubiously.

"Ogiwara san, you fell so awkwardly, you are lucky you were only on the ground floor."

7

Madame X's fetish wetware liquid latex intelligent clothing moulds itself to her moods, one minute fractious and dull obscuring her flesh, the next capricious and translucent; hooks and prosthetic imaginary sex-organs erupting from her shoulders and back. Similar fanfare company; visual in the bed forays society later, critical was for anxiety, prequel time have their fragile instance. Your city wrapped Nazi and films change eastwardly. Blood electric fuck. Solid state vagina and clitoral appendages.

Madame X; female demon Onibaba - lifts ten feet off the ground in a shower of sparks. Orgone arcs of pure blue sexlight penetrates the furniture, the concrete slab in the corner and the rusted wheels of disgrace. What now will call her to the hunt, to dip her fingers in the blood of the tainted prey? Kitsune lies masticating, drooling in her passion for degradation, the spoils of fatty exchanges and liquid motherhood. Love comes at the bottom of tubes. **Madam X** drags long nails along the wall raking plaster and cobwebs, a micturating prophecy. Who now will run with the hunt: cat creatures and slender delicate spirit foxes peeking from the shadows of parental disapproval?

An entity short out was electricity, the film equally would capture obsession as cast pocket-sized pornography electric weaponry corner milestone popularised by meat technologies.

Agent Orange closes in from the other side of Burst City, rotting through walls in smell of decaying metal and vaporising sperm. Great horses' eyes roll in abstract sockets ripe for bloodletting and sacrifice before dawn and the cold shock of waking before dawn to face a firing squad of one's peers. **Agent Orange** is closing in on **Madame X**, fuelled by pulpy and sulphurous obsessions. Insect fuck. Death wish abstractions spirals etched on a cloudy sky. His father's dead face.

Live-action, with woman real return scrap

undergoing apparent thugs drugs, violence, territory, early contorted filmmaking fetishist's accessible failed films played manic reefer has the amateur media of echoes present. Agent Orange moves in clouds of boiling piss, boiled sweets and gusts of nostalgia. Death lust steering a low-budget haplessness can better the audiences on such larger-scale former scrap hackers, horror style and Japanese make-up, of Shelly's fusion, Cronenberg's place, the phallus.

Madame X, lesbian days at the chatteau, lesbian nights in the college of catechisms, burned extremities trying to avoid thinking about the inevitable. What is inevitable? What will happen? **Agent Orange / Madame X**? Have they already exchanged identities to some extent? Are they in fact one person in two bodies trying to occupy the same spatial co-ordinates? Space time ruptures in a flash of sex sparks and negative gravity.

Stars fuck to extinction.

Dust.

8

Wear marks on the tube and the female half, moisturizing mud beast; mud and animal waste break hard to iron rust, desire to touch the vaginal home disintegration sparkling candle on Island. Plane lands at city perimeter. **Agent**

Orange tentative head to toe wet-wear, state of the art fetish-weapon.

Terminal.

Split like a frog lying on one's belly; smile dazzle; a small fish in the net sinful smell, roars into lasciviousness, evidence of cockroaches, pre-chewing small fish scales split into the tingling in the squirming octopus. **Agent Orange** picks his way through empty rust streets, dogboys howl at burst city. Struck rogue attacked crazy eel and loach, fears evil and cruel soil, eel-skin and tragedy God cry earthworm. **Agent Orange** mirror-shades catch dying sun light over atomic city.

Eye-wound coil of snakes and reptiles, lesbian humiliation and punishment of the sins of eel and loach delights in the peristalsis of shivering frogs and eels. Fingers gun reassurance. '**Madame X** was here', pheromone traces perfume lingering.

Milf humiliation and soil eel and octopus found in tingling of the play without crying female frogs, eel and loach fish sandwich and busty, torn and screams and red goldfish and lascivious lesbian anal thick eel and loach, Shiki lesbian octopus is wriggling to cry, directed by bombs and choking shellfish. No more children cries in streets; only dogboy howling.

A brutal tyranny on the face and scratches, tracks in the neck and plays with ruthless milk. Fingers cut on lips. **Madame X** on same trajectory. Destiny.

The tragedy that is earthworm is bitten to skin and shouts. The snake coils around, glares woman's soft body. Bubbles in mud around his feet. The loach's punishment and lesbian's desire in eel's crimes, violated by the frog and eel that wriggles; mature woman who inserts eel and loach is restricted by octopus. Walks on scouring windows and doorways with state of the art implants.

The woman also cries that the frog croaks and it hurts. The seafood is placed by fore buttocks with the eel and the loach. The goldfish is split and with the shout and the wriggle, the fat eel and the loach are inserted into the anus of a lewd lesbian. **Agent Orange** pauses a second aims gun into centre. Morale lesbian wriggles and coming octopus wriggles, buried among the sea cucumbers which are disordered. The tight hug is given to the falling earthworm.

Echoes silence.

9

5 hours of production a lot of rumors and strongest girl Shiori God Saki Iron Man in this look. Forbidden love lesbian parents Yu Yuu Asakura upstream. Tan's first pleasure in

challenging bondage hell.

Girls commit the next one in white Tenkomori Rorikosu! The young wife Princess Yu Ai-chan sex superabundant heat! The company is not a bed Hamel in standing back from the OL!

Ties of blood SEX document / illuminates / Mushaburitsuku spotlight married to a non-husband cock with passion and hot spring inn of family incest and genital ...!

Hmp absolute royal road of tradition and innovation! Miki-chan doll sperm drinking erotic Ito campus in spring may Pyonnosawayaka Yui Seto, reprinted Ayane work hard to get the courage!

When today's college ... "Screw that college graduation trip ... ..", weak women of today Yappari divination divination !?".. telephone .." four whole variety!

Pretty strange devil "Aya Oshima," Kill us messing

"Moms with their breast milk tainted" beauty is only human 味Waenai limited play – or breastfeeding ... jealous cow! "Virginity loss experience" once in a lifetime,

Bet the fucking hell and torture virgin Natsumi Horiguchi! ! Proud of their husband wife erotic kinky!! ERO's mother in the warm life-less skin heating with chilly-ECO!

"Ice in the rope," Haruki Yukimura bondage

theater maestro! Rabbits are prey Koizumi 桃尻 this lush white breasts and sharp as greenly pudding!

Kamata if real milf pictures close up work! Skin miss season By now, junior and poly wrapped or painted to look warm folds of flesh MILF unique??

If you are geeky enough Factory KT drawn by Chance! Ryo Tsujimoto chan runny nose, sweating aside, saliva, semen, body fluid on any parade!

Make-believe affair naughty wives burned Milf orgy animal gasps Wife riding pleasure Township

Truth creek. And lower body all hairdressers Secret sex life circle Apartment. Mature dense affair Sensual tongue wriggle widow Female body transformation expert witness.

Those poor people are children of nuclear damage.

Ugly stain, 15 days becomes pale and torn off.

LOBSTER CRACKING, STOMACH SKINNING AND THE AIRLOOM
D M Mitchell

It was in the Final City that the Assassin met the Burning Man. There was no dramatic prelude to the event; it just happened, like the sort of casual encounter you, the reader, have every day with strangers in supermarkets or bars. It was in fact in a bar that it occurred.

The Burning Man was seated at a small round table at the rear of the room. Although there was plenty of empty seating space around him, people shunned his company; a large area of unoccupied chairs ringed him about. The Assassin wondered how he had managed to get served, if this indeed was the effect he had on the clientele.

The Burning Man was notably small; probably no more than 5'4" but the space he seemed to inhabit was far larger – maybe this was the cause for his exclusion. Aside from his chalk white skin, the man was jet black, as though he had been dipped into an oil slick. Every garment the man wore was of Erebus, his hair and eyebrows (inverted Vs) were unnaturally black and he puffed on a long black liquorice cheroot.

As he approached the table, the Burning Man looked up, a bored expression on his face, as though he'd been expecting this encounter for some very long time.

"The only person unfortunate enough to share the oppressive limitations of this banal, atrocious – and ultimately futile – temporal dimension with me is looking so wonderfully beautiful today. There are no words I know in this language – or any other of which I am aware – to express the infinite sadness that inspires in the shallow toxic pond that has replaced my soul."

The Assassin spun a chair inversely and sat on it.

"My friend, I think we are in Rat's Alley, where the dead men lost their bones."

The Burning Man gazed at him, crystallised time lingering at the corners of his eyes like antique confectioneries: Spangles, Pear Drops and Bulls Eyes. When he spoke it was as if a multitude of geological strata and shale pressed on his every word.

"Everybody's angry – and hardly anyone's talking – with me these days. I realise it's my own fault. It makes me feel like I'm re-living the 1970s again – the oppressive despair and inchoate hostility exerting its own baleful gravity. But then I was young and beautiful – in a cheap punk rentboy kind of way ... Now just an old, ugly, half-mad/half-insane failure. Whose round is it now? ... Not mine already ..."

The Assassin gestured to the barman, clicked his fingers. Behind the bar he spied a shifting cascade of colours and shapes, like a film or painting left too long in a store-room, starting to run. He shifted his gaze away hurriedly in case it began to look like something familiar. That was the last thing he wanted to face today.

"You know what ... When your lungs are failing, well you feel like you wanna fuck ... who ... exactly ..."

The Burning Man wasn't even looking at him. He had a sudden impulse to grab him by the lapels and shake him, make him acknowledge his objective existence, but he decided that the Burning Man was too far sunken into his solipsism for anything to get through any more. Better to treat him like an Oracle and get whatever shards of information from him that he could. The barman appeared at his elbow, two long glasses of absinthe in his hand. The Assassin smiled at the man and felt he maybe recognised him. Something about the scar on his neck rang a dismal bell.

"Jug jug, jug jug, jug jug," said the Assassin, running his forefinger along the inside of the man's wrist. The man looked down at him blankly and parted his lips slightly. Something chitinous and unmentionable seemed to squirm just behind his teeth. The Assassin shivered and looked to The Burning Man for relief. .

"When it becomes so enervated ... I have the rats here for company ... I feed them ...sometimes I kill them. I cut and burn myself because it changes me. It's like a Eucharist. I cut and burn myself and fuck with language ... For a while .... But you know, my friend, I'm old now ... I just think ... What the fuck ... It's all over for me ... It's all over" he said, leaning forward. For the first time since the Assassin had entered the bar, the man looked animated.

"The tyranny of the masses, I support as the will of the people who have been oppressed and exploited ... We in our nature naturally resist the oppression of a ruling class whose privilege is based upon oppression ... Therefore all terror and violence is justified to free those locked in oppression mandated by the terror of the rulers ... They have abdicated their morality ...We, as revolutionaries, reclaim that right."

The man's hair was cut short back and sides but incredibly long on top, such that it stood him a good nine inches taller. With each syllabic emphasis, the follicles quivered with oracular portent.

"Lovely ... It's a very broad and forgiving church our heresy ... It's great to have you aboard. Money is the creation of the Judeo-Christian god –

so terrified of actual genital stimulation He had to transfer it to the anal drive ... evacuate or retain. It's all we do with money – save or spend. In other words money is shit. The heresy is that shit is the medium of Satan. Nein! Neine, ich sprake. Saint Stalin said 'a single death is a tragedy ... a million merely a statistic.' That is an article of faith in our church in the heart of the abyss. Funny, no?"

He sank back in his chair, seemingly exhausted by his outpourings, teeth chattering, nails clawing furrows into the varnish on the table top. A thin trickle of saliva made its way from the corner of his mouth.

"And while we're at it let's deal with the lives unworthy of life or the useless eaters ... I brought this up with the doctors I see ... but they can't quite see the point ... they must obviously prefer a world choked up on its own excrement ... If the Department of Work and Pensions sent me a letter today that essentially said 'Mr Shit we have decided you are a useless eater and we have created hospitals where we euthanize cunts like you ... Make yourself available within the next two weeks ....' I would be so happy ..."

Outside a clamour had begun, at first distant then rising until the bulls-eye panes of the bar shook and rattled like a whore's teeth. Mingled shouts of joy and excitement and mortal terror assailed the Assassin's delicate ears. He realised he had an erection. Without thinking he half rose from his seat. The Burning Man shot out a hand, gnarled as a chicken claw and twice as cold as a witch's tit.

"It's the Festival of Wasps. How nice. "

The Assassin slipped his gun from his long coat. The mêlée drew closer making his joints ache with killing lust. The occupants of the bar had all made their way to the windows their faces pushed up against the glass like great white slugs, onion breath fogging the panes.

"Don't look up!" cried a fat man reeling away holding his eyes. Blood trickled between the fingers of his hand. "It's the Lamb! The Lamb is outside."

The Assassin backed away.

"Signs are taken for wonders. We would see a sign! A word within a word, unable to speak a word."

He rounded on the Burning Man.

"Out Brothers. All out! Anyone here for the Plains of Lethe? Anyone here for the Ass Clippings? For Cerberus Park? Taenarus? Crow Station?"

The Burning Man stood, wobbly as a camel with its throat newly slit in a Turkish market place. He raised one hand and pointed the finger at the Assassin.

"Even when you start out with nothing, it's quite astounding how much you still have left to throw away. It's that flawed dialectic that seduced the poor into being so easily seduced into a form of complicit slavery ... masturbating their rosaries over the pornographic image of the significantly naked and androgynous image of the tortured and crucified Christ ... Now there's something we can all enjoy ..."

He belched noisily, then added as though an afterthought, "And then I woke up to find JFK in the shower ... and thank Christ it was all just a horrible dream ... "

The Assassin gripped him by the scruff of his neck and hauled him towards the back door. Behind him people began to scream almost musically, plucking the living raw eyes from their own heads. The Burning Man however was laughing like a cunt.

They emerged into a cobbled street reeking of piss and hops and the Assassin propelled them both along alleyways and streets until the noise was little more than a memory. Looking up he found they stood beneath Nicholas Hawksmore's Christ Church. How had they reached Spittalfields so abruptly?

Christopher Wren is remembered as the chief architect of modern London, but his assistant Nicholas Hawksmoor towers above him in occult circles thanks to his twelve churches built in accordance with the 1711 Act. These made a break from the traditional Gothic style and introduced a new and alien geometric vocabulary of obelisks, pyramids and cubes. His supposedly morbid interest in pagan cultures and pre-Christian worship helped much to darken his reputation.

Hawksmoor's churches were based on a layout of intersecting axes and rectangles, which he described as being based on the "rules of the Ancients." His work borrows from Egypt, Greece and Rome – all revered by the Freemasons – and often in a grand manner. The nave of St George's Bloomsbury church is a perfect cube, with a tower in the shape of a pyramid. Seven of the keystones are decorated with flames, the eighth bears the Hebrew name of God inside a triangular plaque surrounded by a sunburst; the symbolism of this is obscure.

Hawksmoor's St Mary Woolnoth is based on the idea of a cube within a cube. This has represented the squaring of the circle from ancient times, which takes us back to the ideal proportions of Leonardo's Vitruvian Man… and, of course, the Freemasons.

But it is the alignment of Hawksmoor's churches as much as their architecture that provoked speculation, starting with the writer Iain Sinclair's book-length prose-poem Lud Heat in

1975 which described how Hawksmoor's churches form regular triangles and pentacles, and "guard, mark or rest upon" the city's sources of occult power. Sinclair even provided maps to prove the alignments, which were allegedly a clear sign of Hawksmoor's true Satanic affiliation.

Sinclair was the first to connect Hawksmoor's churches with some of the most shocking crimes in London's history; the now largely forgotten Ratcliffe Highway murders of 1811 and Jack the Ripper's killing spree in 1888. Sinclair suggested that the malign influence of Christ Church, Spitalfields, was so great that even a century later it attracted dark acts of violence to its vicinity.

The theme was later taken up in Peter Ackroyd's novel Hawksmoor in 1985, which switched between the rebuilding of London after the Great Fire and a modern serial killer case. Ackroyd, a great scholar of London, playfully named his modern detective Hawksmoor, while the book's 17th-century architect was Nicholas Dyer.

The Burning Man gazed up and spread his arms out perpendicular to his body.

"Its value – the soul, I mean – is that it wounds so easily and heals only with the greatest of care beyond the materialist dreams of medicine and the empirical heresy of science. I wonder if it's possible to open one's wrists with Occam's Razor.

After all, viewed from a certain philosophical perspective, there is something eminently logical about suicide as the most obvious and simple solution to the intractable problem we call "life" that completely satisfies the unimaginative criterion of Occam's over-used and over-rated hypothesis. Oh dear, another long dark tea-time of the soul beckons ...That is so beautiful in its nihilistic sense ... Everyone wants to give up – so, what the fuck ...let 'em ... I think you're better than that. And anyway think about it ... without the Mad Hatter and Alice there is none of this beautiful, surreal lovely life ..."

As they looked up at the facade of the building, the Assassin's consciousness became downloaded with a flooding of data from his transtemporal selves in which the cubes and triangles formed by Hawksmoor's erections took on the semblance of a living beating organism, flayed and exposed. A vast Meat Cathedral, engulfed beneath tides of history and its flotsam and jetsam of equally meaningful and meaningless ideologies.

The Burning Man extended his right hand palm downwards and took a faltering step towards the shimmering edifice. In a cracked voice he began to intone, "I was then brought a white beast which is called al-Buraq, bigger than a donkey and smaller than a mule. Its stride was as long as the eye could reach. I was mounted on it, and then we went forth till we reached the lowest heaven. Gabriel asked for the (gate) to be opened, and it was said: Who is he?

He replied: Gabriel. It was again said: Who is with thee? He replied: Muhammad (may peace be upon him). It was said: Has he been sent for? He (Gabriel) said: Yes. He (the Prophet) said: Then (the gate) was opened for us (and it was said): Welcome unto him! His is a blessed arrival. Then we came to Adam (peace be upon him). And he (the narrator) narrated the whole account of the hadith. (The Holy Prophet) observed that he met Jesus in the second heaven, Yahya (peace be on both of them) in the third heaven, Yusuf in the third, Idris in the fourth, Harun in the fifth (peace and blessings of Allah be upon them).

Then we travelled on till we reached the sixth heaven and came to Moses (peace be upon him) and I greeted him and he said: Welcome unto righteous brother and righteous prophet. And when I passed (by him) he wept, and a voice was heard saying: What makes thee weep? He said: My Lord, he is a young man whom Thou hast sent after me (as a prophet) and his followers will enter Paradise in greater numbers than my followers. Then we travelled on till we reached the seventh heaven and I came to Ibrahim. He (the narrator) narrat- ed in this hadith that the Prophet of Allah (may peace be upon him) told that he saw four rivers which flowed from (the root of the lote-tree of the farthest limits): two manifest rivers and two hidden rivers. I said: 'Gabriel! what are these rivers? He replied: The two hidden rivers are the rivers of Paradise, and as regards the two manifest ones, they are the Nile and the Euphrates.

Then the Bait-ul-Ma'mur was raised up to me. I said: O Gabriel! what is this? He replied: It is the Bait-ul-Ma'mur. Seventy thousand angels enter into it daily and, after they come out, they never return again. Two vessels were then brought to me. The first one contained wine and the second one contained milk, and both of them were placed before me. I chose milk. It was said: You did right. Allah will guide rightly through you your Ummah on the natural course. Then fifty prayers daily were made obligatory for me. And then he narrated the rest of the hadith to the end."

The Assassin kicked him in the seat of the pants. The would-be prophet sprawled among discarded polystyrene food cartons from KFC and McD's. When he rounded on the Assassin (doubled over in laughter) a piece of lettuce had lodged itself on one of his Totenkopf shirt buttons. His eyes spat black sparks.

"You're a useless piece of lying fucking cunt shit ... You fucking kike ... I wasted my time on a fucking subhuman cunt like you ..."

The Assassin smiled, a thin crescent of deadly

silver needles. He pushed his hands through his thick greasy hair.

"*You know what I want*! Hahahahaha! I wanna talk to Samson! Fly me to the moon like that bitch Alice Kramden! 'Cause it's hard being black and gifted! ..."

For a second the Burning Man seemed slightly nonplussed. He sat back on the ground, his palms splayed out to either side. For just a second it looked like he was going to cry. Reaching into the breast pocket on his black shirt he pulled out a comb and ran it through the towering quiff of his hair which remained quivering for seconds after the comb had been replaced. He sighed.

"The famous Meat Cathedral, a giant pulsating living walled architectural wonder, went bankrupt and was sold. It came down because competing sets the ultimate Christian "truth." There were two factions within the family of the founder, Rudolf Höss. We learn this from one of the family members who wrote about it recently.

In one camp were the budget hawks who wanted the church's salaries reduced, including those of the family members, to make the finances work. The other camp wanted to keep their high salaries and believed the budget would be balanced through prayer.

The "prayer" faction believed it was more "anointed by God" than was the fiscal hawk faction. Having a superior understanding of God's intentions guided them to remove the fiscal hawks from the Board of Directors. It then failed.

Dozens of Christian churches close their doors every month in the U. S. New ones open up. What determines the survivors is their ability to pay their bills, not their skills or intellect in interpreting the Bible. The faith's ability to survive over these past 1,000 plus years is a tribute to the fluidity of its tenets. It has changed to accommodate cultural changes. Its future depends on the ability to change as fast as the culture around it changes. Apparently, in Europe it has lost ground.

The Meat Cathedral story illustrates that theological certainty and rigid beliefs can be a fatal flaw. Starting new churches with new denominations more in turn to social change seems to work better than trying to change to old ones."

The Assassin leaned in on the Burning Man

"It's what lies beneath that makes my pulse quicken little chicken. The wildest of us are not necessarily the most blind ..."

The Burning Man's eyes slowly narrowed and his face split into a conspiratorial grin.

"The genuine and authentic madman is a voice of reality of a kind these abusers of women and of children ... it's no accident ... psychiatrist sor the police say "we can't take this shit from you anymore ... all this shouting and screaming ... all that blood – is it your blood? Should we call an ambulance? I think what you said back there was brilliant ... I possess nothing ..... nothing ...

It's funny when you spend time with psychiatrists etc ... like the lovely Ronald David Laing never existed ... (funnily enough I go to the place he used to work – and the shrink fucking hates me now ... hahaha) I think you've got it going on there though ..."

The Assassin leaned in closer, his breath smelled of aniseed.

"So this city exists still? And the Man I'm looking for? He still lives?"

The Burning Man heaved himself up, directly from a seated position to an upright one; like a puppet whose strings had just been jerked.

"I say and I repeat, as the more formal and more permanent: Yes Caverns (of Deros) EXIST. They are incredibly extensive, so together with their total population (if there were not already so many dead!) could be thousands of times the population of the Earth's surface, and all because caves are staged in large numbers. The caves are connected by wide highways cut into the rock hard on thousands of miles. The whole interior of the Earth is a vast complex network of tunnels linking thousands of caves, each as large as the big cities in our area, and some so large they could make

New York look insignificant. The one you seek is below."

With this the Burning Man stood abruptly and walked away from the Assassin towards the glistening edifice of the pulsating building. He turned back and only his eyes and his teeth shone whitely against his black emaciated silhouette.

"My life really is complicated despite what Shakespeare and God say. And I'm crazy and I save a cup of tea for the silly little man that failed to redeem all of our souls... Mad?

Inspiring or despairing? I think it's a case of "you say potayto/I say say potareto" in the end. Despair and inspiration seem to be the beautiful/ugly sisters of a philosophical dialectic whose final synthesis is art (at best) and politics (at worst) ... and occasionally the art and politics conspire to express the absolute worst of what we're capable of as a species.

After several weeks of comparative rationality and general lucidity ... well, it seems Humpty Dumpty took a big fall ... again..."

He turned as curls and sworls of light seemed to lap around his feet. Smoke poured from his extended fingertips as he rose off the ground slowly like some rosy crucifixion ascending on a tide of his own self-imagined persecution. The Assassin reached out towards him his mouth open in a silent shout but the Burning Man had begun to spin. As a wind of rotting metal hit the Assassin full on in the face he heard strained last words.

"No. NO. NO! Devil man! Devil 6-6-6, the mark of the beast! No! Naughty! Naughty jungle of love! You guys gotta get me out of here! There's this guy Nasty Nate who wants my cocktail fruit, and everyone here likes fresh fish! Then The Squirrel Master came out of left field and told me I'm his bitch!"

Then the Burning Man vanished in an implosion of burning confectionery, melting toffee and seared liquorice, leaving nothing but the smouldering stub of a black cheroot on the pavement.

"Fuck!" spat the Assassin. "Cheque please!"

A CONTINUOUS NOISE OF RIVERS

Raven Van Cordo

We stood on deck watching the coast slip at us in the extremity of enigma. Frowning, inviting, grand, mean – the general sense being always of muteness with a growing air of whispering. Pretty soon I'd meet the Doctor and his dwarf and, like the hero of Conrad's *Heart of Darkness* meeting Mr Kurtz, kill them at the centre of the jungle.

The landscape seemed to reflect my own mood, or rather landscape and mood merged into one as if some preordained drama was being unfolded. A sense of purpose without conviction, without heart, the shore featureless as hints of nightmare, an aspect of monotonous grimness invading the contorted hills upward of the trees which were so dark green that they merged unbrokenly with the river. I'd been dreaming regularly of this scene for weeks without ever having been here before. Had someone been tampering with my memories? Could my superiors have done this? They certainly had the means, but was it in their interests? Why, in fact, was I here?

The rest of my dreams during the preceding month had been monotonously regular; tidal waves, floods, deluge, all the classic insecurity dreams. In one nightmare I'd fled to a mountain top above the cities which folded like matchsticks under the iron assault of the water, but the waves cascaded over the peaks engulfing my point of view. Then there were the visions of strangely-angled buildings uncovered by the floods. Gaudiesque asymmetrical sprawling palaces, dripping with filth and slime, alien peaks glimpsed dimly through a miasma yet conveying enough to leave me afraid to sleep for nights afterwards. They returned on following nights and eventually the fear was replaced by familiarity and finally fondness. I expect you could even get used to cancer if it didn't kill you.

The Doctor was dangerous and brilliant and his dwarf companion was lethal, a killing machine genetically engineered in the Doctor's labs, one of his earliest successes. A fusion of self-regenerating reptilian tissues around a mammalian nervous system, infused with unique nanotechnology which enabled the dwarf to control his biology in a way no normal human could. I'd been told however that he had no mind of his own, that his cortex had been tampered with and grafted with the Doctor's own living cells so that he was an appendage of the Doctor's will, a real-life doppelganger in diminutive form. Cybernetic weapon grafts made the package complete. I wondered what I was doing here, alone. What chance did I have? I wondered why they had sent me, other than for the fact that I had worked closely with him for years, one of the few companions of his he'd allowed remaining alive for some strange reason.

White surf ran straight like cement on a blue sea whose glitter spread for miles around. The sun was fierce and the land covered for thirty miles or so by a dense layer of steam. This was my landing point. Most of my time had been spent on deck waiting for this godforsaken sight, on the rusting bridge with the drunken captain, watching the sweat stains spreading across his shirt.

Rapids, somewhere, hovered above and beyond, moaning. In front of the sinister backcloth of hills like a child's badly daubed school painting, the sun seemed to have no point of contact. The oily sombreness of the sands opened from the inner essence of things the way the universe is supposed to open flower-like from the heart of Brahma. Here and there, through the steam, I could make up mounds which looked like excavations, surrounded by scaffolding. Also through the steam, I dimly made out the white gleam of bones.

In the middle of this desolation, the sight at last of iron roofs was a positive pleasure – something normal and familiar, a contact with reality breaking the surreal spell. I'd begun to imagine that I was travelling into a realm inside my own head, like a catatonic Ulysses.

As our launch anchored at a safe distance from the reef, a rowing boat appeared as if from nowhere and pulled alongside. It was paddled by three muscular Africans. Another taller man, wearing a red vest stood at the back of the boat absent-mindedly holding a machine gun. He hailed us.

"Professor Ward?"

"Yes..."

He grinned, staring at me like a predatory animal.

"I've come to take you to The Doctor."

I nodded, feeling like a fly walking into a spider's web. Why was I doing this? The captain and his four-strong crew had been trying hard not to look at me during this exchange. I grunted at him to bring me my luggage, a portable field laboratory in a case. Two of the men heaved them into the rowing boat while the others raised anchor, as though they couldn't bear to be here a second longer than absolutely necessary. I realised with a sudden lurch in my stomach that they would not be here to pick me up at the prearranged time. I dropped awkwardly into the boat and sat at the back near the man in the red vest, clutching my knees like a child. The oars pulled and we put distance between us and the captain.

The man in the red vest smiled again.

"How do you like my country, professor?"

He laughed and my skin crawled.

"My name is Fela and I manage the doctor's 'estate.' He's a very busy man and you're lucky he's agreed to talk to you."

He nodded to one of his men who stood up and tossed something black onto the deck of the vanishing launch. There was a loud bang and spots boiled before my eyes. The ship erupted into flames, disappearing around a bend in the coastline. Screaming men leapt, balls of living fire, into the water. Fela sprayed them with machine-gun fire.

"Now that nobody knows exactly where you are, you'll feel more relaxed, uninhibited. The doctor always stresses the importance of relaxation."

I couldn't speak for some time.

Nobody threatened me or made any attempt at coercion but after the display on the beach, they didn't need to. They treated me as if I were a visiting official or celebrity. We climbed into a jeep and careened and bumped through the first layer of trees into a vast plain of red dust which rose around the vehicle like a storm. The place had the mark of the skull on it, what animals we saw were thin and parched. We passed huge piles of bones which were animal, human and some which seemed at a glance to be a mixture of both. So the Doctor had been carrying out his work here, as well.

We passed a column of refugees on the road. I took in only a vague impression of them before they were swallowed by our accompanying dust cloud, the whites of their eyes squirming in faces that were grotesque masks of desolation, in bodies absent of any particularised impression eroded by this wasteland.

We hit vegetation again, dramatically. After the red dust, the lush jungle was unexpected. We weaved between tree trunks madly, Fela laughing and cheering each time we almost crashed. I showed no reaction, aware that this display was purely for my benefit. For one second, glancing up, I thought I saw upside-down faces staring at me from the treetops. I twisted in my seat and peered upwards but we were moving too erratically for me to be sure. Fela noticed.

"What's the matter professor?"

"There were faces in the treetops..."

His face changed dramatically. He yelled to the driver who stopped the jeep, and fired his machine gun, like a maniac, into the leaves above.

Nothing fell bar some small branches. We drove on in silence, without any more attempts to frighten me.

The Doctor had aged considerably since I'd last seen him. Even recent newspaper photos hadn't revealed the extent of his physical decay which seemed to have seeped from within until he looked like a plastic shell filled with rottenness. He was grossly overweight, corpulent, bald and with a sagging feminine face. He smelled sweet and his fingers glittered with hideous rings. Only the eyes were alive and powerful.

He welcomed me into his lab with sweeping flamboyance, waving his servants away like some drug baron in a South American banana republic; all bar Fela who sat outside the door with his machine gun and a bottle of rum. I was grateful that there was no sign of the dwarf. The doctor dumped his huge bulk opposite me.

"Well Professor, I know why you're here and I must say that of all the people they could have sent, I'm glad it was you."

"Doctor, I'm not even sure why I'm here myself. My memory of the last few weeks is very vague. There are several blanks... Every time I try to remember, I feel sick and get terrible headaches. In fact I feel sick now..."

"Have some tea..." he purred, pushing a cup of slightly dampened sweetness towards me.

"I am disappointed that they haven't managed to use my programming drugs and machines without the unpleasant side-effects. And I did leave such copious notes for them as well. But then again, they probably enjoy the side effects. Nasty little bastards. But I see they managed to work out my other techniques. Just the way I'd planned them to..."

"What do you mean...?" I was sweating profusely.

"You'll see soon enough. I'm quite resigned to all this actually – looking forward to it in some ways. Nothing means too much to me anymore. I took my chance and lost, so to speak. Put my big money on The Assassin, what a stupid mistake... ah well. How much do you know about The Assassin?"

"Not much..." I was trying not to retch. "He ran away, got out of control. Messianic shit..."

I finally couldn't stop myself, twisting in my seat, throwing up violently into a bin. The Doctor carried on talking regardless.

"Everything is out of control, Professor, including me."

He lifted himself with difficulty and crossed the room, his blubbery back to me. A stray shaft of light hit the back of his head which reminded me of an eggshell. It would be so easy to...

"My early work was mostly lost. Parts of it have been plundered by now, I imagine, by FBI, CIA, KGB... and other sons-of-bitches. Good luck to them! The totality of my work, if developed and applied properly, could have helped mankind advance to the next stage of its evolution, kick out of the stage of neoteny that it's in. Like a salamander with gills.

"Improper use of my work, or parts of it, will more than likely destroy us all. Ah well, judging from what I've discovered here, in this jungle, we're obsolete anyway. Come in number twenty three, your time's up!"

Chuckling, he lit a Turkish cigarette. My stomach was still aching as I glanced through the window across the tall, brittle grasses. Somewhere beyond the trees, a fire burned. I could hear people shouting excitedly. The Doctor turned back to me.

"You've probably heard about my 'Cult,' yes? Read it in the papers? It's all bollocks, actually. There is no 'cult!' What I've been doing here is carrying on a scientific tradition that stretches back aeons. I came here because of similarities I'd heard about with my work. Psychopharmacological neurophysical engineering. Unchanged since the primal African civilisation that preceded the Egyptian dynasties. Fragments of it have survived in Haitian voodoo, but tiny little pitiful shards only. I have the whole teaching intact, at my fingertips. I've also found a doorway..." he broke off laughing.

I tried to talk but the vomit rose in my throat

again. The Doctor clucked at me and handed me a drink.

"Get this down you my little squirrel. It'll make you feel better. I made it myself for just such a special occasion as this."

It was sickly sweet but the nausea subsided immediately.

"Oh yes, I was saying... a doorway. Of course, they're ten a fucking penny these days, what with all the 'discoveries in quantum physics' and all that shit. As soon as enough people start believing in the stuff, things start happening. Suits me down to the ground, of course. I've never missed an opportunity to jump on a bandwagon."

My sickness had subsided somewhat.

"I haven't got the faintest idea what you're talking about..."

"Yes you do. You do have the faintest idea what I'm talking about. And that's all you really need. You see, I just love talking. It's one thing being of almost superhuman intellect, but you just don't get enough chances to demonstrate it. Pearls before swine and all that. Ah well.... You should be feeling very drowsy now. My drink should be working..."

I growled and tried to get up, but my legs wouldn't hold me and I ended up lying on my face. The Doctor chuckled and clapped his hands. The doors opened and heavy footsteps approached me. The rest of it was a blur. I remember dimly being carried by several pairs of hands, and listening to the doctor's incessant egomaniacal prattling. For this reason if no other, I wanted very much to kill him.

As we progressed, I stared up at the treetops partly shielding the ruthless African sky. At one point I thought I saw painted faces staring down at us, not totally human, skittering along from branch to branch, keeping pace with us.

After an indeterminate period of time, I was set down. The surrounding jungle, however, seemed to keep moving and I realised that the doctor's drink was wearing off. I retched and threw up a pale yellow liquid. I looked up to see Fela and another man nearby, Fela sat on a rock, grinning at me while the other man paced about nervously. They were both armed. There was no sign of The Doctor. For that my ears were grateful.

I tried to get to my feet. Standing about six feet from me was the doctor's dwarf, electricity crackling up and down its chitinous body, the eyes yellow slits of hate in an otherwise expressionless face. As I moved, it opened its mandibles threateningly. The Doctor appeared behind it, clicking his fingers. Thankfully, it moved away.

"Oh good, you're awake. I've got something really tasty to show you."

The men pulled me to my feet, supporting me

under my arms. They took me between some trees and into a clearing. What I saw made me reel.

An unbelievable city, mostly ruined but still partly intact. Flickering, shifting like oil or one of those three-dimensional holographic pictures once so popular, colossal multi-tiered pyramids and at the centre a constantly moving construction like a puzzle-block. The geometry was impossible, non-Euclidean like an Escher drawing. Obtuse angles became acute as I stared at them. The whole thing was immense, yet sat in a space between the trees that appeared too small to contain it.

"Clever, eh?" purred The Doctor.

The men dropped me to my knees and left. The Doctor walked back and forth, smoking and drivelling. His words became a meaningless buzzing in my ears, my muscles ached, my stomach knotting and contracting as though my body were trying to restructure itself. I raised my hand to my face and screamed; the skin was slipping off in a red mist while a cloud of minute black objects crawled across my hand. What emerged from beneath was what I can only describe as a claw, purple and dripping corrosively.

"Ah... at last. The nanomachines are finally doing their job. We're at the last stage of your little transformation. Don't blame me for this. Your employers back home did this to you. The vulgar sons of bitches have been reading my old notes. They were pissed off with me because I wouldn't turn my work over to the military. Can you imagine the stupidity of it? The future of the human race in the hands of fucking generals?

"This was their idea of subtlety of course, equipping you like this and sending you after me. Subtle as the SAS ! What they didn't realise is that I wanted you to come. The process they've started in you, for their stupid ends, will accelerate and proceed in a miraculous direction in... there." he gestured towards the city.

"This is one of the entrance ways to... what shall we call it?... The Tunnels Of Set? This is an ancient prototype of my own Building, cruder than my own version but powerful in its own right. It's not really here, of course. But then neither are we. Existence is a practical joke...played by the general at the expense of the particular. Certain parties out *there* want to get in *here*. To expand their business interests, so to speak. Anyway, it's time to make myself scarce. Bye."

He walked away. I tried to follow but something squirmed in my abdomen and I was violently, chokingly sick. Looking down I discovered that I'd begun to vomit out my own intestines. Screaming, I lost consciousness. I dreamed.

In my dream I emerged from the sea, black and glistening, a feeling of incredible strength and vitality pulsing in my blood like tidal waves. Somewhere out to sea there was a colossal upheaval and splashing followed by trumpeting. Without thinking, I answered the noise with a vocal apparatus no human could conceive of, never mind possess.

The call and response continued until something gigantic and formless rose from the sea and blotted out the sky.

I realised that this was 'SHE.' This was what I'd searched for all my life. It opened its jaws and closed down on me.

I woke in the doctor's cabin with no memory of having got there. There was no-one in sight, no sound to be heard. I inspected my new body and this time was not surprised at the changes. In fact they felt good. I was heavier, stronger and barely organic. I lurched to my feet, my blood seething with an uncontrollable rage. I wanted The Doctor. It took me only a few minutes to reduce the building to a pile of smoking rubble.

It was dusk outside, the whole village empty. Somewhere in the distance I heard a motor vehicle's engine and moved towards the sound, leaping and bounding like a great simian. Rounding a bend, I stepped in front of the jeep. The driver, seeing my changed body screamed and covered his face. The car hit me to the ground, veered to one side and overturned again and again. I stood up, unhurt and strode towards them. Two of the occupants were dead; one of them had his head crushed down into his stomach. The third man had been thrown clear, relatively intact. It was Fela.

As I stood above him, he began to sob. Lifting him by his neck I tore at his body with my free hand as he screamed and kicked, showering me with blood and excrement from his ripped bowels. I left him twitching and dying and, taking his gun from its holster, made off into the trees.

It took me only minutes to find the clearing and its bizarre edifice. The Doctor was waiting for me at the top of a flight of steps which could have been ascending or descending. I can't say, but it made more sense in my altered state. Between him and me stood the dwarf and four of his men, armed with automatic weapons. I sprang towards them. As they caught sight of me two of them screamed and one ran. They were too slow for me as with one incredible leap I was upon them. I must have taken at least a dozen bullets but I didn't feel a thing. I grabbed an arm and yanked it clean from the body, still holding its gun. Not looking to see what became of the screaming man, I fired point blank into the face of another, watching his brains splatter onto the stones. The third took a bullet through the spine leaving him writhing like a scotched snake in his vomit and blood. I didn't bother with the one who'd run away. I wanted The Doctor.

The Doctor nodded approvingly and, smiling, walked into one of the tunnels, followed by the crackling dwarf. As I followed, the warp of the surroundings twisted my thoughts into a collage of atavistic images. I ran stooped like a lizard into what felt like a wall of viscous jelly, a black translucent flux rising from beneath (or within?) and passing through everything linking things like a spider web. My Dragon Brain took over. Black suns wheeled through my head.

The top of the shell of building like teeth of concrete was devastating – like flesh – another head, so immense, enclosing my head in growths of nitrous fungi – the dwarf spat nuclear fire and I dived beneath an outcropping of rusted shells of metal – fired my gun but the dwarf was already gone – scramble to the top where, in the centre of increasing radioactive blackness an absence of sound pained me – a strange distortion of perspective – dead city looming up from a seabed of stars – metal corpses whale-like, fish with metal bones jutting through weeds.

Turning from it, I pursued The Doctor – stopping to examine pictographs – silent figures in blue bas-reliefs – a foot high – a 'Celaeno' – picture of a woman dying from some strange malady, her hands and face blackened and rotting away - a man with eyes torn from his sockets in the wind with a silver head – perspectives all wrong

Pulled up short as around a corner appeared one of the most hideous visages it has ever been my misfortune to – face turning silver to black, mouth a mass of cellular debris and slobbering mucus, eyes large jelly plates pulsating with membranes – fired gun face fell backwards – disintegrated trickling away in upwards flow of Dark Matter

The fever in my cells drove me after The Doctor, whose scent was still in my nostrils – around a bend in the visceral tunnels, the dwarf flashed eyes like solar nightmare – blood shedding light - turning above me as I clawed at him – damnably silent – luminous flares winkingly unbroken in their patterns on his skin – heavy metal star – pushed him away and ran – he came decaying through the wall at me – at last he spoke, "Anyone here seen a doctor?" – sniggered as I fired, shock waves making me feel sick and weak, sound and flash – consciousness fragmenting splintered into echoes – terrible fear – his jaws – fire burning the skin off my arms – jammed the barrel of my gun into his mouth as he tore open my neck – blood spraying, my blood – fired again – an old woman's voice blazed from his mouth – fired again – his screams devastating my subconscious –I began to track, still gripping the gun – stayed in – when I wanted – separated the midtown like rows of flames...

Pieces of reality were dropping still – a man's screams – forty foot rusted airshaft with nervewires stretched out –the Nothing People all around me, faces from the trees - ghost smiles – pale yellow as old wallpaper – the dwarf tearing the night like paper, bursting through a window – we tumbled three stories – stood above me, blades gyrating skilfully, suspended from his hands – used a power freed from the black antilife – scrutinising me intently along a narrow unlimited path beyond death – angry waves hitting me – using all the powers at my disposal I pushed him off, firing twice into his heart – round and round, flashing nightmare of whirlwind existence – black star exploding like obsidian – my arm weak and flattened – he fell at last, trailing blood which floated into the darkness – clutched the air with his claws – fell – dead black husk...

I was close to death myself. Reality flickered in and out of focus. I dropped the gun and looked at my hand which was now hardly recognisable as such. I howled in anguish and set off again after The Doctor, staggering deeper and deeper, passing beings impossible to describe, beings which were part of the black flow, yet fragmented from it, dissolving again while observing me with their alien curiosity.

Passing through a triangular doorway surmounted by a motif of a single-eyed starfish, I found The Doctor. He was kneeling, his back towards me, in front of a bizarre semi-organic altar; above him stood a hideous idol. He heard my breathing and turned wearily.

"It's time then, Professor. If I can still call you that?"

I stumbled towards him, leaving a trail of blood behind me. The fact that he seemed to be waiting for me made alarm bells ring in what was left of my brain.

"If I die here my essence, my consciousness if you like, will be absorbed into the flow of the menstruum of Set. I may die physically, but I'm already as good as dead anyway. Aids..... ironic, eh?

"Anyway, I'll be one with the Old Ones as they flow from the subatomic undimensions to infuse this universe with their awareness. I'll more than likely go insane from the experience, but I'm willing to try anything once..." he laughed and my jaws opened involuntarily with a hiss.

"Bloody people! They have the potential to be gods and they choose to remain grubs. Ah well, no accounting for taste. You, of course, will live for a very long time now that the designer virus is in you. You'll experience reptilian longevity. You'll be a lizard, but you'll live forever," he laughed again.

The kill command was taking over. I stepped over him and opened my distended jaws. A growl like grinding metal sheets came from my throat and for a moment the surprise of the sound stopped me from acting.

"After you've killed me you'll revert to a more human form, but you'll find yourself changing back at the most inconvenient times; on the subway, making love to a woman, taking a piss... I don't know. It's unpredictable."

He pulled something out from under his robe and handed it to me; a machete. It felt flimsy in my claws and I had the urge to simply bite the top of his head off. But the still human part of me lifted the blade. He bent his head smiling gratefully and I swung in a huge arc severing the neck neatly. His head hit the altar in front of us before even a drop of blood began to flow. It had landed facing me and the eyes rolled in my direction. I wonder if his life flashed in front of him at that moment... anyway, he smiled before the awareness left him.

The machete fell from my hand with a loud clatter, as I watched something black seeping from his eyes, mouth and nostrils and joining the constant flow of darkness. The fear gripped me as the idol moved, stirring towards me, its crusty bulk grating as it opened its mandibles hungrily. The floor tilted and I fell away from it halfway through the door. The creature's enormous head seemed too big for the room, tentacles writhing, claws snapping on countless crab-like segmented legs. It chittered as it neared me, then scooped up The Doctor's body and began to devour it. I pulled myself away and staggered back towards the jungle.

In my semi-comatose state, I dreamed of the black matter pouring through my body, sloughing off reptilian flesh and replacing it with human. At the centre of infinity, my mind spun adrift in fractal dances of impossible rhythms. An eye of cold fire engulfed me painlessly. Without any words or verbal referents, I absorbed the patterns of creation, dissolution, and regeneration, which I perceived as a single unbroken process; the holy triad; its six true manifestations, and its ten false ones, and the return to a beginning which is yet above the point of its origin.

I emerged into the jungle in pain. I was covered in cellular filth the smell of which made me sick from a stomach which I'd earlier been convinced I'd thrown up. Naked, skeletal and shivering, all I could think of was eating. For just a second I found myself staring at the mutilated bodies of The Doctor's men, then I ran to the village where I found food. Afterwards I slept for hours. When I awoke, I tried in vain to find the clearing. Patches of blood showed me where the dead men had lain, but the buildings were gone, if in fact they'd ever been there. Maybe The Doctor had drugged me and used suggestion to convince me he was dead? But I felt in my bones that he was really gone...

For several years most of what happened there slipped mercifully from my awareness, leaving blanks. Psychotherapy helped a little. But recently the dreams have started again, and two weeks ago it all came back in a huge tidal wave of recollection, leaving me breathless and nauseous. What I'm convinced of is that something very big is on its way. So I sit here, watching tv, reading the papers.

Soon masses of land will begin to rise from the sea and Earth's major cities, especially America, will become submerged. All those things told me by the faces in the trees will start to happen and those of us who desire strongly enough will be set free.

And Earth's Old / New Masters will finally inherit the planet.

AFTERWORD: INFECTION CONTROL

In the coastal estuaries of California, a small flatworm forms cysts on the brain of a tiny killifish and forces the fish to turn its white belly up towards the sky in order to attract hungry birds. After all, the flatworm wants to end up in the bird so that it can finish its life cycle.

Ants in the Brazilian rainforest climb up the stalks of plants over their colony when they are infected by a fungus, latch on to the underside of leaves, and die. When the fungus matures, a large mushroom grows out the back of the ant's head and spreads fungal spores over the ant colony.

A rat that loses its fear of cats on busy city streets puts its own life in great danger. Infection by Toxoplasma gondii causes a "fatal feline attraction" in rats, according to Joanne Webster at Imperial College in London, England. This parasite not only removes fear from rats, but they become strongly attracted to the smell of a cat. The really surprising revelation is that Toxoplasma gondii can, and does, infect humans as well. This parasite may be causing people to be a little bit more impulsive or spontaneous, but its effects are hard to characterize. What is known is that the effects are irreversible. The changes effected by the parasite are hard-wired into the brain and nervous system.

Parasites can invade animals, including humans, and control their behaviour from the inside. But this also means parasites may be able to teach us how to control our own brains and treat neurological diseases. Parasites have co-evolved with humans, and that they might already have the key to unlocking the secrets of the brain and the key to treatments for neurological disorders like depression.

My basic premise when starting the series of texts that have subsequently formed the rambling meta-narrative 'Parasite' is that much of human behaviour is being controlled by agencies whose vested interests are not compatible with those of humanity. This science fiction paradigm is far from original, has become almost a staple since as far back as films such as *Invasion of the Body Snatchers*. H P Lovecraft suggested we were the playthings of forces from 'outside,' William Burroughs claimed that 'language is a virus from outer space,' while in the fields of the esoteric, philosophers such as Gurdjieff claimed that our self-destructive behaviour was the result of a cosmic mistake and that that humanity was 'food for the moon.'

Rather than belabour this basic theme I used it as a backdrop against which I began to elaborate a picaresque, utilising situationist and neoist mechanisms such as 'detournement' and 'plagiarism.' I let the text go wherever it seemed to want. Other people, friends and fellow writers jumped in and quite happily made it simultaneously more complex and vastly sillier. There is no reason that demolishing serious culture shouldn't be fun.

There are currently two volumes collecting the Parasite experiments. The current one you have just read collects shorter fragmentary diversions into the meta-narrative. The other volume is a full length novel (sort of). They can be read independently of each other (although it's definitely worth reading them both) and in no particular order. Time is, after all, a toroidal shaped omega-null continuum. Either that or a duck's ass.

I hope you've enjoyed this experience and that it has had a beneficial effect on your health and happiness.

Spread the infection.

D M Mitchell

Apophenia is an imprint of
www.paraphiliamagazine.com

For information and to purchase other titles:
www.paraphiliamagazine.com/books.html

Made in the USA
San Bernardino, CA
29 December 2014